Readers LOVE Amanda Brittany

'I almost stood up to applaud the author'

'Totally gripping'

'I had to keep turning the pages – I couldn't guess the ending, and I had to know!'

'5 out of 5 stars. A real page turner with a brilliantly executed twist'

'Yet another 5* thriller from Amanda Brittany'

'Brittany is a superb writer, highly skilled at keeping you gripped, staying up late to uncover the secrets'

AMANDA BRITTANY lives in Hertfordshire with her husband and two dogs. When she's not writing, she loves spending time with family, walking, reading, and sunny days at the seaside. Her debut novel *Her Last Lie* reached the Kindle top 100 in the US and Australia and was a #1 bestseller in the UK. It has also been optioned for film. All her eBook royalties for *Her Last Lie* are being donated to Cancer Research UK, in memory of her sister who lost her battle with cancer in July 2017. It has so far raised almost £8,500.

Also by Amanda Brittany

Her Last Lie
Tell the Truth
Traces of Her
I Lie in Wait

Also by Karen Clarke and Amanda Brittany

The Secret Sister
The Perfect Nanny

The Island House

AMANDA BRITTANY

HQ
An imprint of HarperCollins*Publishers* Ltd
1 London Bridge Street
London SE1 9GF

www.harpercollins.co.uk

HarperCollins*Publishers*
1st Floor, Watermarque Building, Ringsend Road
Dublin 4, Ireland

This paperback edition 2021

1
First published in Great Britain by
HQ, an imprint of HarperCollins*Publishers* Ltd 2021

Copyright © Amanda Brittany 2021

Emoji © Shutterstock.com

Amanda Brittany asserts the moral right to be
identified as the author of this work.
A catalogue record for this book is
available from the British Library.

ISBN: 9780008362904

For Ruby

Poison hemlock grows wild on Seafield Island. Proud, white flowering plants dance in the light breeze, reaching for the sun, held upright by purple-spotted stems.

Come closer, it calls to unsuspecting victims, giving away nothing of how deadly it is. *Pick me.*

PART ONE

'Curiouser and curiouser!'
Lewis Carroll

Chapter 1

May 2017

Jan Walker steps into the inky darkness of the lobby at Flynn House, a musty smell snatching her breath away. She fumbles her phone from the pocket of her leather jacket, flicks on the torch.

'It's as though the place is dying,' James says, coming in behind her.

Jan glances over her shoulder at her assistant in the doorway. 'Bit dramatic.' She won't say she feels it too. She wants this commission. But, truth is, stepping into this sad, dilapidated building, after walking across the beach in the brilliant sunshine, has made her uneasy.

'I've got a bad vibe about this place.' There's a tremor in James's voice. He's in his mid-twenties, younger than her by ten years. 'We shouldn't even be here. Let's come back another time with the owner.'

It's true she has yet to be officially invited to view the house. But they were passing through Dunwold, and she wanted to take a look. She swings the torch beam across the hallway. 'It's good money,' she says. 'I can't afford to pass this up.' She lifts the light

3

towards a grand staircase leading to a second floor. A thick, frayed rope hangs from the banister.

'And that's not freaky at all,' James says, not moving from his frozen spot.

Faded gold wallpaper peels from high walls. Cobwebs cling to every surface. The parquet flooring, once beautiful Jan imagines, is scratched, lifting in places, pieces missing, never to be found.

Her gaze glides to a faded framed poster, hanging on a slant. It advertises a performance at The London Palladium. The man in the picture is in his twenties, dressed in a yellow and blue striped jacket, his black hair oiled back from his forehead.

'Felix Flynn,' she says, eyes narrowing. The man is holding a ventriloquist puppet, an exact replica of him, right down to the striped jacket, and oiled-back hair. 'A puppeteer, apparently.'

'Really not helping.' James moves across the hallway, reaches her side – so close she senses him shiver.

A rat darts from the shadows, claws scratching the flooring.

'Jeez!' Jan's heart thuds beneath her fingers, as it disappears into the gloom of a far corner. Clearly, James's nervousness is catching. 'This place is going to need some makeover.'

There's no doubting Flynn House in Suffolk was once a grand property, and Jan knows her company can restore it to the stunning Gothic building it once was. But James is right, there's a foreboding about the place, as though it's crying out to be left alone to decay.

It was built in the late eighteenth century on Seafield Island and can only be reached along a causeway at certain times of day. If she decides to ignore the silent pleas of the house to be left in peace, and takes on the renovation, she'll need to take that into account. The hope is to transform the place into a Gothic boutique hotel for visitors looking for something different, but going by the way James's wide eyes flick over the ground floor, the tenseness of his body language, she knows her team will take some convincing.

'So nobody's lived here for years?'

Jan shakes her head. 'The owner alternates between staying in a cottage on the island and living abroad. Rarely comes to the house.'

They continue to look around the ground floor. A huge room looks out through grubby, cracked windows onto a garden over-run by weeds. The view of the sea is stunning. There's a downstairs bathroom that could be renovated to accommodate guests, a dining area and a run-down kitchen.

Jan turns. 'We should look upstairs.'

'You sure?'

'Don't be a wimp, James. There's nobody here.' She heads towards the stairs. Takes them two at a time, hears James's reluctant footfalls behind her.

There are six rooms on the first floor, set off a narrow corridor, the door to each standing ajar. Jan pokes her head round each one in turn. 'There's a fair amount of work, but the layout is perfect,' she says.

She heads up a further set of stairs, taking in two more bedrooms. 'James?' she calls.

'Yep, coming.' There's hesitation in his voice, as he climbs the stairs, and follows her along another landing.

'The attic room,' he says, looking up a staircase towards a closed door, two brass dogs standing either side – guarding.

'Mmm …' Jan shines her torch up at a peeling red door. 'If we take the house on, we're to leave it locked. The owner doesn't want it touched.'

'Bit odd, don't you think?'

Jan looks about her, flashing her torch into the shadowy corners, and back up at the door. She places her foot on the first step.

'What are you doing?' James says.

She takes another step. The stair splinters and cracks under her weight. She stumbles, grabs the banister for balance.

'Are you OK?'

She ignores him, continues. Reaches for the handle as a thud comes from inside the room – the sound of laughter.

'Someone's in there,' she blurts in a half-whisper. She turns, hurries back down the stairs, heart racing. 'We should go.' She swings back, looks up at the door once more. 'Did you hear that?'

James's eyes are wide, full of fear. 'I didn't hear anything.'

They race down the hallway, away from the attic room. 'I'm sure it's just the old building stirring,' she says.

But she knows what she heard.

They are not alone in Flynn House, and the sooner they leave the better. They won't be back.

Chapter 2

January 2019

Alice

A woman in her late thirties steps into the shop. A slightly older man, putting Alice in mind of a spectacled Gary Barlow, follows.

'Miss Hadley?' the woman says. 'Miss Alice Hadley?'

Alice nods from where she's sitting behind the antique counter in the corner. She can tell they are police. No uniform, but a calm confidence. Shadows beneath their eyes that tell of overwork and lack of sleep. She takes a deep breath, steeling herself for bad news, a heavy feeling, as though a bag of rocks is pressing against her chest, consuming her.

'Your neighbour said we might find you here.' The woman glances about her, studying the shelves full of sculptures.

Alice's father bought her 'Alice's Sculptures in Wonderland' three years ago, with the royalties from his debut novel *Where Doves Fly*. A Victorian building on a cobbled path a hundred yards from the sea, nestled between a bookstore and a jewellery shop selling pieces made from the gemstone Whitby jet.

'I'm Detective Sergeant Barnum,' the woman goes on, showing Alice her badge, eyes now on her. A weak smile appears on her lips then vanishes. 'This is Detective Constable Marsh.'

A prickle of fear touches Alice's neck. Her knees bounce, hitting the desk – *tap, tap, tap*. 'Has something happened?' *Of course something's happened.* Two officers wouldn't track her down, turn up with faces like grim reapers, to tell her she's won the lottery. She lifts her ankle-length cardigan from the back of the chair, wraps it round her shoulders like a comfort blanket.

DC Marsh turns the sign on the door from open to closed. 'Is there someone we can call to come and be with you?'

Alice shakes her head. *Please don't say what you've come to say.*

'There's been an incident in Sparrow Lane, Miss Hadley.' DS Barnum steps closer. 'Your father has been in a hit and run, and I'm afraid—'

'What about Henry?' Alice is stalling. She knows once the officer says the words – *your father is dead* – it can never be unsaid. It would be true. No return ticket. She will have lost him forever, her amazing reclusive father. She will have lost her best friend.

'Henry?' DC Marsh furrows his forehead.

'Dad's dog – did you find him? Is Henry OK? Dad never goes out without him.' She's talking too fast, on her feet now, pacing three steps across the shop, three steps back, her throat drying as she speaks.

DC Marsh turns to look at the DS, moves closer. 'There was no dog, as far as we know.'

'Dad never goes out without Henry.' Her heart kicks against her rib cage. She knows she's being ridiculous – hysteria rising. 'Are you sure it's my dad?'

'Miss Hadley—'

'Alice.' She squeezes her hands into fists. 'Call me Alice.'

'Alice. We are sure the man in the incident is your father. He had his wallet on him.' The DC pauses for a moment. 'Your father didn't survive the hit and run, Alice. I'm so sorry.'

'I need to call Leon.' Her voice cracks, and tears fill her eyes, as she rummages in her bag, and pulls out her phone. But as she stares at the screen, she knows she can't call him. It wouldn't be fair. They've been broken up for three months. Yes, she's seen him a few times since, as friends, but it wouldn't be right turning to him. It wouldn't be fair.

The officers look at each other, and back at Alice. 'Can we call Leon for you?' DS Barnum says.

'No. No.' She shoves the phone back in her bag. 'I should probably close the shop.' She's bewildered, her voice a whisper. 'Check on Henry.'

'Of course. Can we drop you off?'

'I'd rather walk.' She wipes her sleeve across her eyes. 'Try to make sense of this.'

'We will need you to come to the station at some point, just a few questions about when you last saw your father, that kind of thing.'

'Yes. Yes. Of course.' She shrugs the cardigan from her shoulders, and it falls to the floor in a heap, before she grabs her coat from the hook on the wall. She slips it on, flicks her hair from the collar. Pulls on a woolly hat.

'And ... we'll need someone to give us a formal identification,' DS Barnum says, following her through the door. 'Not right now, of course. Tomorrow. If you're up to it.'

'OK.' She sniffs. 'I'd better get to Butterfly Cottage—'

'Your father's house?' DC Marsh says, joining them outside.

Alice nods, in a daze, fumbles with the key as she attempts to lock the door. 'I need to make sure Henry's OK. He'll wonder where Dad is. He's always at home, you see. Dad, I mean. He rarely goes ... went out ... Dad, not Henry. Though Henry only goes ... went out with Dad. Sorry.' The words feel jumbled, messy, catching in her throat, anxiety rising in her chest.

'Will you be OK, Alice?'

'I'm fine. Honestly.' But she's far from it, and knows if she doesn't move away soon she'll break. Fall apart. Sob until there are no more tears left to cry.

'We're sorry for your loss,' DS Barnum says. It sounds heartfelt. 'I can't begin to imagine how hard this must be for you. Please accept our condolences.'

Alice doesn't respond – she can't, her throat has closed. She heads away, into the freezing air. It snowed earlier, and although it disappeared as quickly as it came, the wind is icy, stinging her cheeks. Tears rise inside her, begging to be released. *So this is grief.*

*

Alice opens the front door to her father's rambling old property on the outskirts of Whitby. At the sight of her, Henry wags his silky brown tail, slowly pads over, and looks up with sad, dark eyes. It's as though he knows already that his master won't be back.

'Oh, my lovely boy.' Alice drops to her knees onto the parquet flooring, and hugs the Labrador's thick neck. 'Why weren't you out with Dad, Henry?' Tears stream down her face. A sob catches in her throat. 'Where was he going without you?'

*

'Dad?' Alice whispers into the darkness, seeing the outline of her father sitting on the edge of her bed, his head in his hands.

'Promise me you'll never go back,' he says, lifting his head, turning to look her way. And then he's gone.

'No! Stay! Please.'

Alice's eyes shoot open, her heart thudding as she scans the dimly lit bedroom, the fluorescent green numbers on the clock telling her it's 5 a.m. She hauls herself up against the headboard, wipes away tears from her cheeks.

All her life she has suffered from recurring, bizarre nightmares of being pulled towards a Gothic house near the sea by an

10

unknown force. Alone, she would always take the stairs towards a red door at the top of the house, reach for the handle. Always waking, sobbing, before she could see what was on the other side of the door. But *this* dream about her father was the most vivid she has ever experienced. It was as though he visited her from the grave to warn her.

Warn her about what?

She closes her eyes, searching her thoughts. She has always felt as though a part of her is missing, something lurking in the background that she has never been able to make sense of. She tried talking to her father about it many times – begging him to tell her more about who her mother was, what she was like, about their life before they came to Whitby – but he always shut her off, even got angry on occasions. In the end she stopped trying. Didn't want to upset him. Or was it more than that? Maybe she'd backed down, too afraid to learn the truth.

She forces herself out of bed, grabs her dressing gown, and makes her way downstairs.

'Here you go, boy,' Alice says, placing Henry's food in front of him, her face contorting with tears. He sniffs it and returns to his basket. 'You should eat, sweetheart.' But she knows how he feels. She can't face breakfast either.

She makes a mug of coffee, lets Henry out into the tangled, frosty garden, before turning on her laptop. Everything about today feels slow, sluggish, as though she's entered another dimension.

It doesn't take many clicks on her keyboard to find the news of her father's death and his true identity has broken. Everyone seems to know now that E. H. Membrose – reclusive millionaire and bestselling author of *Where Doves Fly* and *Raging Fires* – was her father – Adam Hadley. It appears to be the most exciting news to break in the literary industry since Robert Galbraith turned out to be J.K. Rowling.

Alice covers her mouth, trying to take in what she's reading – seeing. Her father's face is all over the internet; journalists excited

11

– the secret author's outing seeming on a par with discovering Lord Lucan's whereabouts, or Jack the Ripper's true identity.

Her dad's eyes – one green, one blue – stare out at her from her laptop screen. Every media giant is running the story; #membrose and #secretauthor are trending on Twitter.

'Oh God,' she whispers, her heart thudding as she notices reams of messages on her phone. She grabs a tissue, dabs her face.

A newspaper clatters through the front door. She gets to her feet, makes her way into the hall. The front page covers the same news. Her father's dark collar-length hair with just a sprinkling of grey, his sharp nose that reminded Alice of a ski slope, his chiselled jawline, his unusual eyes all now belong to the world. There are photos of her too. Recent ones of her walking through Whitby yesterday, her blonde hair poking out of the bottom of her woolly hat, her blue eyes bloodshot, cheeks blotchy. Everything her father hid for so long is on display – *including her*.

Alice returns to the kitchen, throws the newspaper on the worktop, buries her head in her hands and sobs.

So this is grief.

Chapter 3

February 2019

Alice

Alice has done little since her father died; even her shop remains closed. But she's read that the funeral will help the healing process – that she might be able to start moving forward after today.

She sits in the lounge at Butterfly Cottage waiting for the cars to arrive. Tears are there, unsteady behind her eyes, but she can't afford to cry. If she starts, she will never stop.

Her speech is folded next to her tissues in her black bag. She took ages preparing it – trying to find the right words to describe her father – her relationship with him. She hadn't realised, until she tried to form those words, how dependent on him she'd been over the years. How desperately lonely she is now.

He would have hated all this fuss. Her getting up in front of strangers and talking about him would have been his worst nightmare. In fact he once said, 'Alice, if you ever find me slumped over my desk – dead – tell no one. Just bury me in the back garden, then carry on with whatever you were doing when you entered the room.'

'Are you planning on dying any time soon?' she said, matching his teasing smile. 'Because if you are I'll need to buy a black dress, and a decent spade from B&Q to clear away the weeds and nettles and dig a hole.'

That was six months ago. At the time, Adam Hadley was a healthy man in his early fifties, considering his only exercise was walking Henry, and the fact he drank far too much red wine. His writing fuel, he called it. So, with recent events, it crosses Alice's imaginative mind that perhaps he sensed, even knew, he wasn't long for this world.

The doorbell chimes. Henry barks, startling Alice from her thoughts. She isn't expecting anyone. Wants to arrive at the funeral alone.

She rises, pushing down a brief hope that it might be Leon. She has spoken to her ex a few times over the past few weeks. He said he was there for her, should she need him. She does need him, but has convinced herself that it's the grief pushing her towards him. It wouldn't be fair to use Leon as her support. He can't be her shoulder to cry on. They want different things from life. He wants marriage, children. She could never see herself as a mother, and has serious commitment issues. He will be at the funeral though. He liked her dad. And she's grateful for that.

She peers through the side window. Tegan Matthews stands on the doorstep. A stunning-looking woman, with tight black curls springing from her head in all directions, and cheekbones that could slice your fingers off. She's tall and strong – does kickboxing and wall climbing – and at thirty – the same age as Alice – she's a leading literary agent with her own company, all due to spotting Alice's father's talent five years ago.

Alice doesn't want or need her here. But she can't hide. The cars are due soon. She takes a deep breath and opens the door. Ice-cold air wafts into the hall.

'How are you, sweetie?' Tegan removes her dark sunglasses

to reveal red eyes. 'I thought you might need someone with you today.' She tilts her head. 'But I can go if—'

'No, no it's fine.' She gestures for Tegan to enter the antique-filled hallway, and as Tegan steps in, Henry lumbers over, sniffs the woman's crotch, looks up at her, tail down.

Tegan grips the dresser next to her, her feet shuffling across the floor, away from the dog. 'He knows I'm not a fan,' she says through a tense smile. 'I was attacked by a dog as a child.'

Alice has heard this story before.

'I can never quite relax around the creatures, though I'm sure Henry is a dear.' She pauses, watching as the dog ambles back into the lounge and flops on his bed. 'Anyway, how are you holding up, lovely?' She touches Alice's arm with the tips of her manicured fingers.

'I'm just about OK.' The words come out fractured. She is far from OK. 'I'll be glad when today is over.'

They move into the lounge, and stand together, looking out of the window, waiting for the cars; Alice lost in thought, imagining going through her father's things in the subsequent weeks, months, his dusty shelves crammed with books, his drawers full of part-written manuscripts. She's dreading it, wonders if she'll ever be up for the task.

Strong-smelling lilies and white roses – a bouquet from Leon's parents – stand in a vase on the table. It's meant to give Alice peace. She caresses the petals with her fingertips. The gesture from the couple she grew so fond of during her time with Leon was a kind one, but she's so far from peace right now, Google Maps couldn't find it.

Further vases of flowers and condolence cards clutter surfaces. The desk in the corner holds her father's closed laptop, reams of paper, and Post-it Notes with jottings – ideas for future novels he will never get to write.

Tegan picks up a condolence card with a dragonfly on the

front. Opens it. Looks inside. 'You've had a lot of support,' she says. 'Everyone loved your dad.'

'Mmm, though I hardly know any of these people, and I'm pretty sure Dad didn't either.'

'Fans of his writing?' She puts the card down.

'Mostly. It's so kind of them. But I wish the press hadn't revealed the address of the cottage.'

'I know. God knows who leaked it.'

Alice turns and heads across the room. Picks up a card from amongst others on an oak table. On the cover is a tiger, mouth open wide in a roar. 'This one came this morning.'

Tegan appears beside her, takes the card from her. *'I'm so glad I've found you,'* she reads, furrowing her forehead. 'That's a bit odd.'

'I know, right? Another fan, probably. Though it's not exactly a sympathy card, and it's not even signed.'

Tegan puts down the card, and they return to the window, where silence stretches – tight – tense – lasting minute upon minute. Tegan pulls a cigarette packet from her bag, shakes one free, rolls it between her fingers, puts it back in the box. 'What time is the car arriving?'

'Not long now.'

'I see the press are here.'

'They've been driving me bloody crazy.' Alice noticed them earlier creeping around, setting up cameras, staring in at her with beady eyes. They've been outside on and off since her father's death. 'If I ever find out who told them my dad's identity, I *will* kill them.'

'You'll have to get in line behind me.' There's no strength in Tegan's words or her attempt at a smile.

So few people knew Adam Hadley was E. H. Membrose, and it's hard to imagine any of them would tell the media.

'They're here.' Alice pulls on her purple, ankle-length coat, and flicks her hair from the collar. 'Let's go, before I run and hide.' She turns to Henry. 'Be good, lovely boy.'

16

He looks up at her for a moment, before flopping his head back down in his basket. He misses his owner as much as Alice misses her father. It has been a struggle to persuade him to even take a walk.

Tegan grabs Alice's hand as they head into the hallway; her fingers ice-cold. 'I have your back, sweetie,' she says, and throws open the front door to a flash of cameras. 'We'll get through this,' she goes on, ushering Alice down the winding path towards the waiting shiny black car.

'*Did you know your father was Membrose?*' '*Have you seen the films?*'

'*Are you creative like your dad, Alice?*' '*I hear Netflix are interested in making a series out of one of his books.*' '*You're an artist, aren't you, Miss Hadley?*' '*Gothic sculptures?*'

'Leave me alone,' Alice cries, as she bends down to get into the back seat of the car, fighting back an army of tears behind her eyes.

'We'll get through this, Alice,' Tegan repeats, before closing the door and dashing to the other side to get in.

But Alice isn't sure how she'll cope.

*

The crematorium is rammed. Some people Alice recognises: her father's publishers; his neighbours; Leon, but most she doesn't know: strangers who knew her father through his words, sharing her grief.

The man the celebrant describes is a stranger. Alice's fault to some degree – she didn't provide enough information for her to go on. Her father wouldn't have wanted her to.

And now she's walking up to the podium on weak legs, gripping the speech she prepared in shaking hands.

Her efforts start well, as she talks about her father's brilliant sense of humour, his creativity, how she loved being home-educated by him, how he made learning so much fun. She doesn't say that however much she loved him, she was often lonely – rattling around Butterfly Cottage playing make-believe with her dolls – while he was absorbed in his writing.

'He wouldn't let me read his novels in my early teens,' she says. '"Far too dark," he would say, totally unaware that I secretly read them under my duvet with a torch in the middle of the night, and scared myself silly.' A tinkle of laughter fills the crematorium, giving Alice time to clear her throat and take a breath. 'He was a wonderful man,' she goes on. 'And a good dad. I feel honoured and incredibly lucky to have been part of his world, when so few were invited in.' The words she's written blur through sudden tears. She knows she can't go on. 'I will miss him desperately,' she says, picking up her scribbled notes, and returning to her seat.

After the service, Tegan grips Alice's arm, and leads her from the building to the sound of Cher's 'If I could turn back time' – one of her father's favourite songs.

Outside, grey clouds skitter across the watery sun. Alice has organised a buffet at the local pub, but she can't face it.

'I need to disappear,' she whispers, a tissue in shreds in her hand. 'I can't face all these people.'

'Then go,' Tegan says, her face wet with tears. 'Everyone will understand.'

I don't really care if they don't.

She pulls free from Tegan, and runs across the lawn towards the waiting black car.

'Take me to Butterfly Cottage, please,' she says to the driver.

As they pull away, tyres slow over cobbles, she glances out of the back window at the swarm of black exiting the crematorium.

Leon is there; tall, handsome in a thigh-length black jacket over black jeans. He looks about him, dragging his fingers through his fair hair. She knows he's searching for her, and places her hand on the window, splays her fingers, desperately needing him.

They'd been together a year when everything fell apart three months ago. He was the best thing that had happened to her, yet she wrecked it. They'd met at the Literature Festival in Whitby. Leon hoped to get a publisher or an agent interested in his fantasy novel. Alice's interest in the event was purely to hear her favourite authors speak. Her dad had instilled a passion in her for reading. Something they'd shared. He'd never go to events though. Rarely left the house.

When it started to rain that day, she ended up in the bar, sitting next to Leon. For a long time after that, he joked that he'd picked her up at a bar. She supposed he had. They began talking. Him telling her about his book, and how, for now, he was a swimming instructor and lifeguard at the local pool. 'Only until the millions roll in, you understand,' he said, and laughed. And she told him about her shop in Whitby, how she was an artist – and he listened. If there's such a thing as love at first sight, this was the closest she ever came to it.

At first it had been perfect. Leon was optimistic, charming, fun. They were so happy. Eventually, he mentioned marriage, having a family, and she knew she wasn't equipped. She adored children, but the thought of caring for a baby, a little boy or girl fully dependent on her, sent her into a cold panic. She couldn't explain why, but she was afraid to commit. Her life hadn't been normal growing up, and her father kept secrets – secrets about his past, the first seven years of her life. Secrets she suspected played a huge part in the woman she was now.

Leon deserved better, someone who shared his dreams.

As she watches from the funeral car, she spots Tegan dashing towards Leon. She takes him in her arms. *When did they get so close?* A memory flies in. 'I'm thinking of changing my agent,' her father said a week before he died. He never did explain why.

Alice turns from the scene unfolding to face forward, the leather seat squeaking under her thighs. The car feels too big. Room enough for seven.

A tear rolls down her cheek, and drips off her chin.

She's never felt so alone.

Chapter 4

Early October 2019

Alice

The envelope feels rough against Alice's fingers. The handwriting is small and spiky, and addressed to Ms Alice Hadley at Butterfly Cottage, where she's been living since her father's death eight months ago. The postmark is Suffolk.

The photograph inside is a black and white study of a Gothic building standing on a cliff edge, grand and imposing, with a steep, high roof rising to a point, and arched windows.

She turns the photo over, her hands shaking. 'Flynn House,' she whispers, reading the words on the back. She knows this house. Has seen it before in recurring nightmares. Her heart hammers against her chest, as she searches the envelope for who sent it. But there's nothing – only the photo.

Her mind flits to ten years ago, when she made a sculpture of the haunting building that disturbed her dreams. Trying to make sense of it through her art.

'Get rid of it,' her father yelled when he saw it, his eyes wild.

She'd never seen him so upset. He left her in tears that day. Slamming his office door behind him.

Later he apologised. Hugged her close. Told her he was having a bad day.

'Why get so angry?' she asked, wiping away her tears.

'Leave it be, Alice. Please,' was all he said. She never discovered why the house upset him so much.

She recalls putting the sculpture in the loft, unable to throw it away at the time, and dashes up the stairs, discarding the photo. Henry lumbers behind, wagging his tail, giving a gruff bark, thinking it's a game.

But this is no game.

She pulls down the loft ladder, takes a deep breath, and climbs the metal rungs.

It's not long before she's lost in memories, pulling out her childhood books, *Alice in Wonderland*, *Alice through the Looking Glass*, pressing them against her nose, breathing them in, before flicking through the pages, imagining her father's melodic tones as he read them to her at bedtime.

She grabs a box of dolls, recalls giving them tea parties, chatting with them, as though they were real – her friends.

Finally, tucked in the top of a plastic box full of exercise books, she finds Gothic House.

There's no doubting the sculpture and the photograph are the same house – the house from her recurring dreams. But Alice had made the clay model long ago, years before seeing the photo. Had her dreams been based on memories? *This doesn't make sense.*

She recalls again her father's outburst when he saw it. He rarely got angry. Her head swims. Had Flynn House meant something to him? Had she been there at some point? There has always been something just out of sight niggling at her subconscious, and it seems even stronger now, since her dad died.

She roots around in a box of cuddly toys, giving her favourite old teddy a hug. She pulls out a tiger. It feels soft under her fingers. A flash of memory – she's a child, clinging to the toy animal, not wanting to let it go.

She turns from her crouched position, adrenaline pumping, and rummages in further boxes. A small tobacco tin grabs her attention. Inside is a passport-sized photograph of a young woman and a receipt. She knows exactly who the pretty young woman, with long blonde hair and bright blue eyes, is. She presses a kiss onto the picture.

'She died in childbirth,' her father told her many years ago, handing her a photo of him and her mother. 'She was amazing. Never forget that. She would have loved you so much, Alice.' He went on to tell her that her grandparents on both sides were long dead, that he was the only family she had. She tried to question him further, but, as always, he closed off.

She turns the photo over. There are no words scribbled on the reverse. But the receipt is for a restaurant in Dunwold, Suffolk, dated 1988. Her parents had shared a steak meal, and a bottle of Mateus Rosé wine.

Alice's mind whirs. The past is calling. Should she ransack the attic for clues? But it's pointless. She's combed every inch of it through the years, searching for answers. Now, without the fear of upsetting her father blocking her way, she feels an insatiable need to know rising inside her.

Who was her mother?

Who sent her the photo of Flynn House?

What secrets had her father kept buried?

She has lived with a big burning question mark over her past all her life, and it seems her father's death has left her with an even bigger puzzle.

Whatever it takes. She needs answers.

*

Alice ends the call with the detective, and is staring down at her phone, fighting back tears, when the doorbell chimes.

'I've brought wine.' Faith stands on the doorstep of Butterfly Cottage, holding a bottle and a bag of cheesy savoury snacks in one hand, a wide smile on her face. Her dark hair is in a high ponytail, tendrils escaping, her thick fringe resting above blue eyes. One of the fastenings on her yellow dungarees hangs open across a checked blouse, making her look younger than her thirty years. She bends to fuss Henry, who wags his tail.

'Sounds good,' Alice says, stepping aside for her friend to enter, pushing down thoughts of the call moments ago.

It's the first time Faith has been to the house. In fact, apart from Tegan on the day of the funeral, and visits from the police about her father's hit and run, Alice has had no visitors. And, apart from a few coffee meet-ups where Faith managed to pull her out of her comfort zone, and regular walks with Henry, she's rarely left the house over the last eight months, preferring it that way.

But things are improving with Faith's constant support. Alice is sculpting again. She's even put make-up on this evening, a first since the funeral.

'How are you, lovely?' Faith leans in and kisses Alice's cheek.

'OK. The grey cloud is lifting slowly.'

'That's good news. You are doing so well.' She smiles, lifts the bottle. 'Shall we get this poured?'

'Of course, yes.'

Faith's eyes flick around the entrance. 'It's such a lovely house.'

'Yes. It needs clearing really ...' Alice pinches the skin at her throat. Sighs. 'It's just so hard ... I can't bring myself to ...' And there's the crack in her voice that's been so common through the months. The sign tears are close.

'Oh, sweetie, come here.' Faith puts the wine down, pulls her into a hug, and doesn't let go for what feels like a minute. 'As I've said before, there's no rush. Baby steps. You'll know when you are ready.'

Wine poured they head into the lounge, clutching glasses and bowls filled with snacks.

Faith sits on the edge of the sofa, her smile warm and reassuring. 'How's the sculpture coming along?'

Alice sinks into the armchair, Henry at her feet. 'I'm hoping to have it finished by Halloween. We normally do well at the shop over that period.'

'That's brilliant. I can't wait to see it.' Faith takes a gulp of wine. 'What are your thoughts about coming back to the shop?' A beat. 'Don't get me wrong. I'm not putting any pressure on. I just think—'

'I hope to. Just part-time to start with, if you can stay on for a bit longer—'

'Sure, but I'm more than happy to back off whenever you feel ready.'

Alice knows her friend will be happy to see her return, that she's been trying coax her out of her grief for a while, without judging her for falling apart, and she's grateful for that. She wouldn't have made the steps she's already made without her.

There were ten applicants back in March for the temporary position to cover Alice's absence while she came to terms with losing her dad. Faith had stood out. She fitted into the shop's Gothic style, and came across as likeable and intelligent when Alice interviewed her. She has never regretted her decision to take her on. Apart from a visit to see family in August, she's kept the shop ticking over so well.

'So, how did the date go?' Alice asks, changing the subject.

Faith has seen two men since Alice met her, both complete disasters, and the one she's presently seeing sounds like a moron. She seems to have a habit of picking arrogant idiots.

'It went great.' Faith's face brightens. She takes a gulp of wine. Grabs a handful of cheesy snacks.

'Should you eat those?' Alice says. Faith is mildly lactose intolerant.

'Of course – it's not real cheese.' She laughs, pops one into her mouth, and munches. 'I like Mitch a lot, actually. He could be "the one".'

'Really?' Alice knows her tone is a little judgemental, though she doesn't mean to be. For all she knows Mitch Fisher could be Mr Wonderful. And it's Faith's life, not hers. She's hardly made a success of her own love life.

'Yes! Really.' Faith laughs. 'Seriously. I like him.'

'Well, that's good. I'm happy for you.'

Alice splashes more wine into both glasses. 'The police called earlier,' she says. 'Just before you arrived.' She takes a breath. 'They're no longer looking into my dad's hit and run.'

Faith widens her eyes, shoots forward in her seat. 'Oh my God, why not?'

Alice shrugs. 'The case is still open.' She takes a gulp of wine. 'But they still have no leads.'

Faith reaches across, takes hold of Alice's hand. 'I'm so sorry.'

'It's fine.'

'No, no it's not fine. It's bloody awful.'

'Maybe something will turn up at some point.' But she suspects they will never find the person who took her father from her.

*

It's gone eleven when Faith gets up and attempts to push creases from her dungarees. 'I should make a move,' she says, as Henry pads over. She gives his ears a gentle rub. 'You're such a lovely boy, aren't you?'

'He is.' Alice rises too, stretches her arms above her head. 'I don't know what I would have done without him over the last few months. He's a good friend.'

Faith's gaze drifts through into the dining room, focusing on Alice's sculpture on the table. 'Wow! Did you make that?'

Alice nods, and makes her way into the dining area, Faith right behind her. She rests her hand on the sculpture she found in the loft earlier. 'It's called Gothic House. I made it a long time ago, when I first started sculpting.'

'Well it's amazing. You're so talented.'

'Thank you.' She feels a blush creeping up her neck. She's never been good at accepting praise – something inside her always saying, *You don't deserve it, Alice.*

'Are you thinking of selling it?'

Alice shrugs. She hadn't thought about it, but maybe it would be for the best. Her father never liked it, and she's not sure she likes it herself. 'I guess I could.' She breaks off, wondering whether to tell Faith the whole story – about the photograph she received in the post that triggered her search for the piece in the first place, but decides against it. Amongst other things it's late. She's tired. 'Could you take it with you?' she says. 'Put it in the shop window?'

'Of course, happy to.'

Alice grabs her phone, and takes a photo of the clay replica of Flynn House. 'I'll put it on Instagram too. It may attract buyers.' She hasn't put anything on her Instagram profile since her father died, a clear reminder that her life has stood still for too long. But something inside her is buzzing, telling her it's about to start moving again.

Faith picks up the sculpture, studies it with a look of fascination. 'It really is amazing.' She lifts her gaze, meets Alice's eyes. 'How much do you want on the price tag?'

Alice shrugs. She doesn't know anymore.

'Tell you what, leave it with me.' Faith leans forward, kisses Alice's cheek. 'I promise I'll get you a good price.'

*

Once Faith has gone, Alice uploads the picture of her sculpture onto her Instagram account:

A piece I made some time ago, available at 'Alice's Sculptures in Wonderland' in Whitby #FlynnHouse #Gothic

Chapter 5

Late October 2019

Alice

There is a ventriloquist's doll in the window of the antique shop down by Whitby Harbour. He sits between a glossy brown Beswick horse with a chipped hoof, and a mustard-yellow art-deco vase. The doll is dressed in a faded-black suit, a red bow tie attached to a yellowing shirt. His black hair is combed back from his frozen face. His shiny red lips want to talk.

As Alice passes by, she feels his stare. 'He's a bit freaky, isn't he, Henry?' she says, as though the dog understands what she's saying. Despite a shiver down her spine, she's drawn to the puppet. In fact, she has always had a bit of a thing for anything macabre. Her sculptures are always dark. She blames her father for that – his influence as her only role model.

'Hey,' she whispers, raising her hand in a wave, as though the puppet can hear her. She glances about to check nobody is listening. The street is quiet. 'I'm as barking as you, Henry,' she says to the dog, ruffling his glossy coat. 'Did you see what I did there?'

She makes her way towards Whitby Bridge, her canvas bag dangling over her shoulder, but she can't resist looking back, just once, half-expecting the puppet to be waving. *Of course, he isn't.*

It's a chilly grey October morning, and the tips of her ears and nose begin to tingle with the cold. The sea air tastes salty on her tongue, as she stops for a moment halfway across the bridge, pulling her woolly hat down over her ears. The sea matches the grey of the clouds like a Fifties twin set. Fishing boats and trawlers bob on the water, lobster pots stacked on the harbourside.

'Dad used to love this place,' she says, bending to kiss the dog's head. 'It was his inspiration. But then you know that more than anyone, don't you, gorgeous boy?'

Before tears invade, she straightens up, and turns from the nostalgic view, taking a deep breath. Yanking on Henry's lead, she pulls him away from a pug he seems to have taken a liking to, and makes her way to the other side of the bridge, before heading up Church Street towards 'Alice's Sculptures in Wonderland', the shop she named after her favourite book, which her father read to her when she was a child.

Once there she stares in the shop window. The shop's woodwork is charcoal black, and a sign – black with gold lettering – is fixed to the wall.

Several of her fantastical sculptures are snuggled into silky black fabric amongst small pumpkins, but there's no sign of Gothic House.

She pushes the door open, and steps inside. The walls seem to wrap around her like a hug, and the slight smell of damp that she can't quite get rid of, and the aroma of coffee percolating, are familiar and comforting. It's good to be back – a step in the right direction.

'Hey, Alice.' Faith smiles from behind the counter, surrounded by her homemade jewellery. Alice agreed a few months back that she could sell it at the shop. 'Ooh, and how lovely to see gorgeous Henry too,' Faith adds.

Alice fishes the sculpture she's been working on from her bag, strips away black tissue paper, and puts it on the counter. 'Ta da! What do you think?'

'Wow! It's amazing,' Faith says, as she strokes Henry, who seems delighted to see her. 'As I've said before, you are one talented lady.'

'Thanks.' Alice feels the usual blush creeping up her neck.

Faith moves her hand from Henry's back, and he sprawls on the floor, and closes his eyes. She stares at the sculpture of a desperate-looking figure made from twisted copper, a man clambering out of a grave, his hands stretching upwards, fingers contorted, mouth wide open as though screaming, flesh torn. 'Though I wouldn't want to spend too long inside your head,' she says.

Alice smiles, and places the piece on the shelf above the counter. 'It's called Zombie.'

'Really? Why?' Faith laughs at her own attempt at humour, but continues to stare up at it, as though mesmerised. 'Someone will bite your hand off for it, Alice – it's truly amazing.'

It is one of the busiest times in Whitby, with Halloween approaching and the Bram Stoker's *Dracula* connection. Alice knows it's a good time for sales.

'We've been really busy over the last few days.' Faith's lips curl into a smile.

'That's great.' Alice tries for upbeat as she shuffles out of her coat and hangs it on one of the hooks by the back door, wishing she could shake the memories of the police coming through the door in January, telling her the awful news about her father.

Faith touches her arm, and Alice startles, realising she's floated away into her own thoughts. 'It's so good to see you here,' Faith says. 'And, just to say again, I can be out of here, as soon as you're ready to return. Just tell me to sling my hook as soon as you are ready to come back full-time. It will make my day to see you back where you belong.'

Alice shakes her head. 'I'm not quite ready to go full-time yet.

I'll take it slow. As I said before, part-time will suit me to start with. It will give me more time on my artwork.'

'Well, whatever is best for you …' Faith smiles. Tilts her head. 'Coffee?'

'Love one.'

Faith rises, goes to head away. 'Mitch would like to meet you, if you're up for it.'

'What? Why?'

'Because you're my friend, and he's my … It's fine if you don't feel ready. I'll completely understand.'

Panic rises inside Alice. Is she ready to start socialising again? She knows she's got to start somewhere, but she's not sure she wants to begin with a complete stranger.

'I've told him so much about you.' Faith heads through the door into the tiny kitchen area, and Alice is relieved she doesn't have to make a decision right now.

Five minutes later, Faith is back, putting steaming mugs onto the counter. 'Ooh, I meant to say, I sold Gothic House this morning.' Her face lights up with pride, as she peers at Alice from under her fringe and blows on her coffee.

'Wow! That's fantastic. I wondered where it was.'

'Some bloke was waiting for me to open up this morning.' She sits down. 'Said he'd seen a picture of it on Instagram. Cameron something-or-other. Loves your work. Didn't even flinch at the price tag.'

What was the price tag? Alice's gaze drifts to the half-empty shelves. She needs to do more work, and a bubble of motivation rises inside her.

'He said he's one of your followers.' Faith sips her drink. 'He's going to direct message you.'

'Is he? Why?'

Faith shrugs. 'No idea, though he's rather gorgeous.'

'That doesn't answer my question.'

Faith laughs. 'He went over the top about Gothic House. Oh,

and he asked if you based the piece on Flynn House in Suffolk, but I—'

She covers her mouth. How is this all connected?

'Are you OK, sweetie? You look like you've seen a ghost.'

Alice lowers her hand. 'The idea came from …' She's not sure how much to tell Faith about her recurring dreams. 'My imagination,' she says, her voice high and shaky.

The door swings opens, and two young women enter. Suddenly the shop feels too warm. Alice grabs her coat. 'Come on, Henry.' She pats her thigh, and he rises and plods over to her – much happier to go on walks now. 'Good boy,' she adds, fastening his lead.

'You off already?' Faith furrows her forehead.

'I've got a bit of a headache, that's all.'

'Well, how about we meet for a drink later?'

'Maybe. Text me.' Alice raises her hand and heads out of the shop, her mind racing. Who is this Cameron? And, more importantly, what is her own connection to Flynn House?

Chapter 6

Late October 2019

Alice

Alice lies on her yoga mat in the lounge of Butterfly Cottage, dressed in lilac leggings and a black vest top, her eyes closed, her hair loose about her shoulders. This is her favourite bit of her yoga routine: the corpse pose.

She barely needs to hear the instructor on the TV; Alice knows this pose so well. But the woman's voice is comforting, reassuring. 'Surrender to the stillness, stretch those legs, relax those ankles. Let your mind and body combine. Find yourself in a beautiful stillness. *Rest in peace.*'

*

Alice sees Faith pushing through the throng with two glasses. It feels strange being in a crowded bar after not going out much for so long. She fiddles with her watch, her anxiety level high. She needs to beat this. Get her life back on track.

'There you go,' Faith says, handing her a glass of white wine. 'Get that down you.'

Alice takes a gulp, the zesty, dry tang of Sauvignon Blanc on her tongue just what she needs.

Faith sits down opposite, takes a long swig from her pint of lager. She's average height, but small-framed. The glass looks too big for her. She glances at her phone, then towards the door. 'He should be here by around quarter to eight.'

'Sorry?'

'Mitch. I told you he wants to meet you. I hope that's OK.'

Alice puts down her glass, rubs a hand across her mouth. She wants to scream that it's not OK– that Faith hadn't made it clear that Mitch would be joining them this evening. But her friend looks so excited. This is important to her. And Faith has been such a support to Alice, the least she can do is take a long deep breath and meet the man of her dreams.

Faith met Mitch Fisher at a Whitby war weekend battle re-enactment. She sets up stalls on Sundays at festivals and events, selling her homemade jewellery and floral headdresses. He approached her wanting to buy one of her necklaces for his mother's birthday.

'I so want you to meet him,' she says now, screwing up her face, hunching her shoulders. 'If I'm totally honest, he's a bit overwhelmed that your dad was—'

'What? Oh God, Faith, you never said that was the reason.' Alice rubs her neck, takes another gulp of her wine. She doesn't want attention being drawn to who her father was. He would have hated it too. She thought Faith knew that.

'I never told him who you were, Alice, truly I didn't.' Faith puts down her pint. 'He saw you comment on my Facebook status, recognised you from the papers. He's a huge fan of your dad's work. He's read all of his books. I wouldn't have …' Her eyes are wide, glazed.

Alice knows Faith feels bad. She touches her arm. 'Don't worry.

Seriously. It's fine.' But it's far from it. The music, chatter, laughter – all sounds too loud, closing in on her. She wishes she hadn't come.

'Hey, Faith.' The voice booms from across the bar. Alice turns to see Mitch heading towards them, and folds her arms like a barrier. She knows it's him from seeing photos on Faith's Instagram and Facebook accounts. From reading his arrogant, sexist remarks – the latest being that men are put on this planet to dominate – she already knows she doesn't like him.

His dark hair, shot through with strands of grey, is tied back in a stubby ponytail. He's closer to fifty than he looks in his social media photos; he's wide-shouldered – over six foot. His lime-green rain jacket is zipped to the neck, his jeans faded, his leather boots battered.

Faith jumps to her feet as he approaches, rises on tiptoe to kiss his dry lips. She grips his arm as though he might escape, and spins round to face Alice. 'Mitch, Alice; Alice, Mitch.'

His brown eyes meet Alice's, as he shuffles out of his damp jacket, revealing a hooded sweatshirt, and he hangs the jacket over the back of the chair. He reaches out his hand, and Alice unlocks her arms, takes his hand. His palm feels clammy, his fingers yellowing, and as she leans forward a slight waft of smoke reaches her nostrils. 'Good to meet you,' he says.

'You too.' Alice feels uneasy, is desperate to make an excuse and run.

He remains standing, eyes still on Alice. Shoves his hands in his jean pockets. 'I was gutted when I heard your father died.'

'Me too.' She sounds flippant, an attempt to keep her emotions in check.

'I've always been a fan. He was a great author.'

'He was.' Her voice cracks, and Faith takes her hand, squeezes, looks at her, wrinkling her brow.

'Though not everyone thought so, did they?' Mitch continues. 'Guess you can't please everyone.'

'No, Dad accepted that. Everyone has a right to an opinion.'

'True. I wonder what he would have made of The Winslow Touch.'

'The what?'

He's fidgety, his eyes suddenly everywhere, flicking around the crowded bar. 'Dane and Savannah Winslow – influencers – they're big on social media. Review everything from restaurants to small shops, films and books. If they like you, great; if they don't – duck.' He drops down on his haunches, pretending to duck under the table, and laughs. 'I could have punched my laptop screen when I heard them say it was a good thing your father was dead.'

'Mitch, maybe you should get a drink,' Faith says.

'Yeah, right, sure.' He straightens up. 'Anyone in need of a top-up?' He points at their glasses with one hand, and takes his wallet from his pocket with the other. 'Whoa, did you see that moth?' He laughs at his attempt at a joke.

Alice looks at her almost full glass. 'I'm OK.'

'I'll have another pint,' Faith says. 'Good to keep them lined up.'

'Not very feminine, babe.' He screws up his nose, which is a little too big for his face. 'Crisps? Nuts? Pork scratchings?'

They shake their heads.

He makes his way towards the bar, pushing through the throng.

'Well? What do you think?' Faith beams. 'I mean, ignoring what he said about the Winslows. I'm so sorry about that, Alice. He's only angry because he loved your dad's writing so much.'

It was tactless. The man's a moron. 'He seems OK. It's a little too early to tell.'

'OK?' Faith's mouth drops open. 'Oh, Alice, I really want you to like him. Is it because he's older than me?'

'No, of course not, I'm not ageist. Just give me a chance to get to know the guy. I'm sure we'll hit it off.'

'Yes. Sorry.' She grabs Alice's arm and laughs. 'But he is gorgeous, isn't he?'

'I guess so. In a man-bear kind of way.' Alice smiles. 'But it's what's inside that counts anyway, Faith. I know you always think you can change these guys but—'

'Mitch is different. He doesn't need changing. He's got his own business, and it's doing really well.' She's rambling, her eyes locking Alice in a stare. She's making a plea for Alice to say, '*You've snagged a good one this time, Faith. Good on ya!*' But Alice won't. She can't say what she doesn't feel – it's not in her nature. She pulls from her friend's stare, and looks around the crowded bar. Mitch has got in a three-deep queue; he's going to be a while.

It's as her eyes move across the bar, she spots him: *Leon.*

'Oh God.' She lowers her head, and slides down in her seat, as though this movement will make her invisible.

'What?' Faith looks about her. 'Alice, what's up, lovely?'

'It's Leon.'

'Your ex? Where?' She's flicking her eyes in all the wrong places.

'Just behind Mitch,' Alice whispers, 'over there. He's …' The person Leon's with is behind a group of noisy men, and Alice can only see her long, slim arms, ringed fingers placed on Leon's hands. 'He's with someone.'

'Oh yes, I see him.' Faith looks at Alice. 'Are you OK? I know you said—'

'I'm fine.' She forces a smile. 'Honestly.' Alice hasn't seen or heard much from Leon since the funeral. Just a few message exchanges that fizzled and died on the screen. But she still has feelings for him, and at the sight of him with another woman her heart decides to dance to a tune of … *What is this feeling? Envy?*

Within moments, Alice has necked back her wine, and is on her feet. 'Listen, I'm really sorry, Faith. I'm going to have to meet Mitch another time. Do you mind? I've got a rotten headache. Sorry.'

She doesn't wait for a reply. Just grabs her coat, and dashes towards the exit, keeping her eyes to the floor. She'll make it up to Faith another time.

It's raining when she reaches the pavement, breathless, the pub door slamming closed behind her. She hasn't got her car, had planned to have a couple of wines. Faith had said she would drive her home to the cottage – though she noticed her friend was about to have her second pint, so maybe she would have ended up walking anyway.

Alice sold her apartment after her father died, deciding to move to the cottage permanently. She's rarely regretted that decision, Butterfly Cottage giving her comfort, but now she wishes she still lived in the centre of Whitby. A twenty-minute walk doesn't look tempting in the rain.

Rain trickles down her collar, as she shelters under the pub's eaves. She shivers and pulls her phone from her bag. The screen is blank – the battery flat. Calling a taxi is out of the question. Still, maybe the walk – even in the rain – will do her good; clear her head of thoughts of Leon, and whoever he's with. She rummages in her seemingly bottomless rucksack for her umbrella, shoots it up, and, head down, sets out for home.

Leon

Leon looks down at Tegan's clammy, shaky hand resting on his, and tries to absorb the shock of what she's just told him. There's a side to this woman that lurks under the surface that he hadn't seen until tonight. He needs to do something about her revelation.

'Hi there.' He turns to see a woman in dungarees he vaguely recognises. 'Faith,' the woman goes on with a bright smile, pressing her fingers against her chest. 'You're Leon, right?'

'Yes.' Still he can't place where he knows her from, wishes she would move away from the table so he can carry on his conversation. Tegan removes her hands from his. Fidgets as she stares at him with worried, drunken eyes. She's had too much wine. It's why she's offloaded. And now she's volatile.

He shakes his head at Faith, trying not to show the irritation he feels. 'Sorry—'

'Alice's Sculptures in Wonderland.'

'Ah. OK. Yes.' He waves a hand in acknowledgement, presses it to his forehead.

'I'm Alice's friend.'

'Yes. Of course you are, yes, sorry.' He went into the shop in May, hoping to talk to Alice. Suggest a drink or meal. But Faith told him she wasn't working and the weak moment that pulled him in to see her passed. *We're not right for each other. She'll never want children.*

Faith looks towards the door, and nods. 'You just missed Alice. She had a bit of a headache. Left to walk home.'

'Really?' His gaze moves to the door, and back to Faith.

A tall man appears by her side, a double brandy in one hand, half a lager in the other. He hands Faith the lager.

'I asked for a pint,' she says, looking up at him.

'If I wanted to date a bloke, I would turn gay,' he says. 'Plus you're driving, babe.'

Faith rolls her eyes. 'Well it was nice to see you again, Leon,' she says.

The couple head away, and Leon turns back to the table. *Shit.* Tegan's gone. He scans the bar, rises to his feet – searching – but there's no sign of her anywhere.

Alice

Alice has been walking for fifteen minutes when the rain stops. She collapses her umbrella, keeping hold of it in a tight grip as she turns into Sparrow Lane. Just another five minutes and she'll be home.

Within moments, the twisting darkness of the lane swallows her. She can't even use her phone to light the way.

Heavy, fast footsteps approach from behind, splashing in puddles, and a beam of light stretches across the tarmac. She picks up speed, heart pounding as she dashes along the uneven surface, glancing back just once to see a man almost upon her.

'Evening,' he says as he passes – a runner – a torch band around his head. He's at the end of the road and disappears from view before her heart returns to an even beat.

She's never liked Sparrow Lane at night, with its overhanging trees and solid darkness, hated walking down here in her teens. And since her father was found dead against the old oak tree with its gnarled branches, she's liked it even less.

She hurries on, wet leaves squelching under her feet. Two-thirds in, a car pulls into the lane behind her. She glances back, squints, dazzled by its headlights on full beam. She picks up speed, something about the slow pace of the car making her uneasy, making her grip her umbrella like a weapon. The car continues, keeping its distance, the hum of its engine menacing. It pulls into a lay-by, headlights highlighting the reds, yellows and greens of autumn, the scattered shiny conkers – some free, some gripped in their spiky shells.

Alice squints once more, before turning the corner onto Bury Road. Detached bungalows, windows ablaze with light, reassure her as she runs along the pavement, ears tuning in to the sound of a car turning out of Sparrow Lane, moving towards her.

Should she stop?

Confront the driver?

Knock on one the bungalow's doors?

Within moments the car pulls up beside her. The window buzzes down. Her heart thuds like crazy.

'Alice.' A familiar voice. 'I thought it was you.'

Chapter 7

Late October 2019

Alice

'Leon!' Alice's heart gallops, the rapid beat pulsing against her fingers as she grips her chest. 'You scared the crap out of me.'

Leon leans across the passenger seat, blue eyes glinting as he looks up at her. 'It's good to see you too, Alice.'

'Seriously, Leon, what the hell were you doing back there? You freaked me out.'

'Back where? I wasn't a hundred per cent sure it was you, if that's what you mean.'

'So that makes it OK?'

'Makes what OK?' He shakes his head. 'Faith mentioned you left the pub to walk home, and—'

'And … what? You followed me like some creepy stalker?' She wasn't sure why she was so upset. But he'd scared her. He pulled into the lay-by, watched her from a distance. *Why had he done that?*

He looks bewildered. 'I've no idea what you're talking about.'

'Back there.' She points towards Sparrow Lane. 'You dazzled me with your headlights.'

'Nope! I didn't see you in Sparrow Lane. Only caught sight of you when I turned the corner.'

She looks back to where she ran from. 'Someone was there … watching me.' Or had someone simply pulled into the lay-by to check their phone or something? Was she acting paranoid? Being unfair on Leon?

'Well it wasn't me.' He looks behind him. 'Do you want me to check it out? See if someone's there?'

'We could both go, maybe.'

'OK.' He stretches across the seat further, flings open the car door. She climbs in, closes the door behind her, and clicks the seatbelt. She feels safe beside him, despite her outburst. How could she have thought he would lie to her? Watch her? Leon's one of the good guys.

Without a word, he spins the car around in the road. Turns right into Sparrow Lane.

'Whoever it was pulled in there.' She points towards the empty lay-by. 'Did you see anyone when you drove up here?'

He shakes his head, and shrugs. 'Not that I noticed.'

'They may have turned out their lights.'

'Why?'

He was right. She was being ridiculous.

He sighs deeply. 'This is where it happened, isn't it? Where they found your dad?'

She looks down at her hands, wanting him to take her in his arms, tell her everything is OK. 'I didn't imagine the car, Leon. If that's what you're saying.'

'Of course you didn't. But this place holds awful memories for you.' He turns the car round in the narrow lane. 'I'll take you home, shall I?'

*

41

'Thanks,' she says, as Leon pulls onto the drive outside Butterfly Cottage. 'So, why were you in Sparrow Lane?' she asks, looking at him.

'I told you. Faith said you'd just left the pub, and I got to thinking about you – us.'

'Faith,' she says, smiling at her friend's clear attempt at match-making.

Leon looks at the steering wheel, then at her. 'I wanted to see you, Alice. Talk to you. There are things you need to know.'

'Like, who you were with earlier?'

'You saw that?' He moves from her gaze.

'Sorry, it's none of my business. You have every right—'

'It was Tegan.'

'Tegan Matthews?'

He nods and shrugs. 'A while back, she said she was interested in my book—'

'Ah, I see. That makes sense. That's good though, isn't it?'

'I guess. We're friends, nothing more.'

'You don't owe me an explanation, Leon. You have every right to be seeing someone.' She turns, climbs out of the car. She hasn't seen Tegan since her father's funeral. A couple of emails flew into her inbox in the weeks following that awful day, but that was it – *so much for having her back.*

She bends, looks back into the car. 'Good luck with your book,' she says. She needs to get away from him, slams the door, heads towards the house.

'Wait up, Alice.' He's out of the car too. Within moments, he's pulling her to him; she doesn't resist. His lips brush against hers. She loves this man. She always has. And tonight she's going to allow herself to be loved.

'I've missed you, Alice,' he says.

*

42

The next morning Leon lies beside her, face wedged in the pillow, his tanned muscular back rising and falling as he sleeps. One arm dangles over the edge of the bed; the other stretches above his head, as though swimming through his dreams.

She throws back the patchwork quilt and pulls herself upright. This was her bedroom growing up, and she loves every square inch of it.

She swings her legs round, slips her feet into her slippers and pads towards the window. Behind the curtains a charcoal-grey sky threatens over Whitby Abbey, the early morning mist surrounding the black tombstones.

Her breath catches at the sight of the Gothic ruins overlooking the sea that inspired Bram Stoker to write *Dracula*.

Leon stirs, and, not wanting to talk right now, Alice leaves the room.

In the shower, soapy water strips away the smell of him from her skin. She has no regrets, but knows they are still miles away from each other with what they want from life – what they want from the future.

Downstairs, Henry plods across the kitchen towards her, tail wagging in a greeting.

'Hello, lovely boy.' She crouches down to snuggle him for a few moments, before opening the back door to let him out.

She plugs in her phone to charge, and once she's made some coffee, she picks up her mug and steps outside into the cool air. 'Henry?' she calls, her eyes flicking over the untidy garden. 'Where are you?'

He appears, a stick in his mouth, and runs towards her, clearly hoping she'll throw it for him. She prises it from his mouth, and lobs the stick. The dog bounds across the mass of weeds. She used to keep the garden reasonable in her teens, but when she moved out, her father let it go.

'I don't want a gardener,' her father said, when she suggested the idea. 'I don't like people.' It always made her smile when he

43

came out with such harsh words. He was an amazing man and *people* would have loved him, if he'd only let them in.

Henry appears to have lost interest in the stick, and is now sniffing along the back fence. Alice turns and heads back into the kitchen, where she fires up her laptop, and picks up her phone, now ten per cent charged. There's a WhatsApp message from Faith:

I spoke to Leon briefly. If you need to talk I'm here. And I really hope Mitch didn't upset you mentioning the Winslows. X

Alice smiles and answers that she's fine.

A speedy response from Faith:

I'll be over later to make sure ☺ x

Truth is, Mitch had been a complete idiot bringing up The Winslows, and Faith bringing it up again isn't helping. It was something she would have rather not known, and now they are fresh in her mind once more.

She heaves herself onto a stool, and keys 'The Winslow Touch' into the search engine on her laptop. Mitch was right – the couple are all over social media. She adds her father's name, and finds a YouTube link, hovers her finger over it, biting down on her lip. Does she really want to hear this couple pulling her father apart? *No.* But her curiosity is too much. She clicks the link.

Dane and Savannah Winslow are beautiful people in their late twenties. They're sitting on a velvet sofa, holding tall flutes of champagne, and tucking into canapés. Savannah's red hair is tied in a messy knot; she's pale, heavily made-up, wearing a sports jacket over a white T-shirt. Dane gives off a sexy vibe, legs spread wide. He's black, lean, muscular, and wearing a navy, clingy silk shirt.

Alice watches and listens as the duo pull her father's books apart. She's heard this kind of thing before. It goes with the territory, her father always said. But then the couple get nasty. Laying into him personally. His appearance – *no wonder he was in hiding with those freaky eyes.* His personality – *he was obviously* some total weirdo hidden away like that. Wouldn't be surprised if he was hiding something dark – really dark, if you catch my drift.

'Good thing he's dead, I reckon,' Savannah concludes, 'spares us having to put up with any more of his books.'

A lump catches in Alice's throat, and tears burn when she sees how many people have viewed the post. She glances at the spiteful comments below, the cruel implications, and anger bubbles. But she's not only angry with this ridiculous couple, she's also angry with her father for dying. That he left her with so many unanswered questions.

A ping on her phone alerts her that someone has sent her a direct message on Instagram. She opens her account on her laptop.

The message is from someone called Cameron88, and she remembers Faith telling her about the man who bought Gothic House. She clicks to accept the message:

Hello, Alice. I hope you don't mind me contacting you. I came across your Instagram account quite by chance, when hunting for things to buy for Flynn Hotel, and couldn't believe my luck when I saw your sculpture. You must have really studied the building to get it so perfect in every way.

I'm the owner of the hotel, and am pleased to say the sculpture now stands proudly in reception.

I would very much like to meet you, and have attached details of a double room pre-booked and paid for in your name for next weekend – please do come if you can.

Here is the website if you would like a further look: www.flynnhouseeast.co.uk

Best wishes, Cameron Patterson.

P.S. There are photos of Flynn Hotel on my Instagram account if you would like to have a look – along with a picture of my new acquisition – your wonderful piece.

She clicks onto his Instagram account, where there are reams of photos of Flynn Hotel. The Gothic building stands on a cliff edge, with a steep, high roof rising to a point, and arched windows. Grooved vaulting, flying buttresses, and a large statue of a dog make the red-brick building unique. This is exactly what Alice created, what the place looked like in the black and white photograph she received – what the place looked like in her dreams.

The latest picture on Cameron's feed is of her sculpture standing on a black-wood dresser. She hovers her finger over the like button for a moment, before clicking it.

She closes Instagram, and opens the hotel's website where a photo of Cameron Patterson smiles out from the screen. He's around thirty, with strawberry-blond hair, and a confident glow. There's a quote in Gothic font saying *'A hotel experience you'll never forget.'* Another click takes her to a photo gallery, with amazing pictures of each room – some she's already seen on Cameron's Instagram profile. There's a promise of isolation and authentic Gothic surroundings – the causeway to the mainland only available for four hours a day. The hotel is on Seafield Island in Dunwold, Suffolk, along the coast between Southwold and Lowestoft. *Dunwold?* The restaurant receipt she found in the tobacco tin was from Dunwold.

Alice goes on a clicking frenzy. A lover of Gothic, she gets this place; can see why people would go there – especially at Halloween – but at the same time it's unnerving how familiar the outside of the building is. She wonders if she's seen the hotel on TV, perhaps advertised on a holiday programme, or even used as a film location. Then why had someone sent her the photo of the place? Why had her father hated her sculpture so much? Why does she feel she's been there before?

'Morning.'

She turns to see Leon in his boxers and a crumpled white T-shirt, running a hand across his stubbled chin, his fair hair pillow-tousled. She observes the taut muscles in his arms, before turning away. 'Coffee?'

'Please.'

Henry bounds in through the back door, and greets Leon like a long-lost friend. 'Hello there, boy,' he says, ruffling the dog's ears. He approaches the breakfast bar, and Henry follows, nails tip-tapping the quarry tiles.

'Weird place,' he says looking over her shoulder at the laptop screen.

'It's Flynn Hotel, on the Suffolk coast.' She rises and grabs a mug from the cupboard.

Leon looks suddenly awkward, as though he's not sure if he should stay or go. He folds his arms high across his chest. 'Looks like the kind of place you'd love.'

'Mmm. I thought that too.' She makes him some coffee, hands it to him. Wants to say so much more. 'In fact, the owner's invited me to go next weekend.'

Leon's eyes widen as he takes a sip of his drink. 'Why?'

'I made a sculpture many years ago. The owner thought it looked like the hotel and bought it.'

'And he invited you to stay because of that?'

'Mmm, it's an extreme gesture.'

'Yeah. Will you go?' His eyes narrow, searching her face.

The truth is, she desperately wants to go. The place is pulling her – begging her to visit. She feels certain she knows the place, that she may find answers there, a connection to her father, perhaps. But, on the other hand, it all feels a bit strange: the anonymous card with the tiger on the front, the photograph of Flynn House, a mysterious man turning up and buying her sculpture, inviting her to the hotel. She's only just ventured out properly since her father's death. Would she even be able to cope?

'Alice?'

'Sorry. No. God no,' she says with a shake of her head.

Their eyes meet, the buzz between them tangible. 'Last night,' she says. 'It was a mistake, right? We want different things, and—'

The chime of the doorbell cuts her off.

'That'll be Faith,' she says, heading for the door, glancing back over her shoulder. 'Maybe it would be best if ...'

He raises his hand, puts down the mug. 'I get it.' He moves past her, his body radiating warmth, and the aroma of sleep. He pauses, touches her cheek, kisses her lips softly. 'I'll sneak out the back way, once I've grabbed my jeans. I'll be gone before we can wish things were different.'

She doesn't want him to go. Seeing him – sleeping with him – has opened up old feelings she thought she came to terms with a long time ago. She wants to talk to him, work this out, but knows if Faith sees him, she will bombard her with questions she doesn't know the answers to herself.

He leaves the room, and she listens for his heavy footfalls on the stairs before making her way to the front door.

Faith stands on the doorstep, staring away from Alice at Leon's car on the driveway next to her Fiat 500. She turns, swinging her ponytail, and smiles; touches Alice's arm. 'Morning, sweetie, how are you?'

'I'm OK.' She fiddles with her earring as Faith stares into her eyes, as though searching for secrets. 'Honestly, I'm totally fine.'

'I was worried when you took off last night. I tried to call—'

'My phone died.'

Faith's eyes are back on the car. 'Got visitors, have we?'

Alice shakes her head, her mind whirring for a way to explain the black Audi on the drive. 'It's the gardener.'

'You've taken on a gardener?' She glances again at the car.

Alice scratches her neck, feeling a rush of guilt for lying. 'Well, I haven't actually taken him on yet … he's just having a look out back so he can give me a quote.' She grabs her friend's arm and yanks her inside. 'Come in for goodness' sake, you're letting the cold in.'

Alice leads the way into the kitchen.

'I'm so sorry again about Mitch—'

'It's fine, please don't worry.'

'He was disappointed that he didn't get to meet you properly.' Faith eases herself onto a stool.

'Another time, maybe.' Alice grabs a mug, spoons in some coffee.

'Wow!' Faith's eyes are on the laptop screen. 'That place looks incredible. It's just like your sculpture.'

'I know. Amazing, isn't it?' Alice moves to the screen, and they stare – mesmerised. 'The bloke who bought it owns the place. It's a hotel, apparently.'

Faith pulls the laptop closer to her. 'It looks … God, I don't know how to describe it.'

Alice nods and smiles. 'Yeah, it really does.'

'So is this where you got the idea for your sculpture?'

'I guess so. I must have seen it on TV, or something.'

'Wow, I'd love to go there.'

'Mmm, well it's certainly intriguing.'

Faith looks up, her eyes locking on Alice's. 'Maybe we could go together sometime.'

'Well, as it happens, the owner sent me complementary tickets.'

'What? Why? Wow!'

'You forgot *when*?'

Faith grins. 'When?'

'Next weekend.'

'What?'

Alice laughs.

'And at Halloween too. Are you going to go?' She touches Alice's arm gently. 'It might do you good to get away. Maybe I could book a room too, come with you?'

'That would be lovely.' Alice's head whirs with the thought of it, wanting to tell Faith about the photo, the strange pull of the place. 'But what about the shop?'

'Oh God. I hadn't thought of that.'

'Listen, if you fancy going,' Alice says, turning to pour boiling water into the mug. 'I'll cover the shop. In fact, why not take my room. I won't be using it anyway.'

Faith furrows her forehead, looks back at the screen. 'That's far too generous, Alice. Are you sure you wouldn't like to go?'

Alice shakes her head, deciding it would be too much. 'I will visit at some point,' she says, 'but not right now. Halloween is the busiest time in Whitby. You go, Faith. I'm happy to run the shop.' The confidence in her voice surprises her. She stirs the coffee, hands it to Faith.

'Well, if you're really, really sure,' Faith says.

'I am, honestly. It will be great to hear what you think of it.'

'Mitch will love it and it's his birthday next weekend.'

The back door clicks closed. Leon's left; but Faith is so engrossed in what's on the screen, she doesn't seem to notice.

Alice gets up the booking confirmation, and is about to print it off when she notices the small print. 'Oh for God's sake.'

'What?'

'This room,' she says. 'It's non-transferable.' She looks up from the screen. 'Sorry.'

'No, honestly, it's OK. In fact …' She opens her bag, and pulls out an old till receipt, flattens it out. 'Got a pen?'

Alice roots around in a pot on the work surface, and hands her one.

'It's short notice,' she says, scribbling down the web address. 'But I'm going to see if I can get booked in for next weekend anyway. I'm all hyped now, and it's the perfect gift for Mitch.'

Alice can't help thinking it's over-generous, but Faith sounds so excited she says nothing.

'If you're really sure you don't mind me taking time off?' Faith says.

'I don't mind at all.' But as Alice says the words, she knows she won't be able to get the place out of her head.

Chapter 8

Halloween Weekend 2019

Alice

It's Friday, the first day of the Whitby Goth Weekend.

At 8.30 a.m., Alice pulls into the long-stay car park, rain bouncing off the roof of her Mazda as though it's taken up tap-dancing. She finds a space, and kills the engine.

It will be the first time she's sat alone behind the counter at 'Alice's Sculptures in Wonderland' since her dad died, but she's certain it's the right time – *she can do this*. She glances in the rear-view mirror at Henry sitting upright in the back, alert, ears pricked, as he looks about him. He will be with her – support her.

It's been half an hour since Faith called, her voice full of excitement, to say she and Mitch were about to head to Flynn Hotel. And Alice had been so close to suggesting closing the shop and joining them – taking Cameron up on his offer. But today and tomorrow will be the busiest days of the year in Whitby. She can't afford to miss sales. Yes, her dad left her a fortune and his cottage, plus his books keep paying royalties, but her sculptures are what she does for herself – her identity. She needs to grip hold of that once more with both hands.

The rain eases, and she gets out of the car, collects a ticket from the machine.

Once Henry's out of the back, wagging his tail, she locks the car, pulls up the hood of her rain jacket, and heads into the town centre.

She hurries past the antique shop. The ventriloquist doll is still there, looking out at her from between the glossy brown Beswick horse and the mustard-yellow art-deco vase. She waves, doubting her sanity for a nanosecond.

The rain stops as she turns the key in the shop door. 'Typical,' she says to Henry, who shakes raindrops from his coat.

It's cold inside, so she dashes through to the kitchen, puts the coffee machine on, and flicks on the radiator, before filling a bowl with water for Henry.

At the counter, a warm mug between her palms, her eyes flick towards the bay window. She startles. A middle-aged couple dressed in black stare in at her. The man is wearing a top hat and cloak, the woman a bustled dress made from satin. Alice's heart thuds, despite knowing they are here for the Whitby Goth Weekend. She should be used to the streets being flooded with people in ghoulish fancy dress and make-up over Halloween; she's seen it year after year. It normally gives her a buzz. In fact, one year she dressed as a vampire, and loved how her customers reacted.

The couple push open the door and smile and nod her way. There's barely room for the woman to turn in her magnificent costume, which is more navy than black close-up and has a slight aroma, as though it's been stored in a musty chest for a hundred years. His top hat almost touches the ceiling as they admire Alice's zombie sculpture.

'We might come back later,' he says, buying a piece of Faith's jewellery: a silver serpent bracelet.

The woman links her arm through his, and as he goes to

open the door, Leon strides in, almost bumping into the couple. Henry greets him with a woof and a wag of his tail and half his body.

Alice hasn't seen Leon since Sunday morning when he sneaked out the back door to avoid bumping into Faith, but he's texted several times. They both agreed to keep things light. *We want different things. We're not right for each other. But there's no reason we can't be friends.* The trouble is her heart says it's so much more than that, but she's got to hold back.

She told him she would be working today, that this was her first day in the shop alone since her dad died, and by the look of the two takeaway coffees he's holding in his woolly-gloved hands, he's here to support her. She loves him for that.

'I thought you'd need this.' He looks awkward as he plonks the cups on the counter, and pulls himself up onto a stool, his eyes on her. 'But I can see you've already got one.'

'Thanks.' She pulls from his gaze. Runs her hand over one of the cups. 'I'll manage both. I need my caffeine fix.'

'Have you heard from Faith?' he goes on, pulling off his gloves and unwinding his scarf from his neck. 'Has she arrived at the hotel?'

'She took off around eight this morning. I'm sure she'll let me know, when she gets a chance.'

'We should go there sometime.' He falters. 'As friends, if that's what you want.'

'Leon, I—'

The door swings open and a woman in a long white satin dress, her face painted to look skeletal, her hair white – a wig probably – enters. 'Your shop is bloody amazing.' She has a Scottish accent, smiles – at least Alice thinks it's a smile.

*

54

Leon stays all day. It's been almost impossible, being so close to him as they sat behind the counter, the woody aroma of his familiar aftershave evoking memories of their early relationship – days spent by the sea; whole days in bed; the candlelight supper he made her in the early weeks that burnt, and they ended up ordering a takeaway. Alice doubts herself now, tries to recall the reasons she pushed him away.

It's been busy though, so they've barely talked; a stomach-churning tension in the air between them, not helped by her invasive thoughts of Flynn House.

By 4 p.m., Alice has sold nearly all her artwork. The shelves are empty, and her resolve to open the shop on Saturday and Sunday wavers. There's little point when she has nothing to sell. Maybe she could work on her latest sculpture over the weekend instead. She hasn't got very far with it, but the plan is in place, fixed in her mind. It's going to be three ventriloquist puppets enjoying a macabre tea party.

Leon heads off at five, brushing a kiss across her cheek before he leaves, lingering for just a moment, before grabbing his jacket. Ten minutes later she fastens Henry's lead. She's about to lock up when a text appears on her phone from Faith:

Oh my God, Alice. You wouldn't believe this place. It's amazing! Scary in a good way. Totally fascinating. You would love it. Please, please come! I love Mitch, but not as much as you. X

Alice laughs and replies:

So glad you love it! I'm not jealous at all! Have you seen my sculpture yet? X

A smiley face pings back, and then another message:

YES! It's in reception. It looks amazing. And there's something else – a painting in the restaurant of a young man who looks so like your dad, even has his amazing eyes! X

Another ping follows. An attachment.

Alice gasps, taking in the photograph. The portrait doesn't only look like her dad, she feels certain it's him when he was young. Central heterochromia – one blue, one green eye – is so rare, and the resemblance to her father is uncanny.

*

Alice and Leon sit by a flickering fire in the Black Squirrel, a pub just outside Whitby, a favourite haunt when they were a couple. Henry is sprawled on the rug in front of them. The sound of The Cranberries plays softly in the background, and a comforting smell of home cooking lingers in the air.

Alice's fingers dance on her phone screen. 'Here,' she says, eyes wide as she hands Leon her phone, the portrait Faith sent frozen on the screen.

He stares for some moments.

'Well?' She takes a gulp of her gin and tonic. 'What do you think?'

'It looks like him. The eyes mainly.' He slides his gaze from the phone to her. 'But it can't be him can it?'

'I don't know.' Her voice cracks, as she takes the phone back. 'It's so like him. But if it is, how did it end up on the wall of a hotel in Suffolk? A hotel I just happen to have been invited to stay at?' She shakes her head. 'This is all too weird.'

'Perhaps your dad had it painted when he was younger and it ended up in an antique shop or something, and the bloke who owns the hotel picked it up because it suited the house. Just like your sculpture.'

'I don't believe in weird coincidences. And Dad was practically a hermit all his life. Why would he have had a painting done, and then get rid of it?' She looks once more at the screen, before putting her phone face down on the table.

'I agree it's odd.'

Alice takes another gulp of her drink, the spirit warming her throat. 'I mean, me making a sculpture identical to the hotel, and the owner inviting me to stay is odd enough. But now there's a picture of a man who looks just like my dad when he was young on the wall there.' She pauses, recalling her dad's strange reaction to her sculpture of Gothic House. 'And there's this.' She fishes the photo she was sent from her bag, hands over the black and white picture of Flynn House. 'It came through the post.'

Leon narrows his eyes, as he studies the grand Gothic building so close to the cliff edge.

'It looks a bit creepy,' he says, turning it over.

She takes a deep breath. Since receiving the attachment from Faith, she's known she has to go there, that the place holds some of the answers she's craved all her life. 'I need to go to Flynn Hotel, Leon. Will you come with me?'

He stares for a moment, his eyes asking her if it's a good idea. She claps her hands together as though praying. 'Please.'

'When?'

'Now.'

'Now?' He hands back the photo. 'Now?'

'Tomorrow then? I've got the free room. We could leave first thing in the morning.'

'But what about the shop? Isn't this your busiest time?'

'Yes. Normally. But you saw how empty the shelves were by the end of today. I've barely done any new work since Dad died.' She leans forward, her emotions controlling her words. 'I need to go there, Leon. Please come with me. You know I have so few childhood memories, that my father kept things close.' Her voice cracks up a notch, trembles a little. 'That sometimes I feel I never knew him at all.' She buries her face in her hands for a moment, before adding, 'I can't explain it, but it's as though Flynn Hotel holds the key. I've got to go there, Leon, and I'd rather not be alone.' She doesn't want to beg, but she will, if she has to.

He bites down on his lip. 'OK.'

'OK?' She flings her arms around his neck. Holds him close for a moment, then releases him. 'Thank you.'

He glances down at Henry, who seems to be listening, sitting upright now, watching them.

'Oh God. Henry,' she says, covering her mouth. 'Maybe we could take him with us.'

'Or my parents could look after him. You know what they're like – the more dogs the merrier.'

Alice feels a pang. She loves Leon's parents, and misses not seeing them. They always made a fuss of her. Made her feel welcome. She loved her dad with every part of her, but her upbringing had been far from typical. She never doubted her father loved her, but she would have given anything to have a brother or sister, cousins, grandparents – a mother; more noise – more life – within the quiet walls of Butterfly Cottage.

The normality of Leon's life was always refreshing: two sisters, two dogs, a dad who taught at the local primary school, a mum who worked as a classroom assistant. Alice loved being part of their world. *If only Leon hadn't pushed for marriage and kids, if it could have stayed just the two of us.*

'Do you think they would mind?' she says. 'Henry's no trouble. But it seems a bit cheeky.'

'They won't mind at all. We can drop him off in the morning.' He shrugs, looks down at the menu. 'Now can we order some food? I'm starving.'

Chapter 9

Halloween Weekend 2019

Alice

Leon's parents' spaniels race to greet Henry, tails spinning like sycamore seeds caught in the wind.

Leon closes the back gate behind him, as Alice strokes the dogs, telling them how gorgeous they are.

'It's so good to see you, Alice,' Leon's mum calls from the back door. She's wearing her usual black leggings, faded at the knees, and a thigh-length sweater, her silver-grey hair pinned up loosely, her face stretched into a wide smile. Within moments she's dashing up the neat garden towards Alice, her arms wide.

'It's good to see you too, Laura,' Alice says rising from fussing the dogs, and falling into the woman's arms, enjoying the warmth of them closing around her. There was no doubting Laura and Joe had hoped Alice and Leon would get married one day, have children.

Laura releases Alice and stares deep into her eyes. 'We were so sorry to hear about your dad, sweetheart.'

'Thanks.' Alice wishes the mention of his name didn't still have the power to reduce her to tears. She coughs to clear her throat, and Leon puts his arm on her back, as though keeping her upright. Laura is simply being loving and supportive, as always – his parents are the kindest people she knows. 'And thank you for the card and flowers.'

'You are more than welcome.' Laura touches Alice's arm, before turning her attention to her son, giving him an equally big hug. 'Have you got time for a cheeky brew? Something to eat?'

'We've had breakfast, Mum, and we should probably head off,' Leon says, as they step into the kitchen, the smell of recently cooked bacon in the air. 'It's a long journey.'

'And the tide is only out between midday and four,' Alice adds, as Joe appears, a hands-free magnifier around his head.

'Alice,' he says, and more hugs ensue. 'How are you, love?'

'I'm good thanks. You?'

'Better since I retired.'

'You're retired already?' She knew he was counting down the days to when he left the junior school where he worked for thirty years, but it had seemed ages away when she last visited with Leon. It makes her painfully aware of the time she's been away from him.

Joe nods. 'And I'm loving every minute. I'm not saying I don't miss the little monsters, but the time was right to hang up my cane.'

'Joe!' Laura says, and rolls her eyes.

'What's with the magnifier, Dad?' Leon opens the fridge door, and peers inside like a teenager searching for food. 'Ooh, fairy cakes.'

'Don't touch those, they're for your nieces. They're coming later.' Laura smiles. 'I've got biscuits, if you're hungry.'

Leon pulls a face, and closes the fridge door. 'So, what's with the magnifier?' he repeats.

'Your dad's taken up stamp collecting,' Laura says.

60

'I have indeed.' Joe nods. He's shorter than Leon, and always seems to be dressed in polo shirts and knee-length shorts, whatever the weather. 'It keeps me off the streets.'

Henry and the spaniels suddenly barge through the kitchen like a herd of buffalo, and into the lounge. 'Oh God, Henry's made them excited,' Alice says. 'Are you sure you're OK to look after him?'

'Of course – he'll be no problem at all.' Laura smiles. 'They'll calm down soon enough.'

'Well, we'd better love you and leave you then, Mum,' Leon says, placing his hand on the back door.

'Where are you off to?' Joe asks, as they head into the garden.

'Suffolk,' Alice says. 'An island just off the coast of Dunwold.'

'How lovely,' Laura says. 'We used to holiday in Southwold when you were young, Leon. Do you remember the multi-coloured beach huts, and the gorgeous pier?'

'I do, Mum. Good times.' Leon nods, and leans down to kiss his Mum's cheek. 'We'll pick Henry up on Monday, if that's OK.'

'Of course, no problem at all.'

'I hope he behaves OK,' Alice says, as the dogs dash into the garden as one.

*

'Hey, Faith, me again, we should be at the hotel around two.' It's the third time Alice has left a voicemail. 'I hope you picked up my other messages, and everything is OK. See you soon, lovely. Can't wait.' She ends the call, and turns to Leon, whose eyes are glued to the heavy traffic building on the A1. 'I still can't get hold of Faith,' she says, moving her gaze up towards the dark sky that looks like a duvet over the motorway.

'She's busy having fun with her bloke, I expect,' Leon says, running a hand over his chin.

'Mitch?' She thinks of the man she met a week ago. 'Maybe.'

61

She bites her bottom lip hard. Turns her phone over in her hands, a weird sense of unease she can't quite explain washing over her. 'But, that's the third time I've called. I texted her last night too, to let her know we were coming, and nothing – zilch. It's not like her, Leon. She would normally send me a stream of smiling emojis and a couple of hearts.'

'Perhaps there's no signal on the island.'

Alice shrugs. 'But she texted me yesterday from there – sent me the picture.'

'Well … maybe the signal's erratic. Why are you making a big thing of it?' He tightens his grip on the steering wheel.

'I'm really not.'

'Yep, you are.' She remembers this side of Leon. He's clearly hungry. She pulls a bag of crisps from her bag. 'Call the hotel if it's bugging you.'

'It's really not bugging me, Leon.' She tries for a smile, opens the crisps, and shoves a handful into his mouth.

'You know me so well,' he says with a laugh, once he's finished munching.

'Are we on target to get there for two?' She glances at the satnav.

'Should be. I'm guessing there's a car park.'

'Yes, on the mainland. We're to park up, and call the hotel. Someone will collect us.'

Leon suddenly brakes hard, and throws his hands in the air. 'Christ, look at this.'

The traffic is stopping, red brake lights flashing everywhere. As they come to a halt, hail, the size of marbles, clatters against the windscreen. 'Looks as though we could be stuck here for a while,' Leon says, taking the bag of crisps from Alice. 'Did you bring a book? Playing cards? Game of Cluedo?'

*

'Alice!' She can hear Leon's voice, but struggles to free herself from her vivid dream, where she's being pulled up a staircase towards a red door. She can't escape. 'We're almost there, Alice … Alice?'

With determination, she opens her eyes, looks up at Leon, and out of the car window at the darkness. 'God!' She pulls up in the seat. 'What's the time?'

'Gone six.'

An accident on the A1 stole four hours of their day. Alice tries to console herself that it was far worse for the poor souls in the minibus that ended up on its side.

As the incredible sight of Flynn Hotel comes into view, a chill trails down her spine, and a strong sense of foreboding washes over her. Should they turn the car round? She looks at Leon. His eyes are fixed on the windscreen as he manoeuvres the final country road. He glances at her and smiles. She's being ridiculous. And anyway, he would probably kill her if she suggested going home now.

There's no doubting it's a stunning view from the mainland, every window of Flynn Hotel lit by an orange glow. The place is balanced on the cliff edge, as though with one nudge it would topple into the restless sea below.

Leon pulls into the clearly signposted car park, where five other cars are parked – Alice recognises Faith's Fiat – she's here, *thank God.*

'Do you reckon we'll meet the Addams family while we're here?' Leon says with a smile, as he pulls on the handbrake.

Alice laughs, grateful for his humour, for being here with her. He kills the engine. 'So what now?'

The shimmering sea separates them from Seafield Island, the causeway covered by the ocean. 'I'm guessing we call the hotel.' She shrugs, peers out of the side window. 'Yes, look.' She points at the contact number on a sign, and takes her phone from her rucksack. She dials the number, holds the phone between her shoulder and ear while rummaging for the paperwork she printed off before she left.

A female voice answers. 'Flynn Hotel, Christine speaking. How may I help you?'

'Oh … hi, this is Alice Hadley. I have a room for tonight and tomorrow—'

'Ah, yes, hello, Miss Hadley, we've been expecting you.'

'We got stuck in traffic, so—'

'No worries at all.' She sounds pleasant and friendly, has a broad Suffolk accent. 'Are you at the car park?'

'Yes, we are.'

'We?'

'Yes, I've come with my … friend. I hope that's OK. Cameron said it was a double room.'

'Of course, no problem at all. I will head over in the boat right away. Should be with you in ten.'

'That's great, thank you.'

'You're very welcome.' She ends the call.

Alice looks across at Leon, and lets out a breath. 'Well, she seems nice enough.'

Leon takes hold of her hand, and furrows his forehead. 'Are you OK? You were dreaming back there. Crying out—'

'A bit nervous, I guess, but fine. Honestly.' Her eyes skitter towards the house on the cliff edge once more. She thinks of her sculpture, the picture Faith sent of the man who looks so like her dad, the photo that was sent to her, the receipt for a restaurant in Dunwold she found in the loft. Suddenly the sirens she heard on the A1 earlier seem to ring in her ears – loud and piercing – and tears she can't quite explain burn behind her eyes. Doubts rise, and she hears her father's voice in her subconscious.

'You shouldn't have come, Alice. I told you to never come back. Go home. Go home now.'

PART TWO

'I am older than you, and must know better.'
Lewis Carroll

Chapter 10

Halloween Weekend 2019

Alice

A powerboat propels through the dark sea, a stream of white surf trailing.

'They're on their way.' Leon climbs from the car, opens the boot, and grabs their holdalls.

Alice takes a deep breath, gets out too, and together – avoiding the many puddles – they head down a slope towards a small jetty lit by swaying lanterns.

'Welcome,' a portly woman, who looks to be in her fifties, calls over the wind. Waving from the boat, arm swishing to and fro, like a windscreen wiper. She's wearing a beanie and sturdy anorak, a scarf wrapped around the lower part of her face. She slows the boat down and aims it towards the jetty, cutting the engine, though leaving the lights on. She climbs out, pulling the mooring rope hard so the white vessel rattles against the wooden planks of the jetty. The sea gurgles and splashes. 'I'm Christine,

Manager of Flynn Hotel,' she says, pulling the scarf from her face, and holding out her hand.

'We're sorry we're later than expected,' Alice says as she shakes the woman's hand. 'There was an accident, and—'

'No worries at all; that's what the boat is for. Have you come far?'

'Whitby.'

After shaking Leon's hand, Christine rubs her hands together as though to warm them up, despite her gloves. 'Lovely place, Whitby,' she says, grabbing their holdalls and putting them in the back of the boat.

Once they are all safely on board, Christine starts the engine once more. 'You'll have to bear with me,' she says, as they pull out from the jetty. 'I only started working at the hotel on Thursday – the day before we opened, in fact.'

'You've only just opened?' Alice looks at Leon, and he shrugs. She hadn't realised.

'Yes. You're Cameron Patterson's first guests. Though he hasn't set foot outside of his cottage on the other side of the island since I arrived. I've received most of my instructions by email.' Alice observes once more the woman's broad accent. 'It's all a bit suck-it-and-see, if you get my meaning. Anyway, enough of my moaning – you haven't come all this way to listen to my problems.' She lets out a strange little laugh.

There's something about the fast-talking woman, the twang of anxiety in her voice, that isn't helping Alice's own jitters about staying over, but she knows it's far too late to change her mind. 'It looks incredible,' she says, unable to tear her eyes from the splendour of the building. It's exactly like the photographs online, the picture she received in the post, how she saw the place in her dreams, yet somehow more haunting. 'Amazing.'

'Oh yes, you'll love it.' Christine nods. 'It has five guest bedrooms – boutique they call it, don't they? And I pretty much do everything. There's Gabriela, of course, who thankfully turned up like some kind of angel on Thursday afternoon asking for work. She tends to the bar, and cleans the rooms. Sweet girl. Though, between you and me, she barely speaks a word of English. Oh dear, I'm not really selling the place, am I? You'll be diving over the side and swimming for the mainland, if I don't stop.'

'It's fine, I'm sure we'll have a brilliant time,' Leon says, gripping Alice's hand, and they exchange a smile.

'I do hope so.' Christine nods several times. 'Just wait until you see inside. It's a cracking place. Mr Patterson bought it in 2017, and renovated the building to a very high standard.'

She revs the engine, and as they speed through the darkness towards the imposing building, the wind whips Alice's hair across her face, and a chill grips her spine.

'We're meeting a friend here,' Alice says. 'I wondered if—'

'All expected guests have arrived,' Christine says, steering the boat towards a similar jetty to the one on the mainland, lined with lit pumpkins, and swinging lanterns. There's a shed nearby, and a steep hill – lined with more lanterns – leads up to the hotel. An expanse of grass in front of large patio windows takes you to the cliff edge, and a pathway leads towards a wooded area. 'Right, here we are then.' Christine helps them onto dry land, surprisingly strong for a small woman, and hands them their holdalls. She moors the boat, then, with quick strides, makes her way up the hill towards the hotel, her head down against the wind. 'I'll go on,' she calls. 'Get ready for you.'

Alice and Leon stare up at the hotel, their bags at their feet. Surrounding mature trees sway, moaning in the wind. A metal sign halfway up the hill, advertising Flynn Hotel, rattles and squeaks in the wind. A stone dog guards the entrance.

As though a door to the skies opens, rain suddenly hammers down – sharp, heavy drops. 'And you wanted to come here, why?' Leon says, with a smile, picking up his holdall.

Alice laughs, but inside she is full of doubt. She looks up, rain stinging her skin. At the top of the building is an arched, barred window in the roof. 'The attic room,' she says, her body stiffening.

Leon's gaze moves to where hers has landed. 'I guess so,' he says. 'Creepy.'

'Mmm,' Alice says, head spinning. She knows already that the walls are muddy brown and the carpet is grass green.

Chapter 11

1976

Verity

The bullies circled, faces menacing. Verity had seen them from the cliff edge, as she leant against the wire fence at the foot of the sprawling lawn at Flynn House.

And now, fists clenched, she raced towards them, black plimsolls sinking into the sand with every footstep, chestnut-brown plaits swinging as she dashed to save her younger brother.

She'll kick the living hell out of each and every one of them. They all deserve to die.

She wasn't tall, but she was older than the brats who targeted her skinny brother. The weight she carried – *not fat, muscle* – gave her an advantage over them. Made her look older than her nine years.

'Hugh,' she cried, as she got closer, her breath raspy. He was on the ground now, and even from a distance she could see he'd peed his grey shorts. She would wash them out when she got him back to the house. Their father couldn't know. He would beat Hugh if he found out.

She continued onwards. Why had Hugh strayed so far? But she knew why. She could see the small red bucket lying on its side, shells strewn across the smooth sand. He loved collecting shells.

One of the kids – there were three in all – looked up. 'It's Verity!' It was the girl who lived above the shop on the seafront. Within moments the nasty kids scattered – scaredy-cats disappearing in different directions.

Hugh was crying when she reached him. She crouched down beside him, began picking up the shells, plopping them back into the red bucket. 'What have I told you?' she said. He was only ten months younger than her, and yet he was so much smaller, a weedy poppet. He was a child and she was the grown-up; she had to be.

'To stay near Flynn House,' he whimpered, wiping his grubby tear-stained face with the back of his hand, spreading his cheeks with sand. 'To never leave.'

'That's right, Hugh. To never leave.' She stood up. Pulled him to his feet. 'Let's get you back there shall we? Before the tide comes in.' And putting her arm around his shoulders, drawing him close to her, she took him home.

Chapter 12

Halloween Weekend 2019

Alice

'Jeez,' Leon whispers in Alice's ear, as they step into the entrance of Flynn Hotel, his eyes widening as he looks about him. 'You've brought me to a Tim Burton film set.'

'Shh.' She nudges his waist with her elbow, and he groans, and laughs. Seeming oblivious to the tension rising inside her.

The high-ceilinged reception has a curving staircase leading to a second floor. Low-voltage wall lights and an elaborate hanging pendant give everything an amber glow. Alice's apprehensive gaze roams the room. Black and white photographs cover one wall, mismatched mirrors another, and through ornate double glass doors there's a bar, luxurious, black satin curtains framing two bay windows. She breathes in the aroma of incense, as her eyes continue to travel, taking in a mahogany colonial grandfather clock with large gold numbers telling her it's a quarter to seven, a pink sofa, a table graced with black fake flowers in pink vases, and finally her sculpture of Gothic House in the centre of a black chest in the corner.

'Miss Hadley?' Christine stands behind a wooden counter, the laptop in front of her seeming at odds with the bizarre surroundings. She's ditched her anorak and beanie, to reveal black hair cropped into a pixie cut, a calf-length black dress over her full figure, cloaked by a silver-weave cardigan. She peers at Alice over red-framed glasses.

Behind her is a rack of keys, and three A4-sized photographs are displayed on the wall in a pyramid. At the top, a picture labelled Cameron – Owner. It's the same photograph Alice saw on the website. Beneath his picture is one of a smiling Christine – Hotel Manager. The third is of a young woman with long, straight black hair, and piercing blue eyes set in a pretty, pale face: Gabriela – General Assistant.

Christine turns from Alice as they approach, and glances through the double doors of the bar towards one of the bay windows. Rain lashes against the glass; lanterns strung along the patio rock and sway in the wind. 'It looks as if you got here just in time. It's getting quite blustery out there.' Her eyes return to the laptop screen. Fingers rest on the keyboard; *tap, tap, tap.* 'Room 2,' she says, stopping to grab a key from a rack. 'It's up the stairs and to your left. A lovely sea-facing room.' A smile floods her round face, her cheeks flushed as she places the key in Alice's hand.

'Could you tell me Faith Evans' room number, please?'

Christine looks at her screen, and back up at Alice. 'Room 4.' She slaps her hand to her mouth. 'Oh my, I probably shouldn't have told you another guest's details.'

'It's fine. She's my friend.'

Christine removes her hand. 'Well, I suppose that's OK then.'

Alice looks about her. 'Is the restaurant open?'

'I can rustle you up something if you're hungry.'

'I'm starving,' Leon says under his breath, jamming his hands in his jacket pockets.

Alice feels his pain. Apart from a bag of crisps, they haven't eaten since breakfast.

'Tonight's film in the lounge is *Halloween*, and there are TVs and Blu-ray players in every room, with a selection of films for your convenience. And a bookcase too, with books personally chosen by Mr Patterson.'

'Thanks. That's great.' Leon is clearly itching to get away.

Christine flaps her face with her hand, her cheeks pinking further. 'Sorry hot flush,' she says. 'I'm at that age, you see.' She leans forward and in a hushed whisper adds, 'I've been thrown in the deep end a bit. Mr Patterson has just left me to it.'

Alice glances at Leon, who is picking up his holdall. 'Well, you seem to be doing just fine,' she says, slightly irritated by the woman's repetitive moaning.

'Well, thank you, I'm doing my best. Ooh, and before I forget,' she goes on. 'If you're interested, Mr Patterson is coming over later to give a tour of the house and a talk about its history. The original owner was a famous magician in the Sixties. In fact, I remember seeing him on television when I was a child. He was an extremely hypnotic character – a bit chilling, in fact. He disappeared mysteriously about forty years ago.'

Leon shifts from foot to foot. Alice knows he's had enough of this woman, and needs something to eat, or a beer, or both. He seems to have forgotten why they are here, that this is the kind of thing she needs to know. That the tour might help. She picks up her holdall.

'And the bar is open now,' Christine continues. 'It doesn't close until eleven. And breakfast in the morning is from seven to eleven.'

It's as though she's ticking off a 'tell the guests list', and sounds hyper and flustered. 'Enjoy your stay with us at Flynn Hotel,' she concludes as they turn and head up the stairs.

The landing wallpaper is patterned – a pale pink rose with black thorns. The carpet is a swirl of pink and black. Like the reception area, the narrow corridor is lit by low-voltage wall-lights. There's another set of stairs leading to a further floor.

'It will be nice to meet up with Faith later,' Alice says as they pass room 1. 'I hope she's OK.' Her eyes fall on a framed poster on the wall, advertising a performance at The London Palladium in September 1960. The man in the picture is in his twenties, dressed in a yellow and blue striped jacket. His black hair oiled back from his forehead.

'Felix Flynn,' she says.

Leon nods. 'The original owner Christine mentioned, the one who disappeared. Looks like he was a magician and a puppeteer.'

She peers closer. Felix Flynn is holding a ventriloquist puppet – an exact replica of himself, down to the yellow and blue striped jacket, and the oiled-back hair. She shivers. 'I wouldn't want to meet him on a dark night.'

'Nor me.'

They walk on. Find room 2.

'Faith's room must be that one,' she says, pointing down the corridor towards room 4. She heads towards it. Knocks three times. 'Faith,' she calls, but there's no reply.

'Shall we freshen up, then grab something to eat?' she says, making her way back.

'Sounds good to me.' Leon takes the key from Alice and unlocks the door.

The room is dimly lit, the furnishings much the same as the rest of the house – pale pink and black seems to be Cameron's favourite colour combination. There's a full-length mirror, a mahogany four-poster bed and ornate wardrobe.

Rain hits the stunning arched window, black drapes pulled back like curtains at a macabre theatre. Alice moves closer, curves her hand over her eyes as she nears the glass, but the world outside the window is black. She can only imagine the choppy sea crashing against the cliffs.

'First or second shower?' she asks, turning to grab her holdall. She throws it onto the bed, and takes off her coat.

'We could be eating sooner, if we share one.' Leon smiles, flops down onto a throne-like chair by the window, and splays his long, jean-clad legs.

She rolls her eyes, her mouth curling into a smile.

'What? You can't blame a guy for trying.'

She should have known this wouldn't be easy. Being close to him is painfully hard. There's only a double bed and the uncomfortable-looking chair. She didn't think this through.

She unzips her holdall, avoiding his eyes. 'Do you think the picture will still be here?'

'I'm guessing if Faith only took the photo yesterday, it will be.' A beat. He looks concerned. 'Are you going to be OK, Alice? We could always get something sent to our room tonight.'

'I'm fine, honestly. I need to see the portrait.' She takes out an ankle-length, yellow dress that she rolled up like a beach towel when she packed her bag. As she unrolls it, she sees her anti-creasing technique hasn't worked.

'I'm going to look a bloody mess this evening if I wear this,' she says, grabbing her soap bag.

'You'll look lovely whatever you wear,' Leon says. She turns to look at him, and for the first time notices his smile doesn't quite reach his eyes. He's as unsettled here as she is.

It's as she heads towards the bathroom, she notices a small bookshelf by the window. She crouches down, eyes flickering over the array of novels. In amongst a whole range of thrillers and ghost stories, are copies of her father's books. 'That's weird,' she says, pulling one out and showing it to Leon.

He shrugs, shakes his head. 'Not really, your dad wrote bestselling Gothic thrillers. This is a Gothic hotel.'

'I guess so.' She shoves the book back on the shelf between

copies of Stephen King's *The Shining* and Robert Bloch's *Psycho*, trying to shake the feeling that something isn't quite right here.

*

The tick tick tick of the grandfather clock echoes into the silent reception area.

'Where is everybody?' Alice whispers, clinging to Leon's arm as they make their way towards the dining room. She's abandoned her yellow dress, and is wearing a purple tunic over leggings. Feels better after a shower. She suits purple, and has plaited her blonde hair – twisted it around her head like a traditional Dutch doll – though a few tendrils have already worked their way loose, spirals of wispy hair floating down her cheeks.

'It's like we're here all alone,' Leon says.

'Mmm, it's a bit creepy, don't you think?'

They're about to enter the restaurant, when a shriek of laughter echoes from the bar, making Alice jump.

'Faith!' She releases Leon's arm and turns. 'I'd know that laugh anywhere.'

Leon grabs her hand before she can head across the chessboard quarry tiles. 'Can we eat first, Alice? Please. I may have to bite my arm off if we don't, and possibly yours too.'

'Go get a table,' she says, pulling her hand free. 'I'll be two minutes. Promise.'

She feels the weight of his hungry eyes on her, as she heads towards the bar.

From the doorway, she struggles to make out the shadowy figures sitting in a booth, but can see a sprinkling of low tables and chairs. The room is dimly lit, with pockets of lighting from wall-mounted lamps and a roaring fire. A young woman with long black hair stands behind a bar at the far end, bright pink lighting around the bar revealing she looks vacant – sad somehow. It's Gabriela, the woman in the photo behind reception.

'Alice!' Faith is dashing towards her, almost toppling over on her three-inch heels. She's wearing a tight-fitting, short black dress, her dark hair loose and curled. She looks stunning, but equally wrong. Faith always wears dungarees and check shirts, trainers, her hair in a high ponytail. 'You came. Yay, it's so good to see you,' Faith goes on, grabbing Alice, and giving her a hug. 'What changed your mind?'

'What can I say? Curiosity got the better of me,' Alice says, as Faith releases her.

'It killed the cat too.' It's Mitch, appearing with a glass of brandy in his large hand. He presses his free hand against Faith's back. 'So be careful.'

'Mitch,' Alice says, and adds, out of politeness, 'nice to see you again.'

He smiles, but there's darkness in his eyes. 'Good to see you again too, Alice.'

'You look lovely,' Alice says, eyes back on her friend.

Faith looks up at Mitch, and tugs at the hem of her dress.

'I picked it out,' Mitch says. 'A woman should look like a woman, don't you think?'

Alice looks from Faith to Mitch, and bites her tongue. 'Listen, I'm about to have something to eat. Are you around after?'

'We'll probably be here until they throw us out,' Faith says with a laugh.

'Great, I'll see you in a bit then.' She turns to go, then spins back. 'I tried to call you a few times to let you know I was coming, but your phone went to voicemail every time.'

'God. I know. I've lost the bloody thing.'

'You've lost your phone?'

'Yep, although …' Faith glances about her, and reducing her voice to a whisper, says, 'I'm not the only one who has had their phone go missing.' She points to a woman in her fifties sitting by an open fire, wearing a satin dress, and strappy shoes. An elaborate standard lamp beams light on the wing-backed chair, as she reads. She's attractive; her thick, chestnut-brown hair swept over one shoulder, silky and straight. As though sensing Alice's stare, she turns quite suddenly, her gaze intelligent, her features sharp. A small smile crosses her lips, as though she realises Alice has seen what she's reading: *Where Doves Fly.*

'Lori's lost her phone too.' Faith's voice sounds far away. 'Which makes it a bit odd, don't you think?' Alice pulls her gaze away from the woman, back to her friend who is still talking. 'Mind you, with this lighting it's easy to lose things, I guess.'

'Have you reported it?' Alice asks.

'Well, I've told Christine on reception. I hate not having it. It's amazing how many times I reach for it.'

Alice glances over her shoulder. 'I better go and order some food, before Leon gets *hangry* and chews his arm off.'

'Leon's with you?' She sounds surprised, her eyes widening. 'Are you guys back together? You never said.'

'No. No, we're not together, just good friends, that's all.' She isn't sure that's how she really feels, but for now it is all Faith needs to know. 'I would have told you if it was anything more, honestly.'

'It's fine, no worries.' She places her hand on Alice's arm. 'I couldn't be happier if you two make a go of it.' She looks over her shoulder, and points towards a booth. 'We'll be over there once you've eaten.'

Leon is sitting by the window in the deserted restaurant. A candle flickers on the table in front of him. He looks up from the menu as Alice approaches. 'I can barely see this,' he says with a laugh. 'But can just about make out burger and chips, so I'll go with that.'

Alice sits down, but before she can tell him she's seen Faith and Mitch, Christine appears. 'Can I get you guys anything to drink?'

'A small red wine please.' Alice scans the menu quickly, trying to decide what to eat, so she doesn't delay things any longer.

'Lager,' Leon says. 'Cheers.'

'And I'll have fish and chips, please.'

'Burger for me,' Leon says.

'Is that the portrait?' Leon says, as Christine walks away.

Alice looks to where Leon is pointing, her hands flying to her mouth. 'Oh my God.' It hangs under a picture-light on the other side of the restaurant. In seconds she's on her feet, dashing between the empty tables. She stops in front of it, stares up at the man in the picture, her heart thudding. She sees her father's unusual eyes, his sharp nose. *This* man in the picture is much younger than her father was, but it's him. It has to be. The resemblance is uncanny. She gazes up at it for some time, emotions rising, before making her way back to Leon, who is shoving his phone into his pocket. 'Everything OK?' she says, sitting down.

'Yeah. Just work. I pulled a sickie to come here – not sure they're convinced. It's OK; there are plenty of stand-ins at the pool.'

'I hope I haven't got you in any trouble.' Leon loves his job; she would hate him to lose it on her account.

'It'll be fine.' He nods towards the portrait. 'So, what are your thoughts?'

She gazes across the room. 'It looks so like my dad.' Her voice cracks. 'One blue eye and one green is so rare.' She turns, glances at their blurred reflections in the window beside them, and back to Leon. 'But why would it be here?'

'It may not be him. People look alike sometimes.' Leon's tone is comforting. He reaches across the table, laces his fingers with hers. 'In fact, I saw a bloke in Tesco once who was a dead ringer for Daniel Radcliffe. I came over all Harry Potter fanboy, but it wasn't him.' He pulls a fake sad face.

'How do you know?' She tries to play along. 'It could have been.'

He shakes his head. 'I asked him to sign my cornflakes.'

'And?' Her lips curl into a smile.

'He signed the box Colin Crumpet. Plus, he had five kids in tow.'

She laughs, knowing he's probably made up the story to lighten the mood. He pushes a straying hair from her cheek with his free hand. 'Are you sure you're OK?' His humorous tone has vanished. 'We can head back to Whitby if you want.'

She takes a deep breath. 'I'm fine,' she says, though feels far from it. 'You're right, people look similar all the time.'

'You might even enjoy the break. It might be good to spend some time together.'

'Yes,' she says, meaning it – relieved he's here with her. 'It will.'

Chapter 13

1979

Verity

'You're a very good girl, Verity Flynn.' Verity placed her palm against the bathroom mirror, splayed her chubby fingers, and leant forward, closer to her reflection. 'You are a very good girl, Verity Flynn.'

This was something she often did. Talked to her reflection. Told herself she was good, because nobody else was going to. Certainly not her father, or the stream of nannies he employed to take care of her and Hugh.

Felix Flynn had brought Verity and Hugh to Flynn House in 1970, aged two and three. Adopting the brother and sister as a gift for his bored wife and stage assistant, Ann Marie Flynn, who hadn't wanted to ruin her exquisite body by carrying children of her own. It was amazing what you could buy if you had enough money and contacts.

Dolls, that's what the children had been initially; dolls for Ann Marie to play with. Dolls she would hand to a nanny when she grew tired of them.

When Ann Marie died of an accidental overdose in 1972, the children became an inconvenience to Felix. Verity learnt early on to keep out of her father's way. Hugh, on the other hand, was full of mischief as a young child. He got in Felix's way, desperate for his father's attention. But Felix had no time for the boy, would grit his teeth, clench his fists, intent on stamping out the bright light that shone inside Hugh, leaving him in darkness.

Tap, tap, tap.

Verity looked away from her twelve-year-old reflection, and up at the ceiling. Hugh was in the attic room again. Locked in the box. Felix would leave him up there for hours sometimes.

The box had been used on stage to give the illusion that Felix was cutting his assistant into three equal pieces. Hugh was petrified of it, certain he was going to be chopped up by their father. It didn't matter how many times Verity told him it was only a magic trick, he never would believe her.

'Wait right there, Hugh,' Verity yelled like she was a superhero, 'I'm on my way.' She dashed from the bathroom, and into the hallway, picking up her diary en route, and shoving it under her arm. 'Here I come.' She couldn't get into the attic, of course, it was always locked, but she could talk to her brother through the red door, be there to comfort him – tell him stories until their awful father let him out.

'Where are you off to in such a hurry?'

She turned to see the latest in a long line of nannies. This one was Nanny Bell. She was younger than some of the others, but still had that sharp, spiteful tone that Felix liked so much in his employees, which Verity hated, and Hugh feared.

'Nowhere.'

'You're going nowhere in a hurry?' Nanny Bell pressed her lips together so they almost disappeared, sucked inside her pretty face. 'What's that under your arm?'

'It's none of your business, quite frankly.' She wasn't about to tell this woman she's been writing about her. Telling her pages how wicked she was.

Nanny Bell's dress was turquoise linen and calf-length, and her tights were sheer. Her shoes shone shiny black, and had small, thick heels. Old-fashioned. Her make-up was thick, heavy.

Verity folded her arms across her chest. She wasn't afraid of this woman. She wasn't afraid of anything anymore. There was nothing Nanny Bell could do that hadn't been done before. She was numb.

'Well, that's where you are wrong, Verity Flynn. Your business is always my business. Your father has made me responsible for you. I'm in charge.'

Verity laughed, a cold chilling laugh, which she could see Nanny Bell didn't like. She saw her body quiver.

Verity looked up the stairs towards the attic room, and back at Nanny Bell. 'Why does my father put Hugh up there all the time?'

'Hugh is a mischievous child – you know that. It's for his own good.'

Verity stepped towards Nanny Bell. 'Is it really, though?'

The woman stepped backwards in her shiny shoes. 'That's what I said.' Her firm voice cracked. 'If he wasn't so naughty.'

'But he isn't naughty. He's never naughty. Felix Flynn is just being cruel, and you could stop that if you wanted to.' Verity stared for some moments, and even though Nanny Bell didn't respond there was something in her eyes. *Fear?* Was she afraid of Felix too? 'I heard you with Daddy last night,' Verity continued. 'Were you having sex with my father?'

The woman's cheeks pinked, and her body twitched. She turned from Verity's gaze. 'Of course not.'

'You are a disgusting woman, Nanny Bell.' She placed a finger against her cheek. 'You make me feel quite sick.'

'And you are a truly horrible child, Verity Flynn.'

'No.' Verity shook her head. 'I am a good girl.' She looked again up the stairs. 'Have you got the key to the attic room? I would like to let my brother out.'

'Only your father has the key.' Her eyes were back on Verity. 'You know that. And even if I knew where it was, I would never go against your father's instructions.'

'Are you afraid of him?' Verity looked about her. 'Why don't you leave? Can't you feel how sad this place is? How desperately, desperately sad?'

'Go to your room, Verity. If your father catches you wandering about the hallways, he'll be angry.'

'If I could get away from here, I would run and run and run. But I can't leave Hugh. You can, though, and yet you stay.'

'I need this job. The experience.'

'And you've fallen for my awful father?'

'No. No, I haven't. You have it all wrong.' Nanny Bell's voice cracked another morsel.

Verity smiled. Had she broken Nanny Bell? 'This isn't experience. This. This place.' She looked about her once more, not moving. 'It's extreme torture. It's hell.'

Nanny Bell turned, and walked away without another word, sashaying down the hallway. Verity felt sure she'd broken her. But it wouldn't matter. Nanny Bell may leave, but another would replace her.

Chapter 14

Halloween Weekend 2019

Alice

Alice stares out of the window at the rain, Leon beside her on a long, cushioned bench, thoughts of the portrait whirring around her head.

Faith is at the bar getting drinks, while Mitch holds court from a chair on the other side of the table, his broad body upright and rigid, his voice low and husky as he tells Leon about LARPing.

Alice turns to face Mitch. She knows what LARPing is. Faith told her about Mitch's obsession with live-action role-play.

'I love it,' he says now. 'Makes me feel like a real man.' His hair is down this evening, resting on his shoulders, and there's still that arrogance about him Alice doesn't like.

'We did a *Hobbit* battle back in August,' Mitch goes on. 'I played Thorin.'

'Thorin?'

'The lead dwarf.'

The irony that he's so tall doesn't go unnoticed on Alice.

Mitch picks up his glass with his yellowing fingers, and drains the remnants of his brandy. 'I was meant to take part in a zombie battle this weekend, but I didn't mind missing it for Faith … and all of this.' He looks about him, seeming impressed by the surroundings.

Alice looks over at Faith who is filling a tray with glasses. She can't help wonder, not for the first time, what she's sees in this man.

The conversation moves on, and Leon, pushing his fingers through his fair hair, tells Mitch that he's a fantasy writer, hoping to be published one day.

Their words fade, as Alice's mind drifts, searching for memories. She's never been able to recall anything further back than the age of six or seven – not helped by her father's silence on the subject, but now she feels sure this place holds the key to unlocking the secrets of her past – her father's past. Yet there's something inside of her that's crying out to leave things be – not to go on.

'That was hard work,' Faith says, tugging Alice from her thoughts, approaching with drinks clanking on a silver tray. Clearly struggling to walk in her heels. 'The girl behind the bar is barely old enough to serve us, and doesn't speak a word of English. Eastern European I think. And she's a right grumpy cow too.' She puts the tray down, and turns to a woman coming up behind her. 'Guys, meet Lori.'

It's the woman who was sitting by the fire earlier reading Alice's father's book. 'She was pretty bored on her own,' Faith goes on. 'So I invited her to join us. Hope that's cool with everyone.'

They chorus greetings, followed by a round of introductions. The woman grabs a stool, and, folding her flowing satin dress under her, sits down next to Alice, picks up a glass of Prosecco from the tray of drinks, and takes a sip.

'Faith said you lost your phone,' Alice says, as a conversation breaker, taking in, once more, the woman's mane of dark hair draped over one shoulder, her sharp nose, her dark eyes. She's attractive, slim, like an ageing film star.

Lori takes another sip of her drink, and nods. 'It's a mystery, really. I left my cell on the table when I went to the bathroom last night, and when I got back it was gone.' She's softly spoken, American, with a confident air. 'I shouldn't have left it unattended, I suppose. But you really don't expect anyone to take it in a place like this.'

'You're from the US,' Alice says.

Lori smiles, teeth white, lips plump, as though she may have had work done. 'What gave it away?'

'Sorry, I didn't mean to—'

'It's fine. I lived in LA for thirty years, but I'm originally from this area. I moved back here a couple of years ago.'

'Have you mentioned your phone to Christine?' Faith interrupts, picking up her pint of lager, taking a gulp.

'Yes, I have. And I've reported it to the phone company too, using the hotel's landline. But there's not much else I can do until I get home. You?'

'Same.' Faith looks about her, as though searching for a kleptomaniac amongst them.

Alice follows Faith's gaze. A couple in their late twenties sit on a velvet sofa, laughing too loudly, a champagne bucket in front of them, as though celebrating.

'You should be like me, Lori,' Mitch says with a sniff. 'I've never had a mobile phone in my life – or should I say cell?' He leans forward, taps his nose. 'Got some inside info years back that they fry your brain. Never looked back.' He lifts his chin and smirks, as though everyone around him is stupid.

Lori takes another sip of her drink. 'Is it what you expected?' she says, moving her eyes from Mitch to look again at Alice.

'Sorry?'

'This place.' Her gaze roams the room. 'Is it what you imagined it would be like?'

Alice shrugs. 'I'm not sure what I was expecting, if I'm honest. I guess it's like the photos on the website and Instagram, so yes, I suppose so. It's certainly atmospheric.'

'Mmm.' She leans close to Alice's ear. 'It's changed out of all recognition.' She smiles, puts down her glass, and looks at her delicate gold watch. 'Cameron Patterson should be over soon, shouldn't he? I believe he's going to do his talk and tour. I'm very much looking forward to it.' She strokes her mane of hair, as though it's a pet. 'I wonder how much will be truth, and how much fantasy.'

'You think he'll make things up?'

Lori shrugs. 'Possibly. The truth about this place is far too dark.'

Alice opens her mouth to question her further. *How does she know about the hotel's history?* But Faith leans across the table. 'Have you met him?'

'Who? The mysterious Cameron Patterson?' Lori shakes her head. 'No, not yet.'

'I have,' Faith says. 'He's rather gorgeous.'

'Faith!' Mitch stares at her, eyes fired, arms folded across his broad body. 'Christ's sake! Way to make me look an idiot.'

'I never meant to.' Faith tugs at the hem of her dress, stares at him for a long moment. Nobody speaks, all clearly feeling awkward about the man's outburst.

Finally Faith takes hold of his hand. 'You know you're the only man for me, Mitch,' she says, and kisses his cheek. But there's a sudden rigidness about her, as though being near him makes her anxious.

Alice shuffles in her seat, wants to shake her friend, tell her to dump Mitch, but she keeps quiet. Faith must see something in him Alice can't – although going by the expression on her face, she may be coming round to Alice's way of thinking.

'Can everyone who would like to take part in the tour gather in reception now.' It's Christine, standing by the door of the bar holding a clipboard, running her fingers through her dark, cropped hair. 'The tour of Flynn Hotel is about to begin.'

Chapter 15

1981

Verity

Nanny Bell held on to her job at Flynn House, despite Verity's efforts to have her despatched from the island. Her father lusted after her, that was the problem, and Nanny Bell seemed to go along with it. Though Verity couldn't be sure she enjoyed his advances. The whole sordid show made Verity feel positively sick.

Today was Nanny Bell's day off. She would spend the night with her mother on the mainland, and return by midday the following day. This was when their father was meant to take care of Verity and Hugh, though of course he never did. In fact, as Verity stood at the window, pressing her fingers so hard on the glass that the tips bleached, she realised she desperately wanted Nanny Bell to stay. At least there was hope with *this* woman who was yet to reach her twentieth birthday. Hope that she may just see how abused Verity and Hugh were, and do something. But Nanny Bell continued on her way across the sand, her bag draped over her shoulder, her dark hair pinned up into a neat

91

and tidy bun. She had a confident walk, Verity thought – a bit like Princess Diana.

It was an hour later that Verity, sprawled on her bed reading, heard her brother cry out. Felix was dragging him up the stairs to the attic room – *thump, thump, thump.*

Although the siblings were now teenagers, Hugh was still a scrawny boy. He hadn't had his final growth spurt, Verity suspected – so Felix, a small man, had no trouble lugging him up the stairs and manoeuvring him into the box. Verity, on the other hand, was hefty. Felix wouldn't dare cross her, *not anymore.*

'You need to keep out of the bastard's way, Hugh,' she whispered to herself, as she heard the red door of the attic room slam. 'When will you learn?'

Once Felix had returned to his room, Verity made her way up to the attic and knocked the door: *tap, tap, tap.* She could hear her brother sobbing inside. 'Hey, Hugh, it's me. Keep strong, little one.'

'It's my arm, V,' he called back, his words bludgeoned by sobs. 'I think it's broken. It hurts so bad.'

'Bastard!' Verity screwed her fists into balls. 'I hate him. I hate him.'

'Tell me the story about Rapunzel, V.' He sounded like a small child.

'OK, but if I do, you have to keep strong, Hugh.' She leant her head against the door. 'Once upon a time, a very long time ago ...'

*

It was dark, gone ten o'clock, when Verity pushed the key into the red door, and turned it in the lock. She'd found it in Felix's room, after searching for almost an hour. 'Hugh,' she said, flicking on the light.

There was movement in the box propped against the wall. A panicked voice from inside: 'Verity?'

She hurried over. A padlock held the box locked. She looked

about her, searching for something to smash it with. She spotted a saw hanging on the wall, lifted it down, and thumped it down on the padlock over and over.

Hugh wheezed, breathless. There were holes in the back of the box, but his air was restricted.

'Felix will never be back, Hugh. He'll never hurt you again.' Another whack – the padlock broke off, wood splintering. She opened the box to see Hugh, eyes red raw from crying. He held one arm limp against his side, taking shaky breaths as he stepped out onto the grass-green carpet, his face contorted in pain. He looked towards the door, fear in his eyes.

'He's never coming back,' she said. 'He's gone forever.' She touched her brother's good arm. 'He'll never hurt you again.'

Hugh smiled as Verity put her arm round her brother.

'Let's see what food there is in the fridge, shall we?' she said, guiding him towards the door. 'You must be starving.'

*

'Do you know where my father is, Nanny Bell?' Verity whispered, a smile dancing on her lips, as the three of them were taken by police car from the island the following day. Nanny Bell had called the police when she arrived just after noon to report Felix missing.

The nanny stared at Verity for a long moment, narrowing her eyes as though trying to weigh the girl up. 'You're a peculiar child, Verity Flynn,' she said.

'Why, thank you.' Verity squeezed her hands into fists. 'That's incredibly kind of you.'

It was clear Nanny Bell couldn't hold eye contact. She pulled from Verity's gaze.

Verity took a deep breath. 'Why didn't you help us, Nanny Bell?' She screwed up her face, angry with herself that she was allowing her tone to weaken – that she sounded vulnerable.

'You do know you'll end up in care, Verity. That nobody will want to foster the likes of you.' Nanny Bell looked at Hugh, knotted up into himself like a tortoise in a shell. 'They will like him, *possibly*—'

'You're wrong. Nobody will come between my brother and me.' Tears burned her eyes. 'No one will ever come between me and Hugh.'

Chapter 16

Halloween Weekend 2019

Alice

'I can come on the tour if you want me to – I don't mind,' Leon says, as Alice rises, about to follow Faith, Mitch and Lori across the bar towards reception. But his eyes look heavy. She knows he's exhausted after the long drive.

'No, it's fine, honestly.' The tour of the hotel isn't Leon's thing. In fact, the whole place is way out of his comfort zone. And the increasing unease she's felt since they arrived is nudging at her too. But she has to do this tour – she's sure her father is connected to this place in some way, and she needs to find out how.

The grandfather clock chimes nine as the guests congregate in reception. The young couple from the bar sit together on the sofa, arms wrapped around each other. The woman giggles, tossing her red bobbed hair. She's dressed in narrow black trousers and a black blouse, her bra visible beneath it. She looks familiar.

Christine gives a little cough, trying to catch everyone's

attention, and Alice's eyes move to where she's standing with her clipboard. 'Is everything OK?' she asks her.

'Yes! Yes …' Christine's eyes are on the paperwork attached to the clipboard. She looks up suddenly, tears forming behind her red-framed glasses. 'Well no, actually.' Her voice is a wobble. 'It's just … well … Cameron hasn't turned up, and his phone goes straight to voicemail … so it looks as though I'm going to have to do it, the tour I mean, and although I have notes, and I know the place quite well from the bumph he emailed to me earlier this week …' She fumbles a tissue from her cardigan pocket, and sniffs into it. 'I'm so sorry, everyone. I realise this is all a bit *Fawlty Towers*, and it doesn't give a good impression of the hotel, but I hadn't realised I would have so much responsibility when I accepted the job.' She's talking fast, her Suffolk accent broader than ever. 'Mark, my son, wondered if it might be too much for me, especially after my Terry's death, and I've been suffering terribly with the menopause. But truth is, now Mark's living in France … I'd become lonely and thought this might be just the ticket. Mark doesn't understand that I need to be doing something with my time, and I would never tell him how I feel. He's got to get on with his own life without worrying about his mum—'

'Don't worry, Christine.' Lori grabs her wrist, as though pulling on a brake, her voice assertive. She's taller than Christine, slimmer, more attractive. Both of a similar age, but so very different. 'The hotel will sell itself. Let's take a walk around the place, and you can tell us what you know.'

'Suck it and see?' Christine takes a breath. 'I have notes.' She taps the clipboard with short fingernails, her face morphing into a smile. 'I can do this, can't I?'

'Of course you can,' Alice says, as Lori releases Christine and steps away from her.

'Well I, for one, can't be arsed with amateurs. Even if this weekend is a freebie.' It's the young woman with red hair, her accent upper class English. Alice stares, her heart thudding. She knows where she's seen her before. 'Let's go to our room, Dane,' the woman goes on, rising, taking the man's hand. He springs to his feet like an athlete, all long limbs – his vest T-shirt clinging to his muscular body. And with a seductive tone she adds, 'I can think of better things for us to do.'

'The Winslows from The Winslow Touch,' Mitch whispers in Alice's ear. 'Small world, isn't it?'

Alice recalls how she watched them pull her father apart on YouTube. She's experienced first-hand how cruel they can be, and vows to avoid them for the rest of the weekend. Cameron Patterson has clearly made a mistake if he's thrown this couple a freebie weekend in exchange for good publicity.

'Take no notice of them,' Faith says to Christine, as Savannah and Dane Winslow head towards the staircase, his arm draped around her shoulders, her high heels clipping the quarry tiles.

'She's got bitch written all over her,' Mitch says, glaring at them as they head up the stairs and disappear from view. 'That kind of woman needs to be taught a lesson.'

Alice cringes, wondering what kind of lesson he means.

Christine leads the group of four over to the photographs on the wall. Most are framed pictures of Felix Flynn performing on stage, either magic tricks, or with his ventriloquist puppets. Alice moves closer. There are several puppets in the pictures, one has wool for hair and is dressed in a checked suit, another has sleek black hair combed away from its face, and is wearing a bow tie. She turns from the pictures.

'Apparently, Mr Patterson found these photographs when he purchased the place,' Christine reads from the clipboard. 'The house was faded and shabby when he bought it in 2017.' Her voice has brightened a fraction, and she seems more confident suddenly, as though the subject fascinates her. 'It was creepy back then.'

'Still is, if you ask me,' Mitch says, his brown eyes scanning the pictures.

'Yes.' Christine looks about her. 'I suppose so. But now it's *meant* to be this way. In 2017 nobody had lived in the house for some time. The owner, Verity Flynn – Felix's daughter – had lived in the cottage on the island, where Mr Patterson lives now.' She pauses for a moment. 'It says here several developers refused to take the place on due to the foreboding atmosphere.' She gives a little shudder.

Alice continues to study the photos, mesmerised, her eyes falling on a black and white head and shoulders photograph of a child of about four with short dark hair. It looks out of place amongst the pictures of Felix Flynn. 'Who's this?' she says, coming over a bit faint, placing her hand on the wall for support.

'Probably one of Felix's children,' Christine says, placing her finger on her chin. 'He had a daughter, Verity, and a son, Hugh. There's a portrait of the son in the dining room, painted by his sister.'

Hugh Flynn? It couldn't be of her father.

'Did Hugh Flynn live here?' Alice asks.

'I believe so.' She's looking at her notes, fumbling. 'The original owner, Felix Flynn, disappeared forty years ago,' she explains to everyone.

'Where are Hugh and Verity Flynn now?' Lori asks.

Christine shrugs, raking through her notes once more. 'I'm afraid I have no idea. It says nothing here.'

Alice's head swims. *Was Hugh her father, and had he changed his name? But why would he? And he didn't have a sister that she knew of.* He'd kept things from Alice, that much was true – but surely nothing this huge. Tears sting behind her eyes. He never told her who her mother was, or anything about her early life. What's to have stopped him hiding a whole lot more?

'Did you see the portrait in the restaurant? The one I sent you?' Faith asks, suddenly beside Alice, moving in close to her ear.

'Mmm.'

'It looks so like your dad, don't you think?'

Tears are nearing the surface. Her father is so clear in her mind it's as though he's standing right beside her. *Go home, Alice.*

'This doesn't look like Hugh or Verity to me,' Lori says, moving closer to the photograph of the dark-haired child.

'You knew them?' Alice says, running her hand across the back of her neck.

'A very long time ago.' Her eyes fix on a photo of Felix Flynn. 'Their father was an awful man.' Lori takes out an inhaler from her bag and shakes it. 'Oh dear, I'm almost out. I'll need to get the spare from my room.'

'Christine!' Everyone turns. It's Dane Winslow standing at the top of the stairs, topless, baring his muscular body with obvious pride. 'We were promised champagne and canapés.'

She looks up at him. 'Yes … yes, of course. They're in the fridge. I'll bring them up after the tour.'

He folds his arms high across his toned chest. 'Now would be good.'

Christine takes off her glasses, rubs her eyes with her fingertips. 'Well—'

'I'm happy to wait if you need to get them, Christine,' Lori says. 'I should probably grab my spare inhaler from my room anyway.'

'I'm happy to wait too,' Faith says with a smile. 'This jerk clearly thinks he's more important than us mere mortals.' Her words are sharp, loud enough for Dane Winslow to hear. He simply scoffs.

'Alice? Mitch?' Christine's eyes dart from one to the other. 'Do you mind?'

Mitch grunts, and Alice shakes her head, drops down onto the sofa. Christine scampers away towards the kitchen, like a frightened rabbit, her flat shoes slapping the floor tiles. Within seconds, Lori heads up the stairs to collect her inhaler, and Dane disappears into the shadows.

'I'm going to get some more cigs from our room,' Mitch says, turning and making his way up the stairs after Lori.

'Are you OK?' Faith says, joining Alice on the sofa, her voice soft and comforting. She puts her arm around Alice's shoulders, and pulls her close. 'I hope this isn't all too much for you.'

'Don't be kind, Faith. Please.' Alice smiles. 'You'll have me blubbing.'

'Is it the portrait?'

Alice nods. 'Yes ... well, this place.' She looks about her. 'It's making me feel—'

A door slams behind them, and Christine appears once more, dashing across reception with a tray loaded with canapés, and a bottle of champagne. 'I'm so sorry about this, ladies,' she says. 'I won't be long.'

As Christine takes the stairs, Alice rests her head on her friend's shoulder.

'You were going to say how it's making you feel,' Faith says. 'This place.'

'It's just the dark atmosphere, I guess.'

'The whole Gothic thing?'

'It's a bit unnerving, that's all.'

After a few minutes, Lori hurries down the stairs towards them, followed by Christine.

'I better see where Mitch has got to,' Faith says, getting to her feet, and leaping up the stairs two at a time.

Alice rises too. 'They're quite something, aren't they?' she says to Christine. 'The Winslows.'

Christine nods. 'I realise they are Mr Patterson's guests, but I've no idea why he would want them here. They're critics, apparently.'

'Mmm, I've seen their awful YouTube channel,' Alice says. 'They can be very cruel.'

'I've heard of them,' Lori says. 'Nasty couple.'

The trio fall quiet for some time. Waiting. Alice is close to backing out of the tour altogether, making her apologies – missing the security of Faith or Leon by her side – when she hears footsteps at the top of the stairs.

100

'We're ready,' Faith calls from the landing. She stands with Mitch, her arm looped through his elbow.

'Great. Shall we begin by heading upstairs?' Christine says, and she and Lori move across reception. The stairs creak as the two of them head for the first floor, but Alice doesn't move, frozen for a moment, staring once more at the solitary child in the sea of pictures of Felix Flynn.

'Alice,' Faith calls. 'Are you coming?'

She tears herself away, and hurries to catch them up. 'Yes, sorry, on my way.'

Leon

The waxing crescent moon is visible through the bay window where Leon sits, his mind whirring. What the hell is he doing here with Alice? It took everything for him to walk away when she ended things, yet here he is, back where he started, and not only that; this time he's keeping a terrible secret.

The bar is deserted apart from Gabriela. The others have taken off on the ridiculous tour of this pretentious house. He rises to his feet, grabs his jacket from the back of his chair, and slips it on. He needs air, needs to think, outside – alone.

Well-placed lanterns and a string of bulbs brighten the patio, but their beam doesn't reach far, and the crescent moon is scuppered by passing clouds. A neat lawn stretches towards a fenced-off cliff edge. The wind is fierce now, howling through the surrounding mature trees. The sound of the sea crashing against the rocks below is atmospheric.

Leon breathes in the cold air, the sensation organising his thoughts. He thinks about Tegan. Their friendship, because that's all it was – he had never promised her anything more. But still she clung to him like a barnacle to a boat – always calling and texting. Had he been wrong to allow that friendship, knowing how she felt about him, knowing she seemed unstable? Had he let it go on too long, hoping she would take on his book? He hated that it could be true. And now she's confided in him, told him things he doesn't want bashing about in his head. Things he doesn't know how to tell Alice. Things he must tell the police.

He heads down the sloping lawn, carried partly by the wind, trying to unclutter his head. He stops yards from the edge and squints out to sea. The lights from the mainland silhouette a boat bobbing some way out on the rough waves. He moves his gaze towards the empty jetty, where lanterns swing to and fro. A gust of wind takes hold of one of the pumpkins, spins it into the air, and out to sea. The boat they travelled to the island in has slipped its mooring. It looks as though they are stuck on the island until midday tomorrow, when the tide goes out, so he'll have to make the most of it. These are the moments he craves a cigarette – wishes he hadn't given up five years ago.

He flicks on his phone torch. The fence that hems the foot of the lawn is flattened in places. He steps back. The wind is fierce. He will struggle if it catches him in its grip. It could take him over the edge. He would never survive the fifty-foot drop.

He looks at his phone. Reads again the message Tegan sent him a few days ago:

Promise me, Leon. Promise you won't say anything. It was an accident.

The wind settles for a moment, whispering through the trees, as though planning an assault. Leon loses himself in thought, unaware he's being pushed forward by the wind.

A gust, like a shove from invisible hands, pounces, takes Leon's body and thrusts him forward. He topples, slips over the crumbling edge. His phone falls from his grip, bounces, smashes against the cliffs.

Heart pounding, he hangs, suspended for some moments. His fingers ache as he clings to the wire fence that stretches and

102

creaks. Rocks and chunks of soil roll down the cliff, tumbling into the sea.

He takes a deep breath, and hauls himself back onto the grass. His eyes dart around the area, stare into the watchful darkness. There's nobody about that he can see.

Panting, he sits on the damp grass, trying to catch his breath, rubbing wet hands on his jacket. Suddenly, a string of lights break free from the patio, one end spiralling in the wind, casting light across the trees – the other end still attached to the building. A flash of yellow streaks through the air; carried fifteen feet off the ground, towards the cliff edge. It twists and turns, floating like a phantom. Leon rises to his feet, his heart thumping as he takes off back towards the house, the wind buffeting him from every side. He's never felt so scared.

Alice

For the last ten minutes, Christine has waffled and bungled her way through the tour, but apart from Lori, who, complaining of a headache, went to her room almost immediately, everyone, even Mitch, has been far too polite to leave the struggling woman, whose short hair now stands on end due to constant run-throughs with her anxious fingers.

As they make their way along an upper floor, an area narrower than the floor below, Alice's legs weaken. She stops, leans against the wall, a heavy feeling of foreboding pressing down on her.

Faith darts back. 'Are you OK?'

'I'm fine, just a bit dizzy.' But it's far from true. A feeling of claustrophobia as they got higher and higher into the house has consumed her, taken her breath away.

Christine and Mitch turn the corner at the end of the hallway, seeming oblivious to her wobble, but Faith stays, concern in her eyes. 'Take my arm,' she says.

Alice pulls away from the safety of the wall, and links her arm through Faith's. They carry on, following Christine, despite her father's voice inside Alice's head shouting for her to turn back.

'I think this must be a photo of Felix's children,' Christine is saying when Alice and Faith catch up.

Alice takes in the black and white study of a boy and girl. The girl is taller, bigger built than the skinny boy – but they look to be around eight or nine. They are standing, hand in hand, faces pale and solemn. Could the boy be her father?

Another staircase leads to a further floor. Alice grips Faith's arm. 'The attic room's up there,' she whispers, hearing her voice tremble.

'That's right,' Christine says, her eyes widening behind her glasses. 'How did you know that?'

'Kind of obvious, wouldn't you say?' Mitch rolls his eyes. 'It's at the top of the house. Duh!'

But he's wrong. Alice knows because she's been in the attic room. She knows she has. It's painted muddy brown. The carpet is grass green. *Outside inside.* Her heart picks up speed, her throat dries. She doesn't want to go up there, where two brass dogs guard.

'You're in for a creepy treat with this room,' Christine is saying, taking a brass key from her cardigan pocket, and making her way up the stairs. And now Faith is following, pulling Alice with her, and she can see the red door, the door of her nightmares. Mitch is behind Alice, and Alice's pulse is racing, her legs trembling. *What is this feeling? Fear?*

'This room has been left exactly as it was when Mr Patterson bought the house,' Christine reads from the clipboard. She pushes the key into the lock of the red door. 'When I first saw it – well I'm not going to lie, it gave me chills,' she goes on, turning the key, and easing the door open. She reaches in as if searching for the light switch. 'I can't wait for you to see it.'

Chapter 17

1981

Verity

Penny and Rowan Campbell were OK. They were in their mid-forties, with no children of their own, but a lot of love to give. In fact, six months after leaving Flynn House, Verity and Hugh's life was almost bearable, even veering towards normal.

They lived in the couple's five-bed detached house in Bristol – an alien experience at first. Penny and Rowan could sometimes foster up to six children at a time, and some were quite rowdy. Mealtimes were chaotic, and Verity would hold Hugh's hand under the table, while the other children bombarded them with questions: *So, your dad disappeared? So, you lived on an island? Is it true your dad was on the stage in London? He was a magician? On the TV? Bloody hell, that's amazing!*

Felix still hadn't been found, and Verity was glad of that. But she understood enough to know his house and money weren't coming to her and Hugh any time soon. It would be tied up for seven years at least, the solicitor had told her, 'or until Felix turns up.'

Going to school for the first time had taken its toll on Hugh at first, but Verity coped well. She had the strength of character that other children feared. She protected Hugh, like she had done all her life. It was clear to teachers that both children were intelligent beyond their years, but Verity was less focused, with a sudden desire to paint, always using Hugh as her model.

'Do you think they are a bit too close?' Verity heard Penny say to Rowan one evening. She had left her room to grab a drink from the kitchen, and been about to enter when she heard their hushed voices. 'She's always painting pictures of him, Rowan. I just find it all a bit … well … I don't know exactly.'

'They've had a weird upbringing, love,' Rowan said over the sound of clanking plates and glasses. And through the crack in the door, Verity could see them washing up. 'They're bound to be close. Need each other, even now. Give the kids time.'

'Yeah, you're right.' Penny dashed her fair hair from her face, her round cheeks flushed as she swirled a glass around in the bubbles. 'They're nice enough kids, they really are. I'm probably over-reacting.'

'And he's so polite.'

She looked at her husband. 'Yes! Scarily so at times – he doesn't seem to have any, I don't know, strength. It's as though he's had the life sucked out of him, poor lamb.'

'His father knocked it out of him from what I can make out. Felix Flynn was an evil man.'

Penny nodded. 'I still think Verity smothers the boy; he doesn't seem to be able to escape her to become his own person.'

'Maybe I'll take him out at the weekend without her. We could kick a ball about. Perhaps go for a burger.' Rowan loved his sport and watched a lot of football on the TV.

'He doesn't look like a footballer to me.' Penny laughed. *She laughed about Hugh.* 'But it's a good idea. I'll try to keep Verity occupied.'

'Well, there's no harm in trying, is there?'

'No. It will do him good to get away from his sister for a bit.'

*

It was midnight when Verity and Hugh left the house, their bags packed.

'I don't get why we're leaving,' Hugh said, as they crept down the path. 'I like Penny and Rowan. I like it here.'

'We can't stay. They're going to try and separate us, Hugh,' she whispered. 'You wouldn't want that, would you?'

'No ... but.' He looked over his shoulder as they padded down the road. 'Where are we going, Verity? They were so kind to us.'

She grabbed his hand. Pulled him along. 'I'll work something out, Hugh. I always do.'

Chapter 18

Halloween Weekend 2019

Alice

'Alice! Alice! Christine!' It's Leon, his panicked voice growing louder, echoing through the hotel, the closer he gets.

Christine's eyes dart to the hallway below. She pulls her arm from within the attic room, and without turning on the light, snaps the door closed, and locks it.

Alice is relieved she hasn't got to face whatever's inside, for now at least, but her stomach knots. She's worried about Leon.

He appears at the foot of the eight-stepped, narrow staircase, bends over breathless, eyes staring up at them, wide and watery. His clothes are muddy and soaked, his jacket dotted with blood.

'Oh, God, Leon,' Alice cries.

'What happened?' Christine says, as they move together down the staircase towards him, and congregate on the lower landing.

'Leon?' Alice puts her arms around him, can feel his heart pounding, his erratic breathing. His forehead shimmers with sweat; his hands are scratched and bleeding.

'I almost fell from the cliff.' His voice is raspy. 'I think the wind pushed me—'

'You think?' Alice says.

'Yes … it's strong out there.' He lowers his head. 'Is anyone else here?' he asks Christine. 'Anyone else in the building, on the island?'

'Mr Patterson's at the cottage, and Gabriela is in the bar, and there's Lori, of course, and Dane and Savannah Winslow, but I think they're in their rooms.' She's talking too fast, her cheeks pink. 'Other than that, it's just us chickens.'

Leon shakes his head, looking at each of them in turn. 'I saw something out there. I don't know, it was ghostlike, somehow.'

Mitch guffaws, the sound inappropriately loud. 'What? You're kidding me, right?'

Leon shakes his head, and takes a breath, clearly narked at being doubted. 'I definitely saw something. Something yellow.'

'Ghosts aren't yellow, are they?' Faith says.

'There's no such thing as ghosts, Faith.' Mitch slaps his hand on his forehead, shakes his head. 'Sometimes you can be so stupid.'

Alice attempts to meet Faith's eye, but her friend seems unfazed by Mitch. Her self-worth must be so low to put up with him, and Alice is angry with herself for not seeing that before. Too wrapped up in her own sadness after her father died to see her friend might need her. She will make it up to Faith. She will get her away from this idiot.

'I didn't say it was a ghost,' Leon says. 'I don't know what it was, but I definitely saw something out there.' A pause. 'Maybe we should check it out.'

'Wait, I'll grab Shaggy and Scooby,' Mitch says with a laugh, 'and I'll be right with you.'

'Stop it, please, Mitch,' Alice says, as Leon wipes his face with the back of his hand. 'Can't you see he's had an awful experience out there?'

'Well that's as may be, but it ain't no ghost.'

'I agree, but Leon's seen something. Someone needs to go out there with him and put his mind at rest.'

'Well don't look at me, Alice.' Mitch splays his hands and widens his eyes.

'Why not? It can be a real-life live-action role-play.' Alice says, fed up with biting her tongue where this moron is concerned. 'It may even make you feel like a real man.'

'Don't take the piss,' Mitch snaps. 'I mean what do you actually do with your life, eh? Faith says you've been stuck in your daddy's house for months doing sod all since he died.'

'Enough!' Leon yells, glaring at Mitch.

'I didn't say it like that, Alice,' Faith says, her eyes darting from Mitch to Alice. 'I said I was worried about you, is all.'

'It's fine,' Alice says. But it's far from it. She's beginning to dislike Mitch with a passion.

'Whatever I saw out there,' Leon says, running his hand over his chin, 'seemed to disappear over the cliff.'

'We should go out there,' Alice says. 'I'll come with you.' She moves away from everyone. 'I'll grab my coat from our room.'

'Thanks,' Leon says. 'I'll meet you downstairs in reception.'

As she heads away, Mitch gives a little cough and says, 'Well as the only bloke with any balls around here, I guess I'd better come too.'

*

Alice closes the door behind her, and places her handbag on the bedside table. She leans against the door for a few moments, eyes closed, wishing she were back in her bedroom at Butterfly Cottage, looking out over Whitby.

She takes a deep breath. Leon's odd experience, on top of the fact the hotel is evoking a strange kind of déjà vu, hasn't helped. But she mustn't let it get under her skin, play with her mind – she needs to keep calm. Not knowing about her past, her father's past, has been a stumbling block all her life, and this place holds the secrets – she knows it does.

She flicks on the light, notices the window is open, and moves across the room to close it. She turns, about to grab her coat.

'Christ!' she cries, leaping backwards. Perched on one of the pillows is a ventriloquist's doll. Its black, oily hair is combed back from its painted face; a red bow tie is attached to a black shirt. It looks familiar somehow. And there's something else that sends a shiver down her spine – the puppet has no feet.

Leon

Christine supplied Leon with a couple of heavy-duty torches, and disappeared into the kitchen, Faith headed into the bar – needing a drink. He's alone in reception, keen to get outside and discover what he saw, adrenaline masking his fear and exhaustion.

His eyes travel over the endless black and white photographs of Felix Flynn. The display says a fair bit about Felix the celebrity. He was clearly talented, a popular act, but it says little about the man behind that persona. Leon peers closer, into the man's dark, emotionless eyes. Christine said he disappeared years ago, and Leon works out that if he is still alive, he would be in his late seventies, early eighties, perhaps.

In the corridor that leads to the front exit, the lounge door stands open – the mesmerising, creepy John Carpenter theme tune of the Seventies' *Halloween* film escaping the room, making him shudder. Leon saw the film a long time ago. Michael Myers, the memorable, chilling killer, had given him no end of sleepless nights as a teenager. He walks over to the door, glances in the room at the forty-inch TV surrounded by empty sofas and chairs, and slams the door closed. He's freaked out enough right now, without a horror film making things worse.

He pads over to the pink sofa, perches on the edge, waiting, the streak of yellow floating in the wind playing on his mind. *Get a grip, Leon.*

Fast-paced footsteps carry above his head, and Alice appears at the top of the curving staircase, her Parka draped over her arm, eyes wide, face pale.

'Hey.' He rises, as she dashes down the stairs and into his arms. She's shaking, her heart beating fast against his chest. 'What's happened? Are you OK?'

Before she can speak, Mitch appears, and thumps down the staircase two at a time in heavy, battered black boots, while zipping his lime-green waterproof up to his neck. He lifts the hood over his hair, now tied in a stumpy ponytail.

'What's up with her?' he says to Leon, as though Alice is invisible. 'If she's got the wobbles, it might be best if she stays behind with the rest of the girlies.'

'I'm fine.' Alice pulls away from Leon, and glares at Mitch, who shrugs, the fabric of his jacket squeaking as he lifts his shoulders. 'In fact, we should go. Now!'

Alice

Alice pulls on her coat, as she leads the way to the main exit and out into the darkness, pushing thoughts of the strange puppet from her mind. She will tell Leon, but now's not a good time.

Leon flicks on one of the torches, hands one to Alice who does the same. 'Let's go to the garden first. That's where I first saw the … well whatever it was.' He makes his way to the front of the house. Alice and Mitch follow.

Once there, Leon points his torch towards the fence. 'That's where I went over.'

'Oh, Leon,' Alice says, taking hold of his arm. 'You could have … are you sure you're OK?'

He nods. 'Yeah, but let's keep away from the edge. The fence is flattened in parts and it's a sheer drop.' He glances towards the tall trees swaying, moaning in the wind, and shudders.

'Let's take a look,' Mitch says, stepping out across the lawn.

'What part of stay away from the edge do you not understand, Mitch?'

He stops and turns back to Leon and Alice, a gust of wind catching inside his hood, making it appear like a bright green balloon at the back of his head. 'Fine,' he says.

'We should head down to the sea,' Alice says. 'Whatever it was, it will be down there somewhere.'

They leave the garden, and make their way down the hill, wind bashing against them, stinging rain coating their faces as they head towards the jetty, where pumpkins are scattered, smashed by the wind.

'Where's the boat?' Alice says, her eyes widening.

'Yeah, I noticed that earlier.' Leon casts his torch across the choppy sea. The boat they'd come in on is further out now, a child's toy on the horizon.

'It must have come free in the wind,' Mitch says, and laughs. 'Looks like we're stuck here until midday tomorrow.'

Alice stares at Mitch for a moment, wondering why he finds everything so amusing. She moves her gaze to Leon, who looks up towards the hotel. Aims his torch.

'There's the flattened wire fencing where I fell.' He lowers the torch. 'Whatever went over the cliff will be round this bend,' he cries over the wind.

'Hang on.' Mitch hurries towards a shed. He drags open the door, and disappears inside, returning with three boat oars. 'If there's a ghost out there, we need to be armed.'

'You can't kill a ghost,' Leon says.

Alice wraps her arms around herself. 'There's no such thing as ghosts.'

A memory flashes in. She's playing on a swing in a garden she doesn't recognise – it's not Whitby, not Seafield Island. Her father watches, smiling from an upstairs window. A woman stares from the foot of the sweeping garden, too far away to see clearly. Suddenly her father appears at the back door, pulls her from the swing.

'Who is that?' she cries, looking over her shoulder as he pulls her inside the house, but the figure has gone.

'You imagined it, Alice,' he says. *'Nobody knows where we live.'*

The memory dissolves, leaving way for the noise of the sea crashing against the rocks loud in her ears.

'Fine, if you don't want one.' Mitch goes to throw two of the oars to the ground, his face barely visible in the folds of his hood.

'I never said that.' Leon takes two from him, hands one to Alice. 'They'll help us walk on the rocks; it's bound to be slippery out there.' He sets off, the rain heavier now, soaking through his jacket, dripping off his hair.

Alice and Mitch follow, and once around the bend it becomes clear what Leon saw.

'Oh my God,' Alice cries, covering her mouth with her hand.

Leon moves forward, crouches down.

'What the hell is it doing out here?' Alice's voice trembles as she comes up behind him.

'I've no idea.' Leon shakes his head, stares up at her with bewildered eyes. He tries to take her hand, but she pulls free, distraught.

'What is it? What's wrong?' Mitch says, coming up behind them.

'It's my dress,' Alice cries, crouching and dragging it from the sea, soaking herself as she tries to wring water from it. 'It's my yellow dress. What the hell is it doing out here?'

Chapter 19

1988

Verity

'Get a room, Hugh, for Christ's sake,' Verity said, hearing the slur in her voice. Drinking too much had become a way of life. She needed to slow up. She knew that. She was twenty-one, no longer a rebellious teenager. No longer the kid who lived on the Bristol streets fighting for survival with her brother.

She flopped her head back on the grass, and stared at the star-dotted night sky. The tang of cannabis, and the sound of Bobby McFerrin's 'Don't Worry Be Happy' floated across the lawns, where students from the university sprawled in clusters.

Verity and Hugh weren't students, though they liked hanging out as though they were. Hugh worked in a factory, and Verity was a shop assistant working on the pick 'n' mix counter in Woolworths, which didn't help her weight problem.

She closed her eyes, wondering how she could prise her brother away from his latest fling, without sounding like the overprotective older sister she knew she was. Couldn't Pippa see he was using her, like he'd used all the others since he'd morphed into a man?

Maybe Verity should go to her lodgings. Leave them to it. He would tire of her soon enough. He always did.

She sat up, dragged on her cardigan. 'I'm going back. You two are making me want to puke.'

Pippa looked up from kissing Hugh, and laughed. She couldn't see how much Verity loathed her. That Verity could happily throw up at the sight of her body entwined with her brother's.

Pippa rolled off of him, falling back onto the grass, her blonde hair splaying around her like it was blowing in the wind. She was more attractive than some of the other young women that Verity had put up with, with her blue eyes, and cascading curls – but still; Hugh was pretty numb to emotion, wasn't he? Much like Verity. Between their father and the awful nannies they'd suffered, any real emotion had been bashed out of them over the years. All they had was their love for each other.

Verity rose to her feet.

A warm evening had followed a glorious sunny Sunday, and they'd been lounging around for most of the day, but now Verity felt as if three was a crowd. But she wasn't the gooseberry, was she? Pippa would soon learn that the bond she and Hugh had was unbreakable.

She grabbed her bright orange rucksack from the blanket she'd been sitting on, and flung it over her shoulder.

Hugh pushed back his dark hair, so like her own, from his face. No longer the skinny sap who peed his pants. He was tall and muscular, his eyes – once a thing of ridicule for the local children – the attraction. Despite the sharpness of his nose, he was beautiful – perfect. 'You OK, V?'

'Yep! Fine!' She stepped away. 'See you tomorrow.' They always met Monday lunchtimes. It was their thing.

'He can't make tomorrow, Verity,' Pippa called after her, her tone assertive. Verity swung round. Pippa was stretched full length on the grass next to Hugh now, propped up on her elbows. Slim and tall, she was so different from Verity, who carried too much weight. 'Hugh and I thought we might go into Bristol for lunch,' Pippa went on, turning to Hugh. 'Didn't we, Hugh?'

Hugh was looking down, fiddling with a blade of grass.

'Hugh?' Verity said. 'Is this true?'

He shrugged, wouldn't meet her eye.

'You two can meet up on Tuesday, maybe. I'm seeing a friend that day.' Pippa paused for a moment. 'I'm sorry, Verity. But the thing is, Hugh and I need some "us" time, and you're always hanging about, and ...'

Verity turned and shot across the lawn at speed, not wanting to hear any more. She hadn't cried for years, her heart too hard for that, but tears burned now, raw and painful behind her eyes. This had never happened before.

Back at her lodgings, she flopped down on her bed, and buried her face in the pillow, memories of childhood sweeping in.

She'd always been the strong older sister. Hugh had been the pathetic fragile child. She'd protected him, hadn't she? Saved him from bullies, punished any nanny who thought they could spank his skinny legs, and so much more. And now – after all she'd done for him – he was about to abandon her. She would never let that happen – never.

*

Hugh and Verity were staying on the outskirts of Bristol. The main house, an Edwardian detached, was owned by Clara McCloud, a pleasant widowed woman in her late seventies. The two annexes where they lived were separate from her house. Clara tended to leave her tenants in peace, which suited the siblings.

It was almost midnight, and Verity had been staring at the ceiling for the last hour, eyes so wide they ached, when there was a knock at the door. 'Verity?'

She flew from her bed, and flung open the door. 'Hugh.' She

117

wanted to take him in her arms, but held back, stepping out of the room, into the night air. 'Where's Pippa?'

'In my bedsit asleep. Can I come in? I need to talk to you. It's important.'

'OK, if you must.'

He moved past her into the room, and perched on the edge of her bed, his head in his hands.

The room was small, simple: a single bed that seconded as a sofa, a laminated wardrobe, a chest of drawers. There was a kitchenette, the sink piled high with mugs and plates, a bathroom barely big enough to turn around in.

'I'm sorry,' Hugh said without preamble.

'For what?' She turned her back on him, picked up a bottle of vodka, and splashed some into a shot glass. 'Want one?'

'No.'

She twisted round to face him, took a long gulp, wincing as it burned her throat. 'What are you sorry for, Hugh?'

He looked down at his hands, entwining his slim fingers until they looked tangled. 'That I love her. That I love Pippa.'

'What?' She slammed her glass down on the worktop. 'You can't do, Hugh. It's lust, that's all.'

'I know you don't like her.'

'She's not right for you, Hugh.'

'All I want is for you be happy for me, Verity.' His tone had become pleading, imploring her to understand. 'You know I'll never push you out. Nobody can ever come between us – you know that.'

Verity's mind spun. She had to play it cool. She had to. 'It's fine, Hugh.' She made her way over to the bed, and sat down beside him. 'I only want you to be happy. God knows life has been hard enough. For both of us.'

He looked up at her, his eyes meeting hers. 'Really?' Sometimes he was so childlike, it was unbearable. 'Because the thing is, V, Pippa and I want to get married.'

She stifled her shock. Tensed. 'Married?'

'Soon.'

'Christ.' She covered her mouth for a moment. 'Are you sure that's what you want?'

He nodded. 'I love her, Verity. She wants kids too.'

Her heart thudded. 'And what about you?'

'Yeah ... I want to give a child everything we never had. Love, security – things we longed for.'

She put her arm around him, and scooped him close. She wanted to scream at him to get rid of Pippa, but bit down hard on her lip. 'Are you sure you're cut out to be a father?' she said. 'I mean we didn't exactly have the best role model.'

'I know, but I think the fact we didn't will make me more determined to get it right,' he said. 'Be happy for me. Please.'

'I am, Hugh,' she lied. 'I am.'

*

Hugh had been gone ten minutes when Verity grabbed her coat and headed out into the night.

'Hello, Verity.' It was the landlady, Clara, dragging a bin from her back garden ready for collection the next day. 'Where are you off to at this late hour, dear girl?'

'Just out,' she said, picking up speed, determined not to let the woman with fluffy white curls and a pastel-coloured dress change her mind, now it was made up.

*

'What's your name again?' The bloke sitting opposite Verity was slumped in his seat, a lit cigarette dangling from his fingers, the sleeves of his denim shirt rolled up to reveal a tattoo of a rose with bloodied thorns on his lower arm. He looked as pissed as she felt. Her ridiculous plan to get absolutely rat-arsed, and screw the first man who paid her any attention was wearing thin now. She'd changed her mind. In fact, she regretted leaving her lodgings. Clara had been right. It had been late, and it was even later now.

This bloke's aftershave was still as strong as when he first joined Verity at the pub table over an hour ago; it was catching in her throat. Her head was swimming. She rested her cheek on the scratched and battered wood of the bar table. It stank of stale alcohol.

'I need to go home,' she said, hating that she sounded so weak – pathetic. 'I feel awful. Can you take me home?'

'That's not what I asked,' he slurred, narrowing his brown eyes. 'I asked what your name is.'

She didn't answer. If he couldn't recall her name, after they'd knocked back shots together, laughed a bit, flirted even – then he didn't deserve to know it.

This bloke – *Pete? Matt? Drake?* Christ, she couldn't recall his name either – was a big chap: tall, broad-shouldered, not bad-looking with dark layered hair to his shoulders. He'd bragged about him and his sister opening a tattoo shop in the town centre, and how his sister was the talent – *dim, but arty* – and he was the brains. He clearly didn't have the same kind of bond with his sister that she had with Hugh. Despite him making her laugh a couple of times, she wasn't keen. A bit of an arse – had a real downer on women. In fact, he could piss off. She'd had enough. She didn't want sex with him or anyone else. She needed to call a taxi.

She rose, stumbled across the room towards the phone in the corner. But he was right behind her, looping his arm around her waist, guiding her towards the exit, and into the quietness of the late hour.

'I need to get home,' she cried, as he dragged her across the silent road, and into the woods opposite the pub. 'No, please. I need to get a taxi.'

*

Water cascaded, cooler now, making her shiver after the deliberately scalding flow from the shower moments ago. Soapsuds snaked down her shaking legs, before spiralling down the plughole towards oblivion, along with the foul, yet fuzzy, memories of the early hours.

A mistake, not rape – Verity tried to convince herself – a hideous way to lose her virginity. She hadn't wanted sex with a beer-soaked stranger. She'd told him no over and over. *Why hadn't he stopped?*

The plan, before her stupid idea to venture out half-pissed, had always been to never lose her virginity. Her petal, as she liked to call it, would stay intact forever, because the only way she'd ever lose it was for love, and she could never imagine loving anyone in the intense way she loved Hugh.

But this, *this* thing that happened on the damp grass, with a bloke she'd just met – with a name she still couldn't recall – was the furthest thing from love that she could get. What the hell had she been thinking? This, *this* had been sordid and cheap, and now she felt unclean – and however long she stood under this pathetic excuse for a shower, it would never wash away her pain, her humiliation, her sadness. This, *this* had been the worst moment of her life, and that was really something, because her whole life so far had been a cacophony of horrendous moments.

Tears rolled down her face. She'd said no. She'd said no so many times.

The phone rang, startling her from her thoughts. She turned off the shower, and the pipes groaned as she grabbed a greying towel from the rack, and wrapped it around herself. It felt harsh against her skin.

'Hello,' she said, once she'd made her way into the bedroom and placed the phone receiver against her ear.

'Verity Flynn?'

'That's right.' She rubbed droplets of water from her face and ear with the edge of the towel. 'Who is this?'

'My name is Marcus Bergman, from Bergman, Smithton and Cavendish Solicitors in Ipswich.'

'It's been seven years, hasn't it?' Her mouth tugged upwards at the corners. She hoped so. She needed something to smile about.

'That's right, I'm—'

'He's legally dead?'

'Yes.'

'Thank God. He was a cruel, arrogant bastard.'

'Well that cruel, arrogant bastard has left you Flynn House, and two million pounds.'

'Oh, well that's all right then, Mr Bergman.' Her voice was satirical. 'Felix Flynn was clearly a fantastic father, and all is forgiven.'

'Could you come to my office? It's—'

'I know where it is. Is the money and house to be divided between me and my brother, Hugh?'

'There's no mention of your brother in the will.'

'So Felix has had the last laugh.' She sat down on the edge of her bed. 'If he couldn't come between us when he was alive, he'll do his best to do so now he's dead.'

'Sorry?'

'It doesn't matter.' And it didn't. Verity would make sure Hugh was well looked after, even if Pippa was part of the deal.

Chapter 20

Halloween Weekend 2019

Alice

Alice leads the way across the main entrance of Flynn Hotel trancelike, the soaked yellow dress draped over her arm, Leon and Mitch behind her. They are all exhausted and sodden, dripping their way into the bar.

Lori is by the fire reading, a glass of brandy in her hand. She lifts her eyes from the pages of her book, jumps to her feet, and dashes over, her dress clinging to her slim thighs, flapping her ankles. 'Christine told me what happened to you, Leon,' she says, touching his arm. 'Are you OK?'

'I'm fine,' he says. 'Thanks.'

'You saw something—?'

'Yeah, but it's OK, panic over,' Mitch says, shaking his head, droplets of water flying from his hair. 'It was only Alice's dress.'

'Seriously?' Alice says. Her plaits have come loose, hanging limp and wet about her face. Her head throbs. Her coat is soaked from the rain and crashing waves. Her dress had somehow ended up

123

on the rocks, and is now sodden, dangling over her arm. There's no quelling the rising fear inside her. She desperately wants to go home, and the thought that they could be stuck here for another fifteen hours is weighing heavy. 'You don't think my dress, which was locked in my room, being found by the sea, is a reason for concern, Mitch?' She detests this idiotic man.

'That is odd,' Lori says. 'You must speak to Christine about this. First our cell phones and now your dress. Who could have taken it?'

The same person who put a ventriloquist's doll on my pillow, Alice wants to say, but bites down on her words. She needs to talk to Leon about it first.

Mitch looks about him, peeling off his wet jacket. 'Where are Christine and Faith?'

'Faith's watching *Halloween* in the lounge, I believe,' Lori says, taking a sip of her drink. 'She said it might cure her angst. Said if you returned, Alice, could you let her know you're back.'

'Well, I've never heard of a horror film curing anxiety before,' Mitch says. 'I'd much rather have a brandy.' He pushes up the sleeves of his top to reveal a tattoo of a rose dripping with blood on his lower arm, and heads away, towards the bar, squelching as he goes.

Alice takes off her wet Parka, and drapes it over her arm with the dress. 'You're right, Lori, I'll talk to Christine,' she says, her voice calmer. 'I need to find out who has a key to my room.'

'Well, she said something about needing to ice some fairy cakes.' Lori furrows her forehead. 'So, I'm guessing she's in the kitchen.'

'OK, thanks.'

'Has Cameron turned up yet?' Leon asks. 'He would have a key to every room, wouldn't he?'

Lori shakes her head. 'Christine said she'd try calling him again, but I don't know if she got through.'

'I think I'll get changed before I do anything else.' Alice shivers, the discomfort of being soaked through to her underwear getting to her. She looks at Leon, hoping he will come with her, the ventriloquist's doll in their room pinching at her anxiety. On top of finding her dress on the rocks this is all too much. She doesn't want to be alone in this place if she can avoid it. 'Are you coming?'

He nods, and they are about to leave the bar when Christine appears in the doorway, looking exhausted.

'Who would have a key to our room?' Alice asks her.

'Only me and Mr Patterson, I believe.' She bites down on her lip. 'Why?'

Alice can't bring herself to explain about the dress. 'Are you sure?'

Christine glances over her shoulder towards the reception desk. 'Well, there's always a spare. I guess ... I'm not always there to keep an eye, you see. There's so much to do. I'm sure my Terry would turn in his grave if he could see me now.'

Alice balls her fists, frustrated by this woman. Though in equal measure she feels for her. This isn't Christine's fault. She's only been in the position for a few days, and, in the woman's own words, she's been thrown in the deep end. Where is Cameron Patterson, after all? Why isn't he supporting Christine? So much money must have gone into renovating the house, and yet he's hired a bumbling woman to run it.

*

'Hey, guys,' Faith says, poking her head out from the TV lounge as Alice and Leon leave Christine adjusting her silver-thread cardigan. Alice wants to keep walking, pretend she hasn't seen her. She wants some time out away from everyone, to get out of her wet clothes – to get her head straight. She's tempted to run up the stairs and into her room, ignore Faith, but she knows she can't. Faith is her friend.

She and Leon pad over to the TV lounge. Faith has changed

out of her heels and little black dress, and looks more like the woman Alice knows, in her dungarees and trainers, her hair pulled into a high ponytail. Is her change of clothes an act of rebellion against Mitch? She hopes so.

They make their way into the lounge, and Faith freezes Jamie Lee Curtis's petrified face on the huge TV screen with the remotes.

'I'll get rid of Jamie entirely, shall I?' she says, looking back at Alice, seeming to pick up on her anxiety.

'Thanks,' Alice says. 'I'm not in the mood for a horror movie right now.'

Faith ends the film, and puts on a news channel, lowering the volume.

'So how did you get on out there?' Faith says. 'You're both drenched.' She peers past them towards the door. 'Where's Mitch?'

'At the bar downing a double brandy,' Leon says.

'Typical, Mitch – he loves his brandy.' She looks at the dress draped over Alice's arm.

Alice fiddles with the damp collar, not in the mood to go through everything that happened again, but knowing she has to. 'We found it down on the rocks,' she says. 'This was the yellow ghost – my dress was the yellow ghost.'

'Oh God. How did it get down there?'

'We've no idea. It was locked in my room.' Alice is trying to be strong, but tears are close. 'I want to go home,' she whispers. 'I hate this place.'

'Oh, Alice, if you hate it here that much you should leave,' Faith says, taking her in her arms.

'We can't,' Leon says. 'It's not as simple as that. The boat has slipped its mooring. It's out in the middle of the sea.'

Faith releases Alice, moves her gaze to Leon. 'How the hell—?'

'We've no idea. We saw Christine tie it up. And from what I remember, she moored it pretty well,' Leon says. 'I'm surprised it worked its way loose, if I'm honest.'

126

'We're going to get changed into something dry,' Alice says, turning to leave. 'Then we'll call someone to get us off the island.'

'OK, well, if there's anything I can do.'

'There isn't. But thanks.'

As they go to leave the room, Faith's eyes drift to the TV screen. 'Oh God,' she whispers.

Alice's eyes dart to the screen. 'Jesus, that's Tegan Matthews.'

Faith waves the remote towards the TV, turns up the volume. There's a picture of Tegan behind a young newsreader, her stunning features and dark curly hair unmistakable.

'Tegan Matthews,' the newsreader is saying, 'the literary agent who discovered E. H. Membrose, best-selling author of *Where Doves Fly* and *Raging Fires*, was found dead in her home earlier today. A friend raised the alarm after not hearing from Tegan for several days. Police are treating her death as suspicious.'

Alice's heart hammers, as the newsreader switches to a story about storms hitting the UK's eastern coastline. 'This can't be right. She can't be dead. She can't be.' She hasn't been a fan of Tegan since she deserted her after her father's death. She even suspected her of telling the media that her father was E. H. Membrose, but to hear she's dead is horrifying. Her chest tightens.

Faith moves towards Alice, puts her arm around her waist. 'God, you're shaking, lovely,' she says. 'You knew her well, didn't you?'

'I thought I did, at one point,' Alice whispers. She turns to Leon, who is drained of colour. He looks as bewildered as she feels. 'We have to go home,' she says. 'We need to call a boatyard on the mainland, or something. Get someone to come and take us off this bloody island.' Alice pulls away from Faith, and races out of the TV lounge, almost tripping over her own feet in her haste to get away. Leon is right behind her.

'I'll see you in the bar in a bit, yeah?' Faith calls after them.

Alice doesn't reply, her breath raspy as she leaps up the stairs two at a time, and heads along the corridor towards their room.

'Are you OK?' Leon says, catching up with her and grabbing her hand.

She stops, bats away the tears now streaming down her cheeks. 'OK?' she cries. 'You did just hear Tegan's dead, right?' She hates that this is turning her into a crumbling wreck. 'You did just see my dress on the rocks, when it should have been in my room?'

'Yeah, I get the dress thing. It's weird. But Tegan's death has nothing to do with your dress.'

'I know.' She looks about her; catching sight of the picture of Felix Flynn on the wall. 'It's this place, Leon. If there's a way we can go home—'

'I agree. I don't like it here either. I don't want to stay here any more than you do.' He takes her in his arms. 'We'll call someone,' he goes on. 'I promise.'

But as he puts the key into the door of their room and turns it, she knows she's yet to face the ventriloquist doll once more.

Leon

Leon leads the way into the room, turns on the light, sensing Alice's tension as she follows him. He wants to talk to her, tell her what he knows about Tegan, what she told him that night in the pub. But now isn't the right moment. It will have to wait.

'Oh God. Where is it?' Alice drops her coat and dress to the floor with a thud.

Leon swings round to see her standing statue-still, eyes wide and watery as she stares at the bed. 'Alice?' He's worried about her. Yes, things have been weird, but it's more than that, Alice isn't herself. It's the possible link this place had to her father too. The sooner they can call the mainland and get off the island, the better. 'Where's what?'

Her gaze is fixed on the pillow. The vacant look in her eyes chilling. He runs his hand over his chin, feels the prickle of stubble, the tension in his jaw. Her anxiety is catching.

She finally looks at him, eyes wide. 'There was a ventriloquist puppet here, and now it's gone.'

'What?' He shudders, the idea making the hairs on his neck stand on end.

'Maybe it was one of Felix Flynn's puppets. It was here in our room, before we went outside.' She runs her hand over the duvet, and up towards the pillow. 'It was right here, staring at me. And the window was open, as though …'

'As though what, Alice? You're officially freaking me out, here.' He rubs his neck. It aches – whiplash? Tension?

She sits down on the edge of bed, and buries her head in her hands. 'It was here, Leon, I swear it,' she says through her fingers. 'When I came up to get my coat, it was here. But now it's gone.'

Leon turns on the spot, dragging fingers through his damp hair. 'There was a puppet in our room?'

She nods. 'Yes. I know it sounds crazy, but I swear it was here on the pillow.'

'OK.' He shudders again at the thought. 'So if what you're saying is true—'

'You think I'm lying?' She looks hurt, her eyes a deep shade of blue.

'No.' He sits beside her, takes her hand, and squeezes it within his own. 'But Alice, if there was a puppet, how did it get here … Where's it gone?'

'It was here. It really was.' A tear zigzags down her cheek, and he holds her close to him for some time.

Once she is calmer, he rises to his feet. 'We need to go home,' he says. 'I'm sure Christine will know who we can call. Let's get changed and go back down.'

'OK.' She rises, pale and exhausted, her face wet from tears. 'I need a tissue,' she says, almost childlike, looking about her.

Within moments, she's frantically looking under the bed. 'My handbag,' she cries. 'It was here, but it's gone. It has my phone in it. Oh God, Leon, what the hell is happening? I'm not sure I can take any more.'

Chapter 21

1988

Verity

Flynn House felt cold and musty after standing empty for seven years – a miserable place, though that was nothing new. Verity had thought she might renovate the place. Cover the past with fancy wallpaper and Dulux paint. She had enough money. But as she rattled around the house alone, the past crawled under her skin, and sucked the small amount of life she had left from her. It was as though Felix was watching, laughing from the grave.

She had hoped Hugh and Pippa might move into the big house with her, but her brother had insisted from the off that the two of them would live independently in the cottage on the island. 'Pippa's got great plans for the place,' he'd said. Verity couldn't help the anger that bubbled inside her. *After all she'd done for him.* She couldn't stay there any longer, watching Hugh and Pippa's love grow stronger. Her stomach knotted each time she saw them together, nausea rising at their happiness, rubbing like sandpaper against her own despair.

It was a month into their return that Verity packed her bags, and left Flynn House. She dropped a note through the cottage door for her brother, explaining how she intended to backpack around Europe. That she wouldn't return for maybe a year.

She hoped the separation might free her mind of him, break the claustrophobic bond they had, because she knew, deep down, it was wrong to be so dependent on him for her own happiness. Time apart was what she needed. Maybe she would find someone – fall in love.

She'd booked a hostel in Paris to kick off her trip. She could afford better, but she wanted to mix with other young people, maybe make friends. She'd picked up brochures from Dunwold's travel agents on the high street, chosen destinations. Cut out glossy photos of the Eiffel Tower, Cologne Cathedral, and Wieliczka Salt Mine, and slipped them inside the pages of her diary.

She would stay in Paris for three weeks, maybe four, then travel to Cologne, and Kraków. She would learn about a world outside of Flynn House and Bristol, outside of England. She would teach herself how to be happy.

But her knowledge of the world was limited, and arriving at Norwich Airport alone felt daunting. She headed straight for the bar. Knocked back two vodkas. This was going to be harder than she thought.

By the time she climbed up the metal steps of the plane, surrounded by couples and families heading off on holiday, her heart was giving out warnings, and Hugh's voice whispered in her head, '*What the hell are you doing, Verity?*'

But as the plane rumbled down the runway, and took off into the blue sky, something happened inside of her. A strong feeling engulfed her: *hope*. She'd never felt it before, but maybe – just maybe – she was leaving the worst of her life behind her.

*

Three months had passed since Verity left the UK. She hadn't made any friends, not really. A few drunken nights with strangers in Paris, and Cologne, but that was it. It was her own fault, she suspected. She wasn't great at letting anyone close. And although she'd left Flynn House miles behind her, the place was still there, inside her head, crushing any attempt to move on. She'd been wrong to be positive, hopeful. She didn't deserve happiness.

She clicked her seatbelt across her lap, and looked out through the round window next to her. The plane would soon land in Kraków. Would Poland be any different? Would she ever be able to let go of her past? Let go of Hugh?

Kraków Airport was tiny, no more than a shed – so much smaller than the airports in England, France and Germany. She'd read somewhere that the airport had once been a military site. She could only imagine how much better it would be for Poland when the new terminal was finished.

She queued for almost an hour for her passport to be checked, before a large woman in military uniform frisked her. By the time she was outside in the cool, autumn air, her holdall by her side, she desperately needed a drink.

Without thinking, still not used to cars being driven on the right, she stepped out into oncoming traffic. A Lada almost hit her, and the driver hooted as she jumped back onto the pavement.

A taxi took her to the main market square, where she bought a bagel from a cart, from an old woman wearing a headscarf. There were a few decent, cheap hotels, and Verity booked a room in one of them for two weeks.

Once showered, she pulled on a black sweatshirt, jeans and low-heeled boots, and headed out once more.

Verity made her way along the pavement looking in shop windows, all closed up for the evening. She slowed outside a shop selling music cassettes, her mind drifting to Hugh – maybe she would buy one for him. He liked Madonna and Cher. The shop was bound to have one or the other. She pressed her hand against the shop window, and lowered her head. God, she missed her brother. She'd only spoken to him on the rare times she could get a call past Pippa, and it was never enough to quench her need.

She headed down some steps into a jazz bar in the basement of a building, approached the bar. 'Vodka, *proszę,*' she said. 'Double,' she added, holding up two fingers.

She found a table in the corner; sat down with her drink. She planned to leave as soon as the music started at nine; unable to cope with happy couples writhing to the sound of a saxophone, the intoxicating voices of jazz singers.

Maybe she should go home to England. Face Flynn House.

An hour later she knocked back her third drink, was about to rise.

'*Czy to miejsce jest zajęte?*' The man was average height, muscular, his dark hair cropped short, his eyes piercing blue.

She knew a little Polish from her phrase book, but he spoke fast. Her face must have shown her confusion.

'Is this seat free?'

She nodded, expecting him to take it to another table. But he sat down opposite her, placed his glass of clear liquid on the table.

She had been about to leave, hadn't she? She should really get back to her accommodation. But something made her stay. This man, whoever he was, stirred something inside her she'd never felt before. She raised her hand to catch the waiter's eye.

'Vodka, *proszę,*' she said as he approached.

The man looked at her smiled. 'My name is Mikolaj.'

'Verity.'

She soon learnt he was a builder, working on the new airport terminal.

'I'm staying in a crappy bedsit nearby,' he said, his English good, his accent twisting her stomach in a good way. She sensed he could see inside her head, knew what she was feeling. And as the evening drew to a close, he brushed her hair from her cheek, and told her she was a beautiful English rose.

*

'Pippa's pregnant,' Hugh told Verity in the December of 1988, his voice full of emotion. 'We're so happy, V. Be pleased for us.'

'I am! That's great news.' She meant it. She was pleased for her little brother, because she now had her beautiful Mikolaj. Hugh and her past were slotted away at the back of her mind. She was happy. Convinced her new lover – *her new obsession* – would never let her down.

Chapter 22

Halloween Weekend 2019

Alice

The tick, tick, tick of the grandfather clock greets Alice and Leon as they make their way back down stairs, his arm around her waist giving her comfort. But still her mind buzzes as she attempts to unpick her thoughts. So much has happened in such a short time: *The portrait of a young man who looks so like her father, a footless puppet in her room, her missing bag and phone, her dress floating in the wind to the bottom of the cliff.*

Did Cameron invite her here for a reason? If he did, where is he? And now Tegan is dead.

The clock chimes once. It's 10.30 p.m. Christine sits behind the reception desk; her head drooped as though she might nod off in a moment, her glasses slipping down her nose, revealing dark pillows of tiredness under her eyes.

As they approach, Alice wonders again about this woman who Cameron has given full responsibility of running the hotel to, despite, it seems, never meeting her. Why had he chosen her? Running this bizarre place seems too much for the woman. She cooks, cleans the kitchen, mans reception, even pilots the boat. She's taken on everything. Is it to simply escape her empty house somewhere on the mainland, where she and her beloved Terry once raised their son? Or is there another reason why she's here?

Leon coughs, and Christine jerks awake.

'Oh my word, I almost dozed off. I do apologise.' She looks at her watch, a cumbersome thing with a huge face and large numbers, squinting her eyes as she peers through her glasses. 'Only another hour, and it will be time for bed.' She gyrates her shoulders and straightens her silver-thread cardigan, eyes back on Alice and Leon. 'How are you both after your terrible shock?' she says. 'Faith mentioned your father's literary agent is dead. Murdered she said.'

'That's right,' Leon says.

Alice stares at the side of Leon's face. 'We don't know for sure she was murdered. They say she died in suspicious circumstances – that doesn't mean murder.'

Leon looks at Alice, takes her hand in his 'And because of that,' his eyes return to Christine, 'we need to get back to the mainland as soon as possible. The police may want to talk to us.'

'What? Like now?' Christine says. 'Tonight?'

Leon nods, and Alice continues to stare at him, comforted by his hand entwined with hers. She hadn't thought the police might want to talk to them, but is glad Leon used it as the reason rather than her fear of this place, her desperation to leave.

'Well, it's still blowing a gale out there,' Christine begins, 'and it won't be the safest of journeys. But I guess if needs must. I'll get the key to the boat.' She eases herself from her stool, and reaches for her anorak and beanie hanging on the door behind her.

'I'm afraid you won't be able to take us.' Leon runs his hand across his chin. 'Has nobody told you? The boat's slipped its mooring. It's a long way out at sea.'

Her eyes widen, as she places her anorak slowly back on the hook. 'Good God, that's all I need. Mr Patterson will—'

'I wouldn't worry about him.' Alice notes the irritation in her own voice. 'He should be here helping you, Christine. Leaving you to cope on your own like this, especially in a storm, is a bit much, if you ask me.'

'Well, I'm sure he'd be here if he could. Let's not jump to conclusions.'

'So why isn't he?' Her voice cracks up a notch. 'Has he given you a reason?'

Christine shrugs, tears filling her eyes, and Alice realises she's been a bit heavy-handed. 'Sorry,' she says. 'I'm just a bit agitated. Sorry.'

'If I'm honest, I can't get hold of him,' Christine says with a sniff. 'I haven't been able to since I arrived. All instructions have been emailed or were left here for me, and—'

'And you're doing a great job.' Leon's voice is calm and even. 'Against the odds.'

She smiles, as though grateful for the vote of confidence, but Alice feels uneasy. *Where the hell is the mysterious Cameron Patterson? The man who invited her here in the first place, praised her sculpture, bought it for a high price?*

Leon looks about him, grabs a pink box of tissues from the chest where Alice's sculpture still stands, and hands them to Christine. 'Do you know if there's a boatyard on the mainland that might send a boat out?'

Christine pulls one, two, three tissues from the box, lifts her glasses, and dabs her damp, tired eyes. 'Well, there's a small boat-yard a bit further down the coast, but they would be closed at the moment, I expect. I can try calling them, but I wouldn't hold out much hope.'

'If you wouldn't mind trying.'

'Of course.' She turns, picks up the land phone, pins the receiver to her ear. 'That's odd,' she says, looking back at them.

138

'The line is quite dead.' She hangs up. 'It must be the storm. Not to worry, I'll grab my mobile.' She reaches under the desk. 'Oh God,' she says.

'What?' Alice makes her way round the desk to where Christine is now crouching. Christine looks up, her red-framed glasses vivid and harsh against her pale face, a severed phone wire in her hand.

'Who would do this?' Christine drops the wire as though it's hot, and rises, straightens her cardigan.

'Something's so wrong here.' Alice hears the tremble in her voice, as she returns to Leon's side. 'We need to get off this island as soon as possible. All of us.'

'That's a bit of an over-reaction, surely,' Christine says. 'A mouse might have bitten through it. I've seen a few scampering about. We really mustn't over-react.' She picks up a black handbag, places it onto the stool she just vacated, and unzips it. 'I'll call the boatyard on my mobile.'

But Alice knows by the bewildered look on Christine's face as she rummages in her bag exactly what the woman is going to say when she looks up, and her heart thuds.

'Problem?' Leon says, as Christine stops searching.

'My phone,' she says, staring at him. 'It was here. It's gone.'

'Not you too.' He sounds agitated. 'This is bloody ridiculous. What the hell is going on here?'

'Maybe Gabriela has a phone.' Alice glances over her shoulder towards the bar.

'Well let's ask her, shall we?' Christine places her hand on her laptop, as though about to close it.

'No wait.' Alice pulls away from Leon's stare. 'Look up the number of the boatyard first. It will save time.'

'Yes, good idea.' Christine picks up a pen and jots down the word 'boatyard' on a Post-it Note, in small, spiky letters. Alice knows she's seen the handwriting before. It's the same as the writing on the envelope she received a few weeks ago that contained the photo of Flynn House.

'You sent me the photo,' Alice says, her tone challenging.

Christine looks up, the pen suspended in her hand, her neck flushing. 'Sorry?'

'The photo of Flynn House, you sent it to me.'

'What's this about?' Leon's eyes flick from Alice to Christine.

'I recognise her handwriting. She sent me a photo of Flynn House, to Butterfly Cottage.' Her narrowed eyes bore into the woman. 'Why the hell would you do that?'

'Is this true?' Leon asks.

Christine puts down the pen. Runs a finger around the collar of her dress and nods. 'I recall sending an envelope to you Alice, to Butterfly Cottage. The address stood out, because it was the home of the author … your father, the one who was in all the papers when he … but—'

'Why? Why would you send it without saying why?' Alice's legs feel weak. This is ridiculous.

Christine shakes her head. 'I didn't. Well I did. But I didn't know what was inside the envelope. You have to believe me. Cameron Patterson left out the envelope and your address, asked me to send it.'

Leon furrows his forehead, takes hold of Alice's hand. 'But you said you've only just started here at the hotel. That you haven't met Cameron.'

'I haven't met him.' She pressed one hand to her flushed throat. 'Officially I've only just started. But he asked me to come here on a couple of occasions before the place opened, to help with the admin, ordering supplies, that kind of thing. I'm so sorry if the picture upset you, Alice.' She sounds sincere. 'But I promise you, I had no idea what was inside the envelope.'

Alice stares at the woman, unsure what to believe.

Christine returns her eyes to the screen, her face tense. 'So, do you want me to search for a boatyard or not?'

Alice's heart is beating too fast. She casts a look at Leon, comforted that he is here beside her, but anger sweeps through

140

her; she's angry with Cameron Patterson, angry with Christine, and angry with herself for being stupid enough to come here.

'I'll try a Google search, shall I?' Christine goes on when Alice doesn't speak. Her fingers tap the keyboard. She pauses, furrows her forehead as she looks at the screen. 'Oh my word.' She rubs her hand across her forehead. 'It seems the Internet is down too.' She taps the keyboard again. Scans the screen, finally looking up at Leon and Alice, shaking her head.

Through the double doors of the bar, rain slashes across the bay windows with enough power to shatter glass. Alice releases Leon's hand, and heads towards the doors to the bar, glancing back once. 'We need to ask Gabriela if she has a phone.'

Leon and Christine catch Alice up, as she makes her way across the bar. Faith, Mitch and Lori are sitting in the corner, but there's no sign of Dane and Savannah Winslow.

Gabriela is standing behind the bar, her blue eyes vivid in the pink lighting. She's tall and slim, her eyes circled by heavy black eyeliner. Her shiny dark hair hangs like curtains about her pale face. Either she's a Goth or has made herself up in a way that suits the hotel.

'Are you OK, Alice?' Faith calls, and Alice turns to see her friend rising. Within moments she's by her side. 'I'm so sorry about Tegan, and the awful way you found out.' She touches Alice's arm. 'I feel so guilty. If I hadn't dragged you into the TV lounge—'

'It's hardly your fault, Faith.' Alice takes a breath. 'I'm sad, of course, but Tegan and I weren't close – not after Dad died.' Her voice trembles, her eyes focused on Gabriela. 'Truth is, I feel drained right now. I'm hoping to go home.'

Faith turns to the window. 'It won't be easy in this weather.'

'No. I know. But we're going to try to get a boat to collect us tonight.'

Faith touches Alice's arm once more. 'I don't blame you, lovely.'

'It's this place, Faith. Don't you feel it?' She looks about her,

her eyes dipping into the shadows, making out shapes in the darkness. 'It's suffocating.'

'I know what you mean.' Faith gives a little shudder of agreement. 'If I'm honest, I'm beginning to wish I hadn't come either.'

'Really?'

'Mmm – though for different reasons.' She glances over at Mitch who is deep in conversation with Lori. 'He isn't who I thought he was. In fact, he's a complete dick.'

'I'm so sorry.' Alice takes her friend in her arms, and her mind briefly drifts from her own worries. She could have told Faith that Mitch was a dick when she first saw him in the pub in Whitby – but would her friend have listened?

'Maybe you can choose the next bloke for me,' Faith says, sounding close to tears, but managing a smile all the same. 'You've got a good one in Leon.'

Alice releases Faith and turns to see Leon standing at the bar with Christine and Gabriela. She knows she messed up the last time they were together, with her fear of commitment, and now she's messing everything up by acting like some kind of crazy woman. 'We're friends, that's all,' she says, but knows, deep inside, she wants more. That she loves him.

'I don't believe you,' Faith says, as though reading her mind. 'You two are made for each other.'

Alice shrugs. 'Maybe.' A pause. 'So, will you tell Mitch it's over?'

Faith looks over at him and screws up her nose. She shakes her head. 'I'll probably wait until I get back now. It'll be easier at home when I can walk away and never have to see him again. Though the thought of spending tonight with him isn't appealing.' She cringes. 'So if there's room for a small one in that boat you're hoping to hire, I'm your gal.'

Alice watches Faith head back to Mitch and Lori, her shoulders slumped as though defeated, before catching up with Leon and Christine at the bar.

The clattering sound of Gabriela rummaging through the

contents of her canvas bag is jarring. *'Moj telefon,'* she cries. *'Moj telefon. Gdzie jest moj telefon?'*

'Let me look,' Christine says, reaching for the bag.

'Nie, nie.' Gabriela holds the bag to her chest. *'Moj telefon.'*

If Alice wasn't sure already, she is now. Someone at Flynn Hotel doesn't want them to have contact with the mainland.

Leon

Everyone is squeezed into a booth near the window, apart from Mitch who is out on the patio puffing on cigarettes, the burning tip glowing, darting up and down in the darkness, as he paces. The rain has stopped for now.

Christine has had her arm around Gabriela's shoulder for some time, and the young woman is now sipping from her second glass of brandy.

'Prezent,' Gabriela says again. *'Telefon, prezent. Od mojego tata.'*

It doesn't take much to work out that her telephone was a gift from her father, and Leon feels desperately sorry for her. He observes her pale tear-stained cheeks, the black smudges of make-up under her eyes. Her black nail varnish is chipped on her short nails. Heavy silver rings clutter her fingers. Faith claimed earlier that Gabriela looked too young to be serving behind the bar, but Leon doesn't see that. Her Goth-like image could be deceiving. Leon's sure this woman is in her mid-twenties. She's one of those people who will be asked for her ID in an off-licence way into her forties.

'Prezent,' Gabriela repeats, her voice less frantic than earlier. *'Telefon, prezent. Od mojego tata.'*

'We will find it, love,' Christine says, as though Gabriela understands what she's saying. 'I promise.'

'Do you think there's any chance Dane or Savannah might have a phone?' Desperation drips from Alice's voice, as her gaze drifts towards the bar doors.

Leon looks at Christine, who didn't seem to hear what Alice said, too wrapped up in caring for Gabriela, and then back to Alice. He rises, rubs his neck. 'Which room are Dane and Savannah Winslow staying in?'

Christine looks up. 'Umm, number 5, I think.'

'Well, we need to ask them if they've got a phone. And if they have, we should call the police. All these mobiles going missing, the cut phone wire, Alice's dress on the rocks—'

'I agree.' Alice rises, and Lori and Christine get to their feet too.

'Not sure it needs four of us,' Christine says looking from Alice to Lori. When they don't sit down she glances at Gabriela. 'Will you be OK, love? We're just popping upstairs.'

'I'll take care of her,' Faith says, putting her arm around Gabriela's shoulder as they walk away.

Leon glances back as Gabriela shuffles away from Faith, looking helpless, her arms knotted across her slim body, as though holding herself together.

On their way past reception, Christine grabs the spare key to number 5. 'Just in case,' she says, jiggling it in her hand.

'In case what?' Alice furrows her forehead, but Christine doesn't answer, just waltzes up the stairs at speed.

A 'do not disturb' sign hangs on the handle of number 5. Christine bangs on the door three times. 'Dane? Savannah?' she calls through the wooden panelling. 'Are you in there?'

'They must be,' Alice says. 'I haven't seen them around the hotel since before the tour.'

'Dane, Savannah, we need to know if you've got a phone we can borrow.' Christine shoves the key in the lock, turns it. 'Hello,' she says edging the door open. 'Dane? Savannah?'

Christine steps into the room and flicks on the light, Leon follows close behind.

'Hello?' Christine peers round the door at the bed. 'Oh my God,' she cries, grabbing her chest, her legs going from under her.

Leon reaches to catch her, sees what she's seen.

'Stay there,' he yells at Alice, raising his hand. 'Don't come in.'

But it's too late, Alice is in the room, has seen the awful sight. Retching she staggers towards the chair. 'Who did this?' she manages, her voice hoarse, thick. 'What sick bastard did this?'

But however much Leon wants to; he can't support her, his mind and body frozen by the horrific scene, and the terrifying knowledge they are sharing the island with a killer.

Chapter 23

1989

Verity

Mikolaj let Verity down – told her their relationship was claustrophobic, that she was obsessive. Said he couldn't live with her
constantly checking up on him, asking him where he'd been, what
he was doing, who he'd been with. He said she was suffocating him.

After he broke things off back in early January, she fell apart.
Spent days waiting outside his work, his lodgings, begging him
to come back to her. She would resort to screaming, sobbing. He
called her a stalker – threatened to report her. *A stalker?* Verity
wasn't a stalker – she loved him – every part of him. She loved
him with all her heart.

And then he was gone, left his job, his lodgings. Nobody
would tell Verity where he was. She searched endlessly, showing
his photo in all the places they'd frequented. She'd lost him. He
was untraceable.

*

She stayed in Poland, facing things alone, until, in early August she couldn't cope any longer, and returned to England, to Flynn House. Her trip to Europe smashed, broken into tiny pieces, her dream of a new beginning gone. Hope shattered.

*

She'd been back at Flynn House a day, when she grabbed her front door keys, the Cher cassette she'd bought in Poland for Hugh, and the tin of fairy cakes she'd made earlier. She stepped into the blisteringly hot day, closing the front door behind her. She wouldn't be gone from the house long. Just long enough to let her brother know she was back.

She knew Pippa's heart would sink at the sight of her turning up unannounced at the cottage, after so long away. She couldn't wait to see her face. Pippa wanted Hugh to herself. Well that was too bad. Verity wanted him back.

She walked round the side of Flynn House and across the lawn towards the wood, pulling on her floppy raffia sun hat over her dark hair.

The wood was gloomy, towering trees blocking out the light. She kept up a quick pace as she pushed through the brambles, excited that she would soon see Hugh for the first time in over a year.

She emerged on the other side of the island to see Pippa in the front garden of the cottage, seeming oblivious to Verity's presence some distance away, frozen as she watched from beside a mature oak tree.

Verity felt dowdy in her long, baggy, grey vest top, and loose-fitting joggers, and couldn't help the surge of jealousy at how beautiful Pippa looked. The woman suited sunny days. Her blonde hair shone like gold. Her pretty floral maternity dress matched the flowering borders, as though she'd planned it that way.

Had Mikolaj left her because she wasn't beautiful like Pippa?

147

Hugh threw open the front door and waved at his sister.

'Hey, V, you're back. Are you coming in, or are you going to stand there all day?' He was happy to see her. And that was good. She wanted *her* Hugh to be happy – just not with Pippa.

'Our plan,' he'd told Verity a few months back when she'd called from Poland, 'is to have three children, a chocolate brown Labrador, and maybe a rabbit called Flopsy. Pippa loves Beatrix Potter.'

Now, Verity hurried towards the house, itching to hold her brother in her arms after so long. Pippa looked up as she opened the squeaky gate, her face dropping for a moment before bursting into a smile. 'Verity. You're back.' She lifted her hands, showing Verity how muddy they were. 'I would hug you, but …'

'It's fine.' *You're the last person I want to hug.*

'I'll be in in a bit.'

*

'I'm so glad you're back,' Hugh said, taking his sister in his arms as she stepped into the cottage. 'I've missed you.'

'Missed you too,' she said as he released her. She touched his face, stared into his eyes. 'I've got so much to tell you.'

'Coffee first?' He led the way into the kitchen.

'Please. Though I can only say for a short while.' She handed him the cake tin, the cassette. 'I've made fairy cakes.'

'Thanks.' Hugh filled the kettle, and flicked it on. 'You look well, V.'

She laughed. 'No I don't. I've never looked worse. I've taken overweight to a whole new level. But thanks.'

He dragged his fingers through his dark hair. 'So how was Europe?'

'Good. You should go sometime. Poland is beautiful.' She stared into his eyes and smiled. She'd read once, many years ago, that his eye condition – central heterochromia – was often genetic. She

148

would dream, back then, when she first learnt from Felix that they were adopted, that their real parents were out there somewhere searching for them, and one day their mystery mother or father or both would spot Hugh somewhere because of his eyes, and they would know it was their lost son, and they would scoop her and Hugh up and take them far away from Flynn House, far away from Felix. But it had never happened. And now it didn't matter anymore. In fact, she didn't care who her real parents were. She would turn her back if they ever appeared. Maybe even kill them for putting her and Hugh through such pain.

Hugh carried the tray of three mugs and the tin of cakes through to the lounge. Pippa had decorated the room in eye-dazzling colours, made cushions and curtains from zingy fabrics. Books were squashed onto bookshelves. Cute ornaments crammed on surfaces. It was ablaze with cheerfulness. It made Verity's head hurt.

'Let me show you the baby's room.' He put down the tray, and headed up the stairs. Verity followed, trying not to show her reluctance.

It was painted pastel lemon. 'We don't know if it's a boy or girl,' Hugh said, his eyes bright. 'I picked up the cot and rocking chair from an antique shop in Dunwold, and Pippa painted them white, and etched them with the lemon roses.' He sounded so proud – excited.

'It's a lovely room, Hugh,' she said, turning and heading back downstairs.

The whole house oozed optimism and exuberance.

Hugh followed her down. And once in the lounge, mugs in hands, they stood at the window. Pippa was rubbing the base of her back. She was big now, the curve of her belly like a balloon waiting to burst, overdue by a week. Pregnancy suited her – made her even more beautiful. Verity envied her for that. *Why couldn't the woman throw up every morning, and look a complete wreck?* 'There's something I need to tell you, Hugh,' Verity began, but his eyes were narrowing as he looked out, his cheeks flushing. Verity moved her gaze to the window. Pippa's face had morphed into a grim stare. Within moments, she was doubled over, crying out in pain. Hugh dropped his mug to the floor with a thud, coffee splattering the wall. He pushed past Verity, almost knocking her over, as he raced for the front door.

Verity watched through the window, as her brother's long limbs took him across the lawn towards his soul mate. By the time he was by her side, Pippa was on her knees, crying out.

Verity placed her hand on the window. Frozen. She wanted to run back to Flynn House – she didn't want to be a part of this, but Hugh was suddenly back.

'Call an ambulance,' he cried, before rushing back out to Pippa.

Verity snapped back from the window, put down her coffee, and picked up the phone receiver. But she knew by the sound of silence on the other end that the phone line was down – it often was, the connection to the mainland poor. She looked towards the front door, her heart thudding, and slammed the receiver down. She knew little about delivering someone else's baby, and Hugh knew even less.

'We need to get her inside the cottage,' she cried, as she hurried through the front door, and across the lawn to where he was kneeling, clasping Pippa's hand. She was on her back now, sprawled on the grass. 'She can't give birth out here in the garden.'

Pippa let out an agonised cry, her face contorted with pain as she grabbed her stomach.

'What the hell do we do?' Hugh's eyes were pleading, as though Verity could make everything right, as she always did. 'Did you call an ambulance?' He looked out across the sea with watery eyes. 'The tide's in. Should we get the boat out?'

'They're on their way, Hugh.' It was a lie. But Verity didn't want to worry him further. They could deliver this child, couldn't they? Everything would be OK. 'We need to get her inside the cottage,' she repeated.

'No!' Pippa cried, as they attempted to move her, fat tears rolling down her face. 'Please. No.'

Hugh had told her once that Pippa hadn't seen a doctor in all the time she'd been carrying the child – insisting natural was best.

'Get some towels, Hugh,' Verity said, her voice shaking. 'Boil some kettles, that's what they do on TV.'

'Christ, you haven't got a clue, have you?'

'I'm a bloody artist, not a midwife.'

'Will one of you please get a grip?' Pippa roared through her tears, squeezing her eyes together, the pain clearly unbearable. 'Help me for God's sake.'

Hugh grabbed Pippa's hand and Verity sucked in a breath. 'OK. Let's both of us calm down, shall we?' she said. 'How hard can it be? People have been having babies since the beginning of time.' She swiped her palm across her forehead. 'Go get some towels, Hugh.' Her voice was low and raspy. 'And a blanket or something, and boil up some scissors to cut the cord, a pillow for her head, maybe.'

'Yes. Yes.' Hugh got to his feet, and raced into the house, and Verity turned her eyes to Pippa. 'I don't like you,' she said, taking Pippa's hand. 'And you don't like me. But we need to get your baby safely into the world for my brother's sake. OK?'

Pippa nodded, her face bright red, her forehead shining with sweat. 'OK.'

Five minutes later, Hugh raced out of the house with a handful of towels, some scissors, a blanket, a pillow wedged under his arm. 'Here you go, sweetheart,' he said, putting the pillow under Pippa's head. 'Now what?'

'Christ! I need to push,' Pippa cried. She released Verity's hand, grabbed her forehead with both hands, and squeezed her eyes together. 'God my head, my head hurts too. Why does it hurt so bad?' She stared up at Hugh. 'Oh God.'

The midday sun pounded down on them, scorching Verity's shoulders as she dragged off Pippa's underwear, and folded the woman's legs at her knees so her floral dress fell about her thighs. 'The head's almost here,' Verity cried, her stomach churning with nausea. 'Pretty sure you need to push again, Pippa.'

'And breathe too, Pippa,' Hugh cried. 'Slow, deep breaths.'

'Which? Which, Hugh? Breathe or push?'

'Both. Breathe and push.' He dropped to his knees near her head, and took hold of her hand.

'The head's out, Pippa,' Verity said, peering between the woman's legs. 'Your baby is about to be born. You're doing great.'

'I don't know. What? I don't know.' Pippa sounded confused. Was struggling to get her words out. 'My head, my head,' she cried.

The baby slid into the world, and let out a cry, and, with shaking fingers, Verity cut the slippery cord, and wrapped the child in a large grey beach towel. 'You need to push again, Pippa. You need to push out the placenta.' She was about to pass the child to Pippa, when the woman's eyes rolled into her head. 'Pippa? Pippa, are you OK?'

Tears rolled down Pippa's cheeks. Her muscles twitched. She was trying to speak, but it was clear she couldn't form any words.

'What the hell is happening?' Hugh cried, grabbing both her hands. He swiped a look at Verity. 'V, help her, please. What's happening?'

'I don't know how, Hugh. She looks like she's having some kind of stroke or seizure.'

'Where's the ambulance, for Christ's sake?' His face streamed with tears.

'They're not coming, Hugh.' She was surprised how calm she sounded.

'What?'

'The phone line is down.'

'Christ! Why the hell didn't you say, Verity?'

'I didn't want to worry you.'

'For God's sake.' Colour had drained from his cheeks, his eyes red from tears. 'She's so still. What's wrong with her? What's wrong, Pippa? Pippa?'

The baby cradled in one arm, Verity pressed her fingertips on Pippa's wrist, searching for a pulse.

'What?' he yelled. 'What?'

'I'm so sorry, Hugh.' She looked up at him.

'No!' He fell across his wife's motionless body, sobbing. 'But that can't be right. Oh God no. No!'

'You need to concentrate on your baby, Hugh.' He hadn't even looked at the child. Asked anything about the little thing.

'No. No. Pippa would still be here if …' He got to his feet, his sobs loud and desperate.

'Hugh. Your baby needs you.' She held out the child wrapped in the towel.

'I can't. I can't, Verity.' He stumbled towards the house, zigzagging across the lawn until he got to the open front door. 'I can't do this,' he said, stepping inside, and slamming the door behind him.

Chapter 24

Halloween Weekend 2019

Alice

Alice buries her face in her hands, her tear-soaked fingers locked against her skin, nausea churning through her body. She knows she will have to look up eventually. See them again: Dane and Savannah Winslow. She can't sit here forever hiding her eyes like a child playing peekaboo. She can't escape this room without seeing them again: the lifeless bodies of the popular influencers.

Memories flood her head of Savannah's nasty jibes, the way she laughed as she said her father's death would save the world from more of his books, Dane with his perfect body, his cock-sure attitude, pulling her father apart so soon after his death like a corpse being torn limb from limb by wild beasts. It had been personal. The words *good thing he's dead* had hurt Alice like hell.

'It goes with the territory,' she could almost hear her dad saying. 'If you dance the polka, Alice, there will always be someone who prefers the foxtrot.'

Alice peels her hands from her damp face. 'No, no, no,' she

whispers as her eyes land on their bodies once more. Their backs are upright against the headboard, arms by their sides. Both have red spots on their cheeks, giving them a fake glow, Dane wearing a red bow tie.

Puppets – someone's turned them into puppets.

Her eyes swoop the half-eaten canapés, the glasses of half-drunk champagne on the table by the window, the pools of vomit on the floor. 'They've been poisoned,' Alice whispers. *How could someone do this?* She looks at Christine. 'Who prepared their food?'

Christine doesn't seem to hear through her own sobs as she frantically searches the room. Opening drawers, bags and holdalls.

'Should you be doing that?' Leon says, seeming to jolt to life. 'I've seen enough TV crime to know you're messing with forensics.'

'We need to find a phone, Leon, call the police,' Christine cries, slamming closed a drawer. She stops searching and stares at the victims.

'Did you prepare the food, Christine?' Alice asks, struggling to pull her eyes away from the couple.

'Cameron did,' Christine says through her tears. 'But why would he kill them? Why would anyone kill them?' She hiccups, wipes her tear-streaked cheeks. 'Who the hell would make them look so bizarre? They barely said a word to anyone since they arrived, kept themselves to themselves. Who would do this?'

'Let's get out of here.' Leon takes Alice's hand, and pulls her to her feet. She's thankful that he's made her move, is getting her out of this room. 'We can't think straight in here,' he goes on, assertive. 'Let's go back down to the bar.'

On the landing, Lori is struggling to breathe. 'Who would do that?' She wheezes, presses her hand against her chest. 'I need my inhaler,' she says, rooting around in her bag. 'I can't find my inhaler.'

'Let me look,' Christine says, taking the bag from Lori, and quickly finding the inhaler.

'Well, I need a drink.' Leon's eyes are wide and fiery. He dashes towards the stairs, pulling Alice along with him. Christine and Lori follow, as though scared to be alone, the sound of their anxious sobs echoing throughout the building.

By the time they reach the bar, Lori's gone into a kind of spasm, bending over making an awful strangled sound.

'Deep breaths, Lori, love,' Christine says, rubbing the woman's back. 'Take a couple more puffs.'

'Is she going to be OK?' Faith says, dashing over, followed by Gabriela. Lori takes a puff, then another, breathes in and out slow and steady, eventually straightening up, her face shiny, her eye make-up smudged.

Leon heads behind the bar, and pours brandy into several mismatched glasses. Everyone takes a glass, before heading across the room towards the table by the window they vacated earlier. Christine, in words that tumble out at speed, tells Faith and Gabriela about the Winslows. Though Gabriela doesn't seem to understand, her face stony pale, her eyes dark.

Leon paces, taking large gulps of his drink. 'Whoever did this is in the hotel,' he says, eyes flicking from one guest to another. 'Can we even trust each other?'

'I think we need to find Cameron,' Christine says as everyone else sits down, banging her empty glass down on the table.

'Do we? Why?' Leon's tone is agitated, his voice trembling. 'What if this mystery guy, who nobody seems to have seen, did this? Killed the Winslows? Or maybe he doesn't exist at all?'

'But, I've seen him,' Faith says. 'Admittedly not since I've been here, which I realise isn't helpful at all. But he exists.'

Lori gets up and makes her way to the bar.

'Bring the bottle over,' Leon calls after her.

Faith's eyes are focused on the window. 'What the hell are we going to do?'

'Well the first rule is,' Leon begins, 'we stay together.'

'Leon's right,' Faith agrees, looking up at him as he continues

156

to pace. 'I've seen enough scary movies to know splitting up gets us killed.'

A stab of fear pierces Alice's heart. 'Oh God, please don't say that.' A tear rolls down her cheek. 'This is too much.'

Leon crouches down by her side, and takes her hand, laces his fingers with hers. Their eyes meet. 'We'll be OK, Alice,' he says, pushing a damp strand of hair from her cheek. She wishes she could believe his words.

Faith gets up as though something has struck her. 'Talking of going off on our own. Where's Mitch?' She walks towards the French doors, and looks out. 'He was out there earlier having a ciggie, wasn't he?' She opens the door. The wind takes it from her hand and it jerks back on its hinges, bangs hard against the wall. 'Mitch!' she calls. 'Mitch, are you out there?' She turns back, looks at the others, wide-eyed.

'Boo!' He appears behind her, and grabs her shoulders with heavy hands.

Faith screams, clasping her chest. She shrugs his hands away, a flash of anger in her eyes. 'What the hell did you do that for?'

'You're edgy, babe.' He lumbers into the bar, and approaches the table looking windswept, and bringing with him a waft of cigarette smoke. 'What's up with you lot? You look as though you've seen a ghost.'

'It's Dane and Savannah Winslow … They're dead.' Alice doesn't meet his eye, is surprised how calm her voice sounds. 'Murdered.'

'The Winslows?' He scans the gathering. 'Christ! Is this true?' Everyone nods.

'Where? How? Have you called the police?'

'We can't,' Alice says. 'The landline is down, and everyone's phones have gone missing.'

He looks towards the window. It's the first time Alice has seen him lost for words, a flash of fear on his normally arrogant face.

'I've been thinking. I reckon our only hope is the cottage,'

Lori says, returning with the bottle of brandy, and still sounding breathless. She sits down and splashes some of the amber liquid into her glass and Leon's. 'Whoever took our phones must be here – in this house.' Her frightened eyes skitter across the bar. 'Surely, whoever it is, they wouldn't have thought to take Cameron's phone.'

Leon nods. 'Good point.'

'Unless the killer is Cameron,' Christine says. 'We can't rule that out.'

'Yes, but there may even be a landline over there,' Faith says, pushing back her fringe.

'If we head over there together, we'll be safe,' Lori goes on, picking up the glass, and taking a swig of her drink.

'Sounds like a good plan. I'm up for going to the cottage,' Leon says.

'Me too.' Faith rises. 'Alice?'

'OK.' Alice reluctantly rises.

Lori goes to get up, but it's clear she's still having problems catching her breath, and lowers back down in her seat. 'Oh God. I'm not sure I'm up to it, if I'm honest.'

'I'll stay with Lori.' Mitch has been to the bar, grabbed himself a glass. He fills it with brandy, so full some spills over the top of the glass, and splashes the table.

'Surely if we can't all go, none of us should,' Christine says. 'You just made a big thing about us all staying together, Leon.'

Lori looks over at Gabriela, who has moved away from everyone, and is now sitting on a stool at the next table, her head in her hands, her dark hair hanging over her face. 'Maybe if Gabriela and Mitch stay with me … Gabriela doesn't seem to know what's going on anyway, and it will confuse her further if she goes with you. We'll stay here in the bar together.'

Alice furrows her forehead, stares at the woman who is stroking the thick mane of hair hanging over her shoulder. 'Are you sure?'

Mitch drops down in a seat next to Lori with a thud. 'I'll take good care of her,' he says, as Gabriela gets to her feet and heads back behind the bar. 'I have the feeling it's going to be a long night,' he goes on, as everyone heads away. He gulps back the brandy, drains the glass. Picks up the bottle and takes a long swig from it.

Chapter 25

1989

Verity

Verity was surprised by the pang of sadness she felt when Pippa Larkin died. Though, if she really thought about it, it wasn't exactly a pang. A pang would imply a shock-like feeling, a pinball ricocheting through her body bouncing off her emotions, tears maybe, heart thumps, even tremors. She certainly hadn't felt any of that nonsense. A tingle then – yes, she'd felt a tingle of sadness that her brother had lost the love of his life.

But, for the main part, Verity was glad Pippa was out of her life – gone. Vanished in a puff of smoke, the way her father had made women disappear in his magic tricks. Though Pippa hadn't exactly vanished. Pippa was buried in the wood. A cross, which Verity had made, placed on her grave. Not that Verity or Hugh were religious. How could they believe in a God who had dropped them into Felix Flynn's world when they were too young to fight it? But the cross felt like the right thing to do, for Hugh's sake. Verity was a good person like that. The thing was, Pippa had

160

no family. She had nobody to miss her but Hugh, so it seemed foolish to involve outsiders in her loss. They might even blame Verity for Pippa's death, and she couldn't have that.

What Verity hadn't expected when Pippa died, was how devastated her brother would be. The way he was drowning in unbearable, inconsolable grief had come as a shock. She would have expected him to be sad, yes. That she would have to care for him as she always had done, yes. Rebuild him, yes. But this was different. This was a road – Anguish Avenue or Bereavement Boulevard or Sadness Street – and he was travelling it alone, on a desperate journey without her.

*

'Are you going to name the child?' she asked her brother, when the baby was two weeks old, but Hugh, cocooned in his duvet, humming of body odour, didn't reply.

When the baby was three weeks old, Verity stood in the doorway of Hugh's dark bedroom once more. 'The child needs a name, Hugh,' she said.

He peered out from under his duvet, still sick with grief, his face pale; cushions of darkness under his eyes and said, 'I can't do it, Verity. I want to. But I can't.'

The baby was a month old when Verity took hold of her brother's hand and squeezed. He was flopped on the sofa, had been drinking heavily. 'You still need to give your child a name,' she tried once more, showing him the baby pressed against her body in a sling.

'Tiger,' Hugh said, his voice a slur.

'Tiger?'

'Strong. Brave. A survivor.'

'Really? You want to call your baby after a wild animal?'

He turned to face Verity, looked deep into her eyes. 'Yes.'

'OK, but it's not enough to just name the child after a predator, Hugh. This baby needs you.'

He stared long and hard at the child snuggled against Verity, his eyes – *those eyes* – melting her stone heart. He was the only one who could do that. He looked up at Verity. 'I'm sorry, I'm going to be a crap dad for a while,' he said. 'I don't even know how to begin. Give me time, V. I will get there. I just need your support. Help me get through this, and when I come out the other side, we'll be a family – you, me and Tiger. Will you do that for me?'

'I will,' she said, her mind churning, spinning, planning. 'If you're sure it's what you want.'

'It is,' he said. 'It really is.'

Chapter 26

Halloween Weekend 2019

Alice

Christine shuffles into her anorak, pulls on her beanie, and grabs two torches from behind the reception desk. She tests they both work, and says, 'Right, I'll wait here for you folks, while you get your coats from your rooms.'

Once upstairs, Faith continues along the landing to her room, as Alice and Leon unlock the door to theirs. 'See you in a bit,' Faith calls, raising her hand in a wave.

'I'm so sorry this has turned into a nightmare,' Leon says, once they are inside.

Alice turns. His eyes are wide, helpless. 'It's hardly your fault.' She takes his hand, and he pulls her to him. 'This was about me searching for my past. I was a fool, and I'm scared, Leon,' she whispers into his chest.

'It's going to be OK,' he says, but his rapid heartbeat tells her he's worried too. 'We'll find a phone, get help.'

'Are you sure going to the cottage is such a good idea?' There's a tremble in her voice. 'I just thought if we stay in the bar over-night – all together—'

'But there could be a landline.' He releases her, looks towards the window. He's pale, his fair hair tousled. 'We need to get off the island, Alice. As soon as possible.'

'I guess.'

They leave the room, and head down the stairs, Alice pulling on her Parka, still damp from earlier.

They stand with Christine, who is togged in her anorak and beanie. The tick, tick, tick of the grandfather clock telling them it's twenty-five to one in the morning. And as soon as Faith appears, they head towards the main entrance.

'Jeez,' Alice says, as she opens the door, and the wind grabs it with force. 'Are we really sure this is a good idea?' She stands in the doorway, watching the others head into the blustery night, Faith's ponytail thrashing across her face. 'It's getting worse,' she yells above the wind sweeping through the trees, and rattling the metal sign, confirming Alice's doubts.

'At least it's stopped raining,' Leon cries.

Alice darts from the doorway to catch them up, and Christine hands her a torch. She flicks it on, slicing the beam through the shadows, her stomach churning as she imagines a killer lurking in the darkness.

They make their way across the front lawn, past the French doors to the bar. Mitch and Lori sit behind the glass, appearing to be lost in their own worlds, Lori's elegant posture juxtaposed against Mitch's body slumped in the chair, legs splayed, still knocking back brandy from the bottle.

Alice's gaze moves away from the window and across the area, past the flattened wire fencing where Leon almost lost his life, imagining her yellow dress floating across the night sky in the wind. She swallows her fear, and takes hold of Leon's hand.

As they step onwards, she catches sight of an amber glow radiating from the attic window. 'The light's on,' she says to Leon.

He looks up. 'Is that the attic?'

She nods. 'You didn't turn on the light when we were up there, did you, Christine?' she calls out, trying to make herself heard over the howling wind. But she knows the answer already. When Christine locked the door to the attic room earlier, the light was out. *Muddy-brown walls. Grass-green carpet. Outside, inside.* She pushes away the invading confusing thought.

Christine glances up at the window. 'That's odd. Maybe the storm's messing with the electrics.'

They pick up pace as they make their way through the wood, Alice still clinging to Leon's hand. He's jittery, his palms sweaty. She wants to say something to comfort him, but has no words.

'The cottage isn't far,' Christine calls, her voice shrill. 'Come on, you two. Keep up. We must stay together.'

There are lights up ahead, and, as they emerge into a clearing, a pretty cottage appears, every window glowing orange, beautiful, yet there's something equally eerie about the place that Alice can't put her finger on.

The gate squeaks as Christine opens it. She hurries up the path towards the front door, and starts to hammer on the rusty knocker. 'Cameron! Cameron! Are you in there?'

Leon and Alice join her on the doorstep, as Faith steps over a small white picket fence onto the lawn. She presses her nose against the window, and rests her fingertips on the glass as she peers in. 'There's someone in there,' she says, her voice quivering. She looks about her, as though searching for something to use to break the glass.

Christine continues to bang the knocker. 'Cameron. It's me – Christine. Please let us in.' She presses the heavy wrought-iron handle down. The door eases open. 'It's not locked,' she says, entering the house, everyone close behind her. 'Cameron?' She switches off her torch as the brightness of the lounge engulfs them. 'Cameron?'

165

'There's nobody here,' Leon says, looking about him. Under different circumstances, the room might seem cosy, if a little dated and worn. Two floral sofas and a wing-backed armchair cup an open fireplace. A small TV stands in the corner, and a lamp gives off the orangey glow they'd noticed from outside. A heavy-wooden sideboard under the window has a photo of Cameron and a woman smiling from a silver frame, and there's a shelf full of books. Leon peers closer, noticing all of Alice's father's novels.

He turns and takes the narrow staircase two at a time. 'Cameron,' he calls, peering into a bathroom, heart thudding. He steps into the room, which smells faintly of bleach, and yanks back a stained, polka dot shower curtain stretched full length across a lemon-coloured bath. There's nobody there.

Floorboards creak as he makes his way across the landing towards three more doors. Two stand open with lamps on inside the rooms. The third is closed.

'Is there anyone up there?' Alice calls from the foot of the stairs. 'I don't think so.'

He searches the first bedroom decorated in blues and yellows, pine furniture, and a double bed. It's homely, yet gives nothing away about the cottage's owner.

The second room is empty apart from an easel, and a desk and chair facing the small square window looking out at the sea. A palette of paint, and a jar full of brushes are on a small table; paintings are propped against the wall. He steps closer, and stares at one of the paintings. 'Oh God,' he whispers, as he takes in the portrait. It's Alice's father – but this time there's no doubting it's him. It's exactly how he looked when Leon first met him. How he looked just before he died. This painting isn't as good as the one in the hotel dining room. It's as though the artist in still honing their skills. He grabs it, relieved it's not wet, and shoves it under his arm.

The third room is locked.

'There's nobody up there,' he says lumbering down the narrow staircase, and into the lounge. He looks at Alice, and opens his mouth, ready to tell her about the painting, when Christine appears in the doorway that joins the lounge and kitchen.

'Nobody in the kitchen,' she says, hands on her hips, eyes flashing behind her glasses. 'The back door's unlocked, and I've checked outside, couldn't see anyone.'

'That's weird, because I could have sworn I saw movement when I looked in through the window,' Faith says, eyes leaping about as though she thinks someone will jump out of the sideboard, or from behind the floral curtains that drape each side of the window. She shakes her head. 'I must have been mistaken. My mind playing tricks.'

'Not surprising with what we've all been through, love,' Christine says, touching her arm gently. She looks at Leon. 'What have you got there?'

He tugs the painting from under his arm. 'I found it upstairs.'

Alice stares at it, tears filling her eyes as she clearly recognises her father's face. 'What the hell's going on?'

Leon wishes he could transport her far away. Make everything right. He hands her the picture, and she continues to stare at it.

'Look, a phone,' Christine says eyes widening. She points to a small table in the corner, where a cumbersome old-fashioned phone sits. 'Is it for real or some kind of ornament?'

Faith dashes over, picks up the receiver, and pins it to her ear. 'Thank God, there's a line.'

A collective sigh of relief echoes through the cottage, as Faith taps the phone keypad set in a panel resembling a dial. She waits for a moment, biting her lip. 'Hello, my name is Faith Evans. I'm a guest at Flynn Hotel on Seafield Island, just off the coast of Dunwold.' Her voice wobbles, her eyes darting from Alice to Leon to Christine. 'We're cut off from the mainland, and need police here urgently. Some people have been murdered … Dane

and Savannah Winslow. They are, *were*, guests at the hotel …
There are seven of us … maybe eight; we can't be sure.' Her voice
cracks at the mention of the invisible Cameron. She listens for
a moment. 'I really don't know.' She gulps back tears, drags the
back of her hand across her nose. 'Yes, yes we will. Thank you.
OK. Yes.' She hangs up the phone, and drops down on the sofa.
'They're sending help.'

'Oh, thank God,' Alice says, propping the picture against the
wall. Leon moves closer to her, takes her in his arms. He's relieved
when she rests her head against his chest. That she lets him hold
her. Her thundering heartbeat telling him she's far from OK.

'They said we're to stay together until they arrive,' Faith says.
'So we should probably head back to the hotel and wait.' A crash
of thunder rattles the house, and heavy rain follows, splattering
the window.

Faith gets to her feet and heads towards the door, 'The sooner
the better,' she says.

Chapter 27

1990

Verity

The birth of the now chubby-limbed infant with bright blue eyes and a tiny rosebud mouth – a beautiful creature so totally help-less and dependent on Verity – evoked feelings that had confused Verity at first. But now, six months after the baby's birth, she was aware that *this* love – *this* feeling – was as intense as the love she'd always felt for her brother. It was a protective kind of love, an unbreakable love. She knew, even then, she would do anything for this child. That she would never let her go.

*

Over the months, Hugh hadn't wanted to see Verity or his baby, so when he called, quite out of the blue, and asked her to bring his daughter to the cottage, Verity had felt a surge of happiness.

She bundled the baby into her little white coat, and pulled up the fur-trimmed hood. 'You are so beautiful, my precious girl,' she said, kissing the child's tiny hands.

Frost crunched under Verity's boots, the cool air nipping her cheeks. Her little Tiger propped on her hip, cooing, and gurgling, blue eyes absorbing nature, tiny hands grasping Verity's hair. 'We're going to see your daddy,' she said, kissing the baby's feathery dark hair, breathing in the sweet smell of the infant as she walked through the wood towards the cottage. 'I've never been this happy,' she whispered close to the child's ear.

This life – her life with this child – was almost perfect.

'We're nearly there, sweetie,' she said, pushing through brambles, the winter sun's rays slanting through tall trees, brightening their way.

Finally the cottage came into view.

A few paces on, she opened the squeaky gate. The garden was over-run with nettles and weeds – poison hemlock rife. Verity smiled at the thought of Pippa looking from beyond the grave, seeing the state of her precious garden. 'This is where your daddy lives, Tiger,' she said as she walked up the path.

She knocked three times and waited.

When Hugh finally opened up, she gasped at his scrawny body, the wild beard covering his chin. How had he let this happen? How had *she* let this happen? His creased, grubby T-shirt, hung over baggy jeans. His feet were bare. It seemed, despite her leaving a box of groceries on the step of the cottage once a week for the last six months, he hadn't been eating properly and looked so much older than his twenty-two years.

'So this must be Tiger.' His dull eyes lit up briefly as the child threw him the brightest of smiles. Verity couldn't help but hope they were on the verge of getting through this. That Hugh was about to emerge strong for the baby's sake. And maybe, just maybe, they would become a family. A funny kind of family some might say – not the kind Hugh and Pippa dreamed of – but a family all the same.

She stepped into the cottage, straight into the lounge. The floral curtains were pulled closed, half hanging from the rail, no light coming in from outside. The room was lit by a standard lamp in the corner, the pale green shade lopsided. Dirty cups and glasses were strewn over every surface; dust, as thick as insulation, covered the sideboard under the window, and the bookshelves.

'Such a beautiful child,' Hugh said, closing the front door behind them; a heavy sadness in his voice that Verity had feared for so long he may never lose. *Will his grief always be so raw?* 'Come here, Tiger,' he said reaching out his arms to the child. 'Come to your daddy.'

As he hugged the baby close to his chest, tears filled her eyes.

'To new beginnings,' Verity whispered.

But Hugh was silent, and within moments, he handed Tiger back to Verity. 'I'm sorry,' he said. 'I just can't do this.'

Chapter 28

Halloween Weekend 2019

Alice

Tension surges through Alice's body. Rain stings her cheeks like nettles. She holds onto Leon's arm, her fingers pressed deep into the fabric of his wet jacket, as they hurry through trees that rock to and fro, their heads down against the blustery wind. And each time the wind settles for a brief moment, the *tick, tick, tick* of leaves falling through the branches is haunting.

The journey back to Flynn Hotel seems longer than the walk there, intermittent flashes of lightning, and crashes of thunder not helping Alice's anxiety. She sighs with relief as they push through the last of the bushes and brambles, onto the hotel grounds, their shoes squelching into the grass as they dash towards the main entrance.

Christine and Faith turn the corner, disappearing from view, but Alice slows on the lawn, releasing Leon's arm, her eyes moving up towards the attic window once more. The light is still on. Perhaps Christine was right and the electrics are playing up. Leon stops too, glances back at Alice, concern in his eyes.

'You OK?' he calls, the wind snatching his words, making them small. 'Stupid question, I know.'

Alice nods, catches him up, pointing the beam of her torch towards the endless sea. Waves are high – abandoned – casting shadows like frolicking demons. She's never seen the sea so out of control. She shivers, raindrops rolling down her cheeks, her neck. Her eyes skitter towards the wire fence waving in the frenzied wind like it's alive. She takes hold of Leon's arm once more, hating how close she came to losing him.

'We should go inside.' Leon pushes back his soaked hair from his face, and she sees the fear in his eyes. He's scared too.

Inside the hotel, the grandfather clock tells them it's twenty-five to two. Christine, Faith and Lori have congregated near the reception desk, talking in hushed, anxious voices.

'Where are Mitch and Gabriela?' Leon says, as he and Alice approach, interrupting their conversation.

Lori looks up at him wide-eyed. 'I don't know,' she says. 'I was just telling Christine and Faith, I haven't seen either of them for ages—'

'So much for everyone staying together.' Alice grabs a handful of her own hair and squeezes, water spilling to the floor.

'Well I'm sorry, Alice.' There's firmness in Lori's softly spoken American twang. 'I didn't realise I was left here to babysit.' Her smooth cheeks flush pink. 'And I might add, that they left *me* on *my* own. I've been in a terrible state ever since. It's playing havoc with my asthma.'

'Sorry.' Alice unzips her sodden Parka, and removes it. 'I didn't mean to … This is all so awful. Sorry.'

'It's fine.' Lori's voice softens further. 'We're all very stressed out, and it's not surprising. But please let's try to support each other, shall we?'

Leon removes his jacket too, and throws it down with a thud onto the sofa. He looks bedraggled, exhausted, and Alice wishes she could turn back time to the moment when they were sitting

173

in their favourite pub in Whitby, Henry sprawled by the fire at their feet. If she could turn back time, never have come here, she would. This was all her fault.

'So, when did you last see Mitch and Gabriela?' Leon asks, his eyes steady on Lori.

'About ten minutes after you took off,' Lori begins. 'Mitch went upstairs to his room. He'd had a fair few brandies.' She bites down on her full lip, pulls away from Leon's gaze. 'Was worse for wear, stumbling around the place.'

'And Gabriela?' Christine chips in. 'Where is she?'

'I don't know.' Lori clears her throat, her cheeks flushing. 'I hadn't taken much notice of her. She was behind the bar, and what with the language barrier, well it meant we couldn't really have a conversation. I noticed she'd gone, just after Mitch went to his room.' She looks down as though the chessboard floor has the answers, stroking her thick swath of hair that's draped over one shoulder. 'I hate this place, always have,' she says. 'When I found myself alone here, I wanted to cry. I don't think I've ever been so afraid.'

'Oh, love.' Christine touches her arm gently. 'It must have been so frightening for you.'

'It was.' Lori sniffs and nods, her voice a wobble. 'What happened to the Winslows was playing on my mind like a horror film on repeat. I couldn't get the fact they were upstairs …' She looks towards the staircase and shudders. 'I thought if I sat here in reception, I could have eyes everywhere. I've been a complete mess, quite honestly. I just thank God you're all back safe.'

'Well, we don't have to worry for much longer, Lori,' Christine says, her voice even as she pulls off her sodden beanie and wrings it out. 'The police are on their way.'

'Really?' Lori's eyes widen. 'Well that's fantastic.'

'I called them,' Faith says. 'They'll be here as soon as possible. But, we still need to make sure Mitch and Gabriela are OK.' Her eyes drift up the staircase. 'I'll go and check on Mitch.'

Before Alice can open her mouth to suggest Faith shouldn't go alone, her friend heads up the stairs and disappears onto the shadowy landing.

The silence stretches, tension building, seconds turn to minutes as the grandfather clock tick, tick, ticks into the quiet.

Finally, Alice looks at Lori, narrows her eyes. 'You said you've always hated Flynn House. Have you been here before?'

Lori looks flustered, rubs a hand across her chest. 'I have, yes. A long time ago.' She clears her throat.

'Really?'

'I was Hugh and Verity's nanny in the late Seventies, early Eighties. It was my first job. I was here until their father disappeared.'

Alice stares at Lori, trying to imagine this attractive American woman as a nanny, her heart racing once more. 'If you hated the place, what made you come back?'

'Panic over!' It's Faith galloping down the stairs. 'He's passed out on the bed – I couldn't stir him, so I've locked him in.'

'That's a relief,' Alice says, as Lori moves away, their conversation over, for now.

'It is.' Faith nods. 'I mean he's a complete prick, but I would hate anything awful to happen to him.'

'Let's make sure Gabriela's in her room, shall we?' Lori says, her voice sounding stronger. 'Make sure she's OK too.'

'Good plan.' Christine moves across the lobby. 'I'll grab the spare key to Gabriela's room.' She leans over the desk, and picks it off a hook. 'Let's head upstairs together,' she goes on, tucking the key into her cardigan pocket.

'Gabriela's room is on the upper floor,' Christine says, leading the way towards the next set of stairs. 'Her room is next to mine.'

Once there, Christine knocks on the door of room 6. 'Gabriela, it's Christine.' She presses her ear to the door. 'Gabriela, I have a key and I'm coming in. I hope you're decent.'

'She won't understand a bloody word she's saying,' Faith whispers into Alice's ear.

'Gabriela, I'm coming in after the count of three … One … two … three … here I come, ready or not.' Christine unlocks the door, pushes it open, and heads inside. 'Gabriela?' she says, flicking on the light.

Within moments, Christine is back on the landing. 'She's not there,' she says with a shrug.

'We should go downstairs until the police come,' Alice says, her voice firm – she turns, makes her way down the corridor. Everyone follows as she descends the two flights of stairs and heads into the bar, where they congregate, seemingly afraid of losing one another, afraid of becoming prey to a killer. But as Alice looks at each of them in turn, she can't help but wonder if the killer is one of them.

Chapter 29

1991

Verity

Verity sat cross-legged on the rug in Hugh's lounge, watching the toddler dressed in jeans with an elasticated waist, and a bright yellow T-shirt, wander back and forth, clasping a yellow Duplo brick in each tiny fist.

Hugh leant forward on the sofa, elbows on knees, dragging his slim fingers through his hair. 'I'm sorry, Verity,' he said, the pain in his voice tangible. 'What more can I say? I can't help who I am. How I feel.'

'But, I still don't get how you can reject your own child.' Tears shimmered in her eyes. She so wanted – needed – him to love Tiger. Then they could be a family.

'Not reject. You've got it wrong. I'm incapable, that's all. I detest myself, the person I've become. I hate that I feel so little for the kid. But we had a crap upbringing; you more than anyone know that. What do you expect from me? Felix battered any true feelings out of me.'

'But you loved Pippa.'

He nodded. 'Yeah, and look how that turned out.' He stared at Tiger, who dropped down on her bottom in front of the TV, eyes glued to a kids' programme, two puppets living on a canal boat.

'Rosie! Rosie!'

'Yes, Rosie and Jim,' Hugh said, his voice dull and low. 'Puppets.'

'Puppets!' Tiger said, looking over her shoulder at Hugh, her cheeks pink, eyes bright.

Hugh turned to Verity. 'I can't invent feelings, V, and I can see the kid is cute. I get that. But I'm never going to be a good father; I don't know how to be.'

Verity's heart sank. Hugh had barely wanted to see Tiger over the past year. In fact this was the first time they'd been to the cottage in ages. It was clear he was still mourning that ridiculous woman. How had this happened? They were meant to be together – happy – the three of them.

'You're a brilliant aunt, Verity. I thank God the kid's got you.' His eyes filled with tears. 'I'm going to bed,' he said, getting up. 'See yourself out.'

'How can you turn your back on us, like this?' Verity cried, as he padded across the room.

'I'm sorry,' he said.

Verity scooped the scattered Duplo into the yellow bucket, and stood it in the corner of the room. 'Let's go home, little one,' she said, lifting Tiger into her arms. 'It's OK, you have me, and I will love you always. And one day, you will have a daddy too, and we will be a family. I promise.'

PART THREE

'I can't explain myself, I'm afraid, sir,' said Alice,
'because I'm not myself, you see.'
Lewis Carroll

Chapter 30

1994

Tiger

'Tiger?' Aunt Verity shouts from the kitchen.

I like being called Tiger. Daddy named me after a wild animal because I am strong and brave. He says I am a survivor, but I don't really know what that means.

One time, I drew a picture with my blue and yellow and black and orange crayons. It was of my daddy and my mummy and a tiger. 'That's me,' I said to Aunt Verity, pointing at the tiger, when she leant over my shoulder to look at my picture.

And she said, 'And is that me?'

And I said, 'No, that's my mummy. Her name is Pippa.' I know that because Daddy told me her name, and he said I must never forget her. Ever. So I don't.

But then Aunt Verity cried. Big fat bubbly tears rolling down her face.

'It is you,' I said, because I don't like it when she cries. 'I love you.' I said that too, because I do.

181

And she pinned the picture to the cupboard. 'I love you too, Tiger,' she said.

'Tiger,' she calls again from downstairs. 'It's time for tea.' I smile and think of my very favourite book *The Tiger Who Came to Tea*, which Aunt Verity bought me when I became five years old.

I'm not that hungry right now, and want to play with my red bus. It's got one, two, three, four yellow wheels. I know all of my numbers, and Aunt Verity says I am very clever. She says I am a brilliant artist too – just like her. She paints all the time. She likes painting pictures of Daddy.

'It's hereditary,' she said about me being an artist. At least I think that's what she said. I don't know what that means, but I think it's good because she was smiling.

I jump up when she calls me again. My arms out like an aeroplane, I whiz and whirr and whoop from my bedroom and down the stairs, 'One, two, three, four, five, six, six, eight, twelve … what's for tea?' I say, running into the kitchen.

Aunt Verity has made me baked beans on toasty soldiers. I jump onto the chair at the table. Pick up my knife and fork. I like toasty soldiers. Aunt Verity has cheese on hers. I don't like cheese. It makes my tummy feel sick.

While we eat she tells me about my grandpa – her daddy, my daddy's daddy. 'He's dead now,' she says, as I munch – dead means he's not here anymore so I can't see him or talk to him – 'but when he was alive he was on TV. His name was Felix Flynn and he did magic tricks. He had puppets too and he could make them talk.' She tells me this story a lot.

I like my grandpa's puppets, and, even though he's dead, his puppets talk to me.

'Grandpa used to get cross with your daddy,' Aunt Verity says. This is always when her voice goes sad and crackly. 'And one time he hit your daddy so hard he broke his arm. That's why we have to look after your daddy.'

I want to hug my daddy all of the time, because he's sad all of the time, and it makes me sad that his arm got broke. But Aunt Verity says he doesn't want to see me too much.

'He's fragile.' She says this a lot too, especially when her voice goes all slurry. Aunt Verity says fragile means breakable, and I don't want to break my daddy, so I stay away – even though I want to be with him all of the time.

'Maybe, you can see your daddy later today,' she says as I carry on munching. 'If you are very, very good.'

'I will be good.' I nod one, two, three, four, six, seven times, knowing I will be very, very good for the rest of the day.

'But first we need to go across to the mainland, to stock up,' she says.

I don't like the mainland anymore. I used to like going to the village shop, as everyone was friendly there, and people would ruffle my hair and say, 'How are you today, Tiger?' But we're not allowed to go there anymore. Not since the boy with the strawberry-blond hair kicked me. He was much bigger than me, but I wasn't scared, I spun round and kicked him back very hard, and he toppled over onto his big fat bum.

'If you come in here again, you little rat,' the shop lady yelled, hugging the big boy with the strawberry-blond hair as he cried, 'it will be the last thing you do.'

'I'm Tiger, not Rat,' I said, but she grabbed a broom and shooed us out onto the pavement, and everybody looked at us, and the nice people who said, 'How are you today, Tiger?' shook their heads and pulled angry faces.

'I'll set my Terry on you if you ever come back,' the shop lady said before slamming the door.

So that was that.

I wasn't sure what a Terry was, but I think it might be a big dog.

I cried, and I needed a wee wee badly, but when Aunt Verity cried too, I had to stop crying and cheer her up. I had to be strong and brave, just like a tiger.

So now we go to a big supermarket called Tesco. It's scary

there as there are lots of people who never look down, or smile at me and say: 'How are you today, Tiger?'

Sometimes, as Aunt Verity pushes the trolley up and down and up and down, I pretend I'm invisible. But nobody notices. Not even Aunt Verity.

'Go and get your trainers on,' she says now.

I slide down from the chair like a slippery snake. 'OK,' I say, but I really don't want to go to the supermarket. I want to stay here with the puppets.

I don't like Tesco very much.

Chapter 31

Halloween Weekend 2019

Alice

Faith presses her nose against the window, eyes skittering across the darkness. 'It's still raining, but looks calmer out there.' She glances over her shoulder at Leon. 'Should we go out there and look for Gabriela?'

'Yes, we really ought to find her,' he says, his voice heavy with tension. 'Make sure she's OK.'

'I'm not sure we should go outside anymore tonight,' Christine says, shaking her head and lifting her palms as if to say, *I'm out.* 'Shouldn't we wait for the police?' She drags her fingers through her hair, making it spike. 'Two people murdered, one gone AWOL, Cameron nowhere to be found. I just don't think going out there again is the best idea. We should all stay in here, together.'

Faith rubs the back of her neck. Her dungarees are crumpled, and tendrils of dark hair fall loosely from her sagging ponytail. 'I still think we should look for her, is all. She's only young. Doesn't

185

understand English.' She opens the French doors, letting cold air in, and steps out onto the terrace. Leon follows.

Alice looks at Christine and Lori who don't move. She shrugs and follows Faith and Leon out into the darkness once more.

'Gabriela!' they all yell, Faith veering away from Alice and Leon, heading towards the wood and disappearing into the shadows.

'She's not out here is she?' Alice looks up at Leon, her arms around herself like a straitjacket, shivering from cold and fear. 'This is so awful. I'm so sorry I dragged you here.'

Leon takes hold of her hand. 'You weren't to know, Alice. You can't blame yourself for this.'

They continue across the lawn. 'Gabriela!' Leon cries once more. Alice strains her ears for a response, but there's only the sounds of the trees, branches creaking, leaves whispering, and an animal cry somewhere in the distance.

Faith appears, running back towards Alice and Leon. 'God knows where she is,' she says, panting. 'If she headed into the woods, we'll never find her tonight.' But her eyes have focused on the wire fence. 'Should we check on the rocks below?'

Leon shakes his head. 'There's no point. I know this sounds cold, but if Gabriela went over the edge, and we've no reason to think she would have ... she wouldn't have survived.' He pauses for a long moment, as they all stare out to sea. 'Let's go inside. Stay together.'

*

Later, back in the bar, Christine and Lori sit opposite each other in a booth, upright and serious, as though they're about to play a game of poker. Alice and Leon are on the sofa, silent, their faces pale like ghosts, eyes heavy. Faith is looking out of the window, eyes flicking across the darkness.

It's a long ten minutes before Christine speaks. 'What exactly did the police say, Faith?'

Faith glances back over her shoulder. 'They said they'll send someone over to the island as soon as possible.'

'By boat?'

Faith shrugs, and shakes her head. She looks back through the glass and whispers, her voice sounding defeated, 'They didn't say.'

'Helicopter maybe?'

'I wouldn't have thought so. Not in this weather.' Faith, cups her hands over her eyes, and continues to look out. 'A boat seems the likely option, but I can't see any sign of one, and it's still pretty rough out there, even though the storm's died down a bit.' She turns and heads towards the bar. 'Anyone else need a big drink? Because I do.'

Leon

The grandfather clock chimes three. Time is passing painfully slowly – as though every second is a minute, every minute an hour. Christine is dozing in a chair by the window, talking in her sleep, mumbling something about fairy cakes, though most of her words are inaudible. How she can sleep at all is beyond Leon's understanding. The thought of closing his eyes against this fear feels impossible. His whole body is on hyper-alert, his eyes darting the shadows.

Lori and Faith lie stretched full-length on benches like corpses, one each side of a table. Both awake, but so still and silent.

There's no sign of Gabriela, *or Cameron*, and Mitch is still in his room.

Alice and Leon sit on a sofa, his arm draped around her shoulders. Her head is pressed against his chest, and he wonders if she can hear the fast thud of his heartbeat, or the sound of his mind whizzing and whirring with everything that's happened – not only since they arrived at Flynn Hotel, but also before – long before. Despite this awful situation, he knows he must tell her what he knows. They haven't been this close in so long. If he keeps *this* from her, it could ruin everything; though if he tells her, could it be worse?

He takes a deep breath. 'There's something I need to tell you, Alice,' he says quiet enough so the other women can't hear. What he has to say is for Alice's ears only. 'It's never going to be a good time,' he goes on, 'but I need you to hear what I have to say, before we get back to Whitby. Before the police come. Before it all comes out.'

'What are you talking about?' She peers up at him with worried eyes. 'You're freaking me out, Leon.'

'It's about Tegan ...' He stops, takes a deep breath.

'Tegan?'

'The thing is, she told me she was in love with your dad.' It comes out fast, the words falling over each other – as though they've been crammed into a dark cupboard, and the door has finally opened, springing the contents free.

'What?' Alice pulls herself upright, away from him, stares deep into his eyes. 'What are you talking about? Of course Tegan wasn't in love with my dad. She was his literary agent, for God's sake.'

'It was more than that, Alice.' He tries to order the words he knows he has to say. 'Apparently they had a thing.'

'A thing?' She screws up her nose. '*A thing?*'

'A brief relationship – a fling – I don't think your dad thought it was serious, but—'

'No, no they didn't have a fling.' She shakes her head. She would have known. 'That can't be right. He would have told me.'

'I'm only telling you what Tegan told me. That your dad broke it off with her the day he died. That's where he'd been that evening, to Tegan's apartment, to tell her it was over. She was gutted, thought he loved her, that it was more than it was, and—'

'This can't be right.'

'Think about it, Alice – Henry wasn't with him.' He tries to take her hand, but she shakes it free. 'Your dad never went out without him. Tegan was scared of dogs.'

She shakes her head again. 'No, you've got it wrong, Leon.'

He runs his hand over his chin, takes a deep breath. 'There's more, Alice, much more—'

'I don't think they're coming.' It's Christine. 'The police, I don't think they're coming.' She's awake, standing by the window, her voice a blade cutting off Leon and Alice's conversation. 'It's been well over an hour since Faith called them.'

'What, Leon?' Alice whispers, clearly trying to ignore Christine's invasion. 'What else is there?'

'The rain has stopped,' Christine goes on, turning to Leon and Alice. 'Maybe we should go out there now. Go down to the jetty and wait for the police.'

'Or, Christine,' Leon snaps, 'we can stay here where it's safe.'

'Leon?' Alice's eyes are locked on his. But Christine is heading over to them with quick steps, and Lori and Faith are sitting up now, Faith stretching her arms above her head and yawning.

'I'll tell you everything later, Alice. I promise,' he whispers, as guilt surges through him that he's still keeping things from her. But he can't say any more, not now Christine is beside them, her plump body a shivering wreck. The words he wants to say to Alice have stumbled and fallen in a cluttered heap in his already confused brain.

Alice

'When will they be here?' Christine's voice is rising in volume; she wrings her hands. 'The police – when will they be here?'

'I'm sure they're doing their best,' Alice says, Leon's words playing over in her head. *Did her dad have an affair with Tegan?* She tries to recall times she was with the two of them. Had looks passed between them that she'd missed? Had there been a spark of chemistry she didn't register at the time? She can't recall anything of the kind. Perhaps she hadn't wanted to see it. Had she been in denial, not wanting to share her father with anyone?

'So where the hell are they?' Christine continues, her body twitching.

'I'm guessing the storm has made it impossible for them to get here,' Faith says, stretching her arms above her head once more, before getting up, and making her way over to the rest of them. 'But I'm sure we'll be fine, if we stay together in the bar until the tide goes out tomorrow.'

Christine nods and looks at her watch. 'It's gone three. Only another few hours before daylight.'

'What was it like here when you were a nanny?' Faith asks Lori, after a long silence. 'What were the children like?'

The woman looks agitated by the question. 'Let's just say they had a difficult upbringing.' She rises to her feet. 'I'm afraid you'll have to excuse me, I desperately need the loo.' She grabs her handbag, and goes to make her way across the bar.

'Christ's sake,' Leon whispers, dragging his fingers through his hair.

Lori flashes a look over her shoulder. 'I heard that, Leon.' But she continues on her way.

'You really shouldn't go alone,' he calls after her.

Lori swings round. 'You're right. What am I thinking? But you can't all hold my hand. Christine, will you come with me?'

'Of course.' Christine jumps to her feet. 'I could do with going too, if I'm honest.'

'That's incredibly kind,' Lori says, with a smile, as Christine catches her up.

'But what if one of you is the killer?' Alice's eyes move from one to the other, as they stop and turn, looking awkward.

'Well, don't look at me,' Christine says, her face a mask of indignation. 'I'm no killer.'

190

'Well, I'm not saying it is you, Christine, but we have to keep an open mind here. Two people are dead.'

'There's a ladies' room in reception,' Christine says. 'Let's all go together. That way we'll be safe.'

Alice feels her body wobble as she stands up. Everything's so bizarre. A party of five are about to trot to the loo together, for fear of being bumped off one by one by an invisible killer stalking a Gothic hotel on an island in the middle of nowhere. You couldn't make it up. How the hell had it come to this? A bubble of hysteria rises inside her, and as Leon takes her hand, she begins to laugh. Loud. Hysterically.

'Alice?' Leon says. 'What's up with you?'

'What's up with me?' she cries. 'What's up with me?' Her laughter turns to tears, as she bends over, holding her stomach, bile rising in her throat. 'What the hell are we going to do?' Once she's sure she's not going to be sick, she straightens. 'We're all going to be murdered aren't we? Whoever's doing this is going to pick us off one by one. Kill us all.'

Leon pulls her to his chest, strokes her hair. 'Try to calm down, Alice. This really isn't helping.'

'Yes, calm down, Alice,' Faith spits, her eyes wide. 'We're all in a state here – all in the same boat. You don't see the rest of us acting so bloody crazy.'

'Bit harsh,' Leon says, as Alice falls silent, her heart thudding. 'This is going to affect us all differently, Faith. You need to allow a little.'

'OK. Sorry.' Faith raises her palms as though surrendering. 'I'm just a bit …'

'Crazy?' Alice whispers, throwing her a daggering stare.

'Give me time,' Christine says with a forced smile. 'I might be swinging from that crazy chandelier with you girls soon.'

'Sorry to interrupt, folks, but I still need to use the loo,' Lori says, and heads out of the bar. They all follow.

Once in reception, Lori takes the three steps down to the

191

ladies', straightening her flowing dress, and pulling her thick hair over one shoulder as she disappears from view, a door squeaking closed behind her.

'Wait up,' Christine says, following.

Alice, Leon and Faith wait on the sofa, not making eye contact – none of them speaking. The house seems to be closing in around them.

Eventually, the door to the loos squeaks once more, and Christine reappears, climbing the steps, tugging at her underwear.

'I think I'll go too, while we're here.' Alice gets up, passes Christine, before descending the steps.

The ladies' is immaculate. Black tiles on every wall, two pink sinks – the colour theme matching the rest of the house. Alice goes to the loo then washes her hands with the pleasant-smelling soap. She catches sight of her reflection in the oval mirrors above the sinks. If she had any doubts that this evening has taken its toll, her reflection confirms it has. Her hair hangs lank and damp, her eyes are bloodshot, her skin pale, all smacking of anxiety-fuelled exhaustion.

She sets the dryer going, and moves her hands under it.

'Everything OK, Lori?' she calls, over the whirring dryer, glancing over her shoulder at the closed cubicle. When there's no reply, she feels a small sensation of panic. She crouches down, peers under the door, sees Lori's bag propped against it, and relief surges through her. 'We'll wait for you outside,' she says, straightening up.

She exits the ladies' and goes to sit with the others. Faith jumps to her feet – almost as if she has taken a baton from Alice in a relay race. She makes her way down the steps.

'Should we check on Lori, do you think?' Faith says when she returns five minutes later. 'I called out to her, but she didn't reply. She's been in there a long time.'

Alice shrugs. 'I think she may have a tummy upset, or something.'

'Too much information,' Leon says, but he doesn't smile.

Faith and Alice head back to the ladies', leaving Leon and Christine in reception.

'Lori? Are you OK in there?' Alice calls, her head close to the cubicle door. She crouches once more and peers underneath. 'Her bag is still there.' She rises, using the door for support, and it eases open. 'Lori?' She looks round the door. 'Oh God, where is she?'

'What the …?' Faith cries from behind her.

Alice covers her mouth with her hands. There's a small window behind the loo, but hardly big enough for Lori to climb out of. And anyway, why would she?

Faith, eyes wide, spins round and bangs open the other cubicle.

Feeling cool air on her neck, Alice turns. 'Was the window open when you came down here earlier?' She can't recall if it was when she was there before.

'I don't think so.' Faith moves towards it, bites down on her lower lip. It's only open a few inches, but it isn't latched. It's big enough to climb through.

Alice pads across the room, approaches the open window. Her head spins. Has Lori climbed out? Has she left of her own accord through this window, or has someone taken her?

She thinks back to when Lori didn't respond when she called out earlier. Had she been lying in the cubicle then? Had someone attacked her? *Cameron? Mitch? Gabriela?* Everyone is suddenly a suspect. And worse, did Alice miss her cry for help?

She pushes open the window, letting a whoosh of cold air in. Looks out into the darkness, a shiver trailing down her spine as she scans the area. There's no sign of her.

'The window's cracked,' Faith says, and Alice's gaze moves back to the glass. There's a smear of blood on the frame. She goes to touch it, but Faith grabs her hand, and pulls it back.

'Don't,' she says. 'The police will be here soon. It's evidence.'

193

Chapter 32

1994

Tiger

I still don't see Daddy much, and that makes me sad. But Aunt Verity says he loves me, and I must believe that, and never forget it. One day, she says, he will wake up and smell the roses, and we will all live happily ever after as a family. The trouble is, I *do* worry about this very much, because there are no roses at Flynn House, and there are no roses in Daddy's garden either. There are only spiky, stingy bushes that prickle and burst my skin, and the poisonous white flowers with purple blotchy stems that I must never ever touch.

Today I am happy because I am in Daddy's garden, and it's just Daddy and me. And I'm wearing my red shorts. And I'm wearing my yellow T-shirt too. Aunt Verity has never bought me swimmies. She says the sun will burn me and make my skin crispy if I don't wear shorts and a T-shirt.

'The sun has got its hat on, Tiger,' Daddy says, and I look up at the bright blue sky. The sun is big and shiny, and because it might make me blind, I squeeze my eyes so they are nearly closed. I can just about see through the slits.

I'm having the best fun ever in my paddling pool, *splashing, splashing, splashing.* I can't actually swim in the pool because it's too small, but quite a long time ago, Daddy took me down to the sea. And I swam and swam, and he clapped his hands and said I was amazing. I like it when Daddy calls me amazing. And I like days when it's just Daddy and me, when Aunt Verity is busy at the big house doing her jobs, like washing or mowing the lawn – or she's painting her pictures.

'Can you hear the birds singing, Tiger?' Daddy says, looking up again from writing in his notebook. He likes to write. He says it makes him feel better, and one day, when I'm bigger, he says he'll read all of his stories to me. But for now they are a bit too scary. Instead he reads me fairy tales. My favourite is Rapunzel.

'Shh, Tiger,' he says, when I splash again. 'Stop and listen to the birds.'

So I stop splashing, and look up at the trees. 'Chirp, chirp, chirp.'

*

Later, when Aunt Verity comes to get me, she starts shouting at Daddy, her face turning red, and she throws a whole deckchair and its leg breaks off, and Daddy marches like a soldier up and down the garden, rubbing his head, and making growly noises like a big bad bear.

'I don't want Tiger to end up like us, V,' he yells.

'And you think you have a right to an opinion? I can count on my hand how many times you've seen Tiger in the last five years.'

I grab my cuddly tiger, that Daddy bought me for my birthday, and curl up into a ball and roll under the hedge, like an invisible hedgehog. Listening.

Daddy shouts that he wants me to go to school, to be normal.

Be like other kids. But I know what school is like because I've seen *Grange Hill* on the television, and I don't want to go there, not one little bit.

'Home schooling will work out fine,' Aunt Verity shouts. 'Tiger is so clever, Hugh.' And then she shouts some more about how she looks after me all of the time, and that Daddy rarely sees me. And that it will be her decision, and hers alone. And Daddy says it isn't up to her, and that he is my daddy, so he chooses what happens to me. He says he will come to Flynn House and take me away if she isn't careful.

But Aunt Verity says, 'You know you'll never set foot in the place, Hugh. You're too afraid of the past.' And I realise Daddy has never been to the big house, and that makes me sad.

And then Aunt Verity grabs my arm and drags me out from under the hedge, and all the prickly branches scratch my arms and legs and blood bubbles everywhere.

'Aunt Verity!' I scream, and then I cry so hard my nose runs.

'Oh, Tiger,' Aunt Verity says, and she wraps me up tightly in a grey beach towel. 'Let's get you home, sweetie. Let's get you away from Daddy; he's in a very grumpy mood.'

*

I like making fairy cakes with Aunt Verity. It's my third favourite thing in the whole world. My first is being with Daddy, my second is being with the puppets, but this is my third.

'Are you OK now, Tiger?' Aunt Verity says, as I spoon the mixture of eggs and sugar and flour into paper cases, and lick my fingers.

I nod. 'I like making cakes.'

'I'm sorry I got cross with Daddy earlier. And I'm so sorry you hurt your legs and arms.'

'It's all right.' I scoop more mixture onto the spoon. 'When the cakes are cooked, please may I have three?'

She smiles. 'That's a little bit greedy, Tiger.'

'But I have got sore legs and arms.'

'Well just this once, then,' she says with a big smile.

I plop the mixture into the last case, and Aunt Verity puts the tray into the oven while I lick the bowl. It's not long before the whole kitchen smells sweet and sugary and my tummy grumbles.

*

Later, in my room, Aunt Verity straightens my yellow duvet, and karate chops my pillows, and lays my cuddly tiger on top of my red pyjamas.

'What's that noise?' I ask, looking up from building a house out of Lego on the floor. I hear it a lot. *Tap, tap, tap* above my head.

'I can't hear anything, sweetie,' Aunt Verity says, bending down and stroking my cheek. She says this every time I ask her about the *tap, tap, tap*. 'You're imagining things again, Tiger. You have a good imagination, just like your daddy.'

I like it when she says I'm like my daddy.

Maybe it's the puppets in the attic, I nearly say. But I know I can't say that because Aunt Verity doesn't know I go up there to see my puppet friends, and, if she did, she might be cross, and take away the key.

The noise gets louder. *Why can't she hear it?*

'Dinner will be ready in an hour, darling.' She leaves the room with a wave. 'I'm going to have a little drink now.'

Tap, tap, tap.

*

When Aunt Verity is flopped on the sofa asleep, with an empty glass in her hand, up the attic steps I go – one, two, three, four, five, seven, eight, nine.

'Hello,' I say to the brass dogs that guard the room.

197

I open the red door, and look inside.

Aunt Verity comes up to the attic lots of times, and one time I saw where she hid the key, and ever since, I've been coming too. Aunt Verity doesn't know I'm here, behind the red door, and neither does Daddy. They have no idea at all.

I sit down, happy here on the grass-green carpet. I like the muddy-brown walls too. It's like being outside inside. I don't like the bars at the arch-shaped window, but I love the shelves full of magic tricks. There's a huge red box that Grandpa Felix used to put ladies inside and cut them into three bits with the saw that's hanging on the wall. I know he did that, because there are pictures all over the walls downstairs. But it's OK. It wasn't real. It was just pretend. Magic.

There's a top hat too, but no rabbit, and there are lots of sparkly clothes that were my grandmother's. And then there are the puppets. The puppets are my friends. Not my real friends. I haven't got any real friends. But I know what friends are from watching children's television.

I scratch my arm. The blood bubbles are now crusty scabs. I like to pick them off. See the blood again.

At this very moment exactly, I'm going to have a picnic – outside inside – with my puppet friends. I've brought them each a fairy cake.

I pour Rosie a cup of tea first because she's my favourite. I named her after *Rosie and Jim* on children's television. *Rosie and Jim* are puppets and they live on a boat on the river. My Rosie doesn't live on a boat because she lives in the attic, and she doesn't look like Rosie on the television either. Rosie on the television has black hair and black eyes, but my friend Rosie has yellow hair and her eyes are blue and her lips are shiny.

Then I serve Paulo some tea. I know his name is Paulo because Aunt Verity showed me pictures of him once and told me his name. I don't like Paulo very much; he has a very cross face. But I mustn't leave Paulo out of the picnic, because that would be unkind.

'Would you like a fairy cake?' I ask Ralfie, my third puppet, and he nods his head, and smiles. I named him Ralfie after a dog I saw on the beach once. Woof, woof, woof. He was a fluffy brown dog that jumped up at me and made me laugh. Puppet Ralfie has freckles across his nose and cheeks, and red hair made of wool, and he's dressed in a black and white checked suit. I serve him his cake onto the plate, and he gobbles it down. 'It's fun being outside inside, isn't it?' I say to him.

I turn. 'What about you, Rosie? Would you like a cake?'

I love being up here in the attic with my friends, outside inside.

Chapter 33

Halloween Weekend 2019

Alice

'Lori's disappeared,' Alice cries, arms flailing, cheeks flushed as she dashes up the steps from the ladies' and into reception, Faith right behind her.

Leon and Christine jump to their feet, eyes wide.

'We can't go on like this,' Faith cries. 'Christ! We have to do something.'

'I agree.' Leon massages his temples as he paces the chessboard floor tiles. 'But what the hell can we do, but wait?'

'The police should be here soon,' Alice says, but she doesn't believe her words, not anymore. Surely they would be here by now, if they were coming.

Christine takes off her glasses, rubs her watery eyes. 'What are we going to do if they don't?' she says.

Faith flops down on the sofa, looks up, as though the ornate ceiling has the answers. 'I keep going over and over the call I made at the cottage. Whoever answered the phone said, "Hello."' Her eyes dip, land on Alice's face where they lock. 'I mean, wouldn't they have asked which service I require? That's what they say, isn't it? The emergency services. I've seen it on TV; they ask what service you require?'

Alice nods slowly. 'I guess so.'

'So, now I'm wondering if the call ever went through to the mainland. What if I didn't speak to the emergency services at all?'

Alice's eyes widen. 'Why wouldn't it have gone through, Faith?'

Faith bites down on her lip. 'I know it sounds far-fetched, but hear me out. It was a man who answered, so what if it was Cameron Patterson? What if he pretended to be the emergency services?'

'That makes no sense, Faith.' Alice shakes her head, doesn't want to believe her.

'I think Faith could be right,' Christine says, folding her arms around herself. 'What if he set up the phone to go straight to his mobile, or something? I think they can do that, can't they?'

'You can do anything, if you want to bad enough,' Leon says, but he's shaking his head, as though he doesn't believe it.

'He would have known we would go to the cottage eventually, what with everything that's been happening here at the hotel,' Faith goes on.

'But why would he play games like that?' Alice says. 'And anyway, if he was pretending to be the emergency services, he would surely keep up the pretence and get it right, and ask what service we required.'

'I don't know, would he?' Faith shrugs.

'But it doesn't make sense, Faith. He could have just disconnected the phone.'

'Not if he's playing games with us.'

A chill darts down Alice's spine. Could Faith be right? Could Cameron have set this whole thing up? Taken their mobile phones? Cut the phone line?

'What if he killed the Winslows?' Christine says, covering her mouth with her hand, her eyes shimmering as she looks about her. 'What if he's going to kill us all?'

'But why?' Tears prick Alice's eyes. 'Why would some man none of us know kill the Winslows? Do all of this?' She looks around too, a stab of fear almost knocking her off her feet. She grips Leon's arm, and he turns, stares deep into her eyes.

'I have to get help,' he says.

'What? No, Leon, we need to all stay here, together,' Alice cries, tightening her grip on his arm. 'There's no way to get back to the mainland until tomorrow. The boat's gone, remember? The phone lines are down.'

'I have to do something.' He shakes off her hand, makes his way into the bar, and everyone follows, as though attached to him by invisible leads. He heads across the room, and throws open the French doors. 'The storm's almost over now,' he says. 'I reckon I can swim back and get help. It's not that far.'

'You can't!' There's panic in Alice's voice, the thought of him leaving sending a bolt of fear through her body. 'What if the storm returns, Leon? You won't be safe out there.'

He glances over his shoulder, meets her eyes once more. 'I'm a good swimmer, Alice. You know that.'

'I think it's a good idea.' Christine puts her arm around Alice, but she shrugs her away.

'He's a lifeguard,' Faith says. 'He can do this.'

'While he's getting help, the three of us can lock ourselves in one of the bedrooms,' Christine goes on. 'We'll be safe together.'

'It makes sense, Alice,' Leon says. 'You've got to see that.'

Alice shakes her head, her throat closing. 'Please don't go, Leon. The four of us can stay. We'll be safe here until morning.'

'I really think Leon should try to get us help, Alice,' Christine says. 'If he can.'

'No!' Tears fill her eyes. 'Leon, please, this is ridiculous.'

But she knows from his determined look that Leon thinks he's doing the right thing. He leans in, kisses her cheek. 'I have to do this,' he says. 'Stay with Christine and Faith at all times. Go up to one of the rooms as soon as I leave, and don't come out until I'm back with the police, whatever happens.'

He walks away, and as he disappears through the double doors into reception, Alice's body shakes, memories of losing her father filling her thoughts. She can't lose Leon too. She just can't.

*

Alice unlocks the door to her room, and is about to press down the handle when it hits her, 'Oh God, we should probably check on Mitch first.'

Faith slaps her hand to her mouth. 'I totally forgot about him.' She looks towards the end of the dimly lit hallway. 'And if I'm honest, I don't fancy checking. I mean, what if he's ...?'

'What? Dead? The killer?' Alice's voice is high-pitched – neither option sounds good, and she doesn't fancy finding out.

'Well I'm not going down there.' Christine pushes past Alice, opens the door. 'He's locked in. We should lock ourselves in too, like we planned.'

Faith and Alice look at each other for a moment, before following Christine into the room.

Once the door is locked and bolted, Alice lowers herself down onto the hard, wooden floor, but she feels far from safe. Safe would be sitting in the tangled garden of Butterfly Cottage, Henry sprawled in the sunshine, her father, very much alive, telling her about the latest book he's working on, her telling him how well her little shop in Whitby is doing. She loved it when they talked in the moment, not looking back, or forward – just that precious, safe moment in time – just the two of them.

She rests her back against the wall, and lowers her head, hair falling over her face. She cradles her knees, her mind drifting to Leon; still unable to believe he's taken off, left her here in this nightmare, putting himself in danger.

Five minutes later, Christine is sprawled on the double bed, staring up at the ceiling. She looks different without her glasses – now on the bedside unit – her eyelids heavy. It's the first time Alice has properly studied the quaint little woman who chirpily greeted them in the white boat, what now feels like weeks ago. Her face is lined by life, her eyes carrying dark shadows. Her cropped hair and trendy red-framed glasses gave her a younger vibe when they first met her, but now the harrowing day seems to have aged her a decade.

'Do you live nearby?' Faith asks, turning from where she's sitting in the throne-like chair facing the window, to look at Christine. Alice can't help thinking she's trying to kill time, fill a void with pointless conversation until Leon returns.

'I've lived in Dunwold on the coast all my life,' Christine says, sounding nostalgic. 'I remember Flynn House fascinated me as a child, but none of us kids ever went too close.' She half-laughs. 'The thought of Felix Flynn catching one of us trespassing – and putting us in one of his wooden boxes and chopping us up – was a pretty good deterrent.' Her smile says she's back there in the past, a child once more running along the beach without a care. 'The place had a mysterious vibe back then.'

'Still has,' Faith says, turning her eyes back to the window and the view of liquid black, her blurry reflection in the glass haunting.

'Do you remember the children, Verity and Hugh?' Alice asks.

'No, not really, they rarely ventured out – kept under lock and key by Felix.'

Alice picks up on something dark in her voice, or perhaps it's the heavy mood in the room.

'Hugh was a sad little creature, I vaguely remember,' Christine goes on. A brief sigh seems to hold a note of regret. 'I was strangely excited when I got the opportunity to work here. To finally set foot inside Flynn House, find out what it was like inside the mysterious mansion that fascinated us as kids.' She paused for a moment, wrapping her arms around herself. 'Though I still miss working in my little shop on the mainland.'

'You owned a shop?' Alice asks.

'Mmm, for many years – my parents owned it before me. Happy times. But when my Terry died six months ago, and my son moved away—'

'I'm sorry to hear about your husband,' Faith says, glancing over.

'It doesn't get any easier. Grief.' Christine pulls herself up to a sitting position, her eyes shimmering as she props herself against the baroque headboard. 'He had terminal cancer. Though the irony is, it's not how he died.' She looks down at her hands, entwines her chubby fingers. 'He was on medication when we went for a break in Cornwall, and I wonder now if that's what made him unsteady on his feet ... He went out for a walk along the cliffs and ... well ... he lost his footing, tumbled to his death.'

Alice covers her mouth, holding in a gasp. 'I'm so sorry,' she says, hearing the pain in Christine's voice.

'A blessing some might say.' Christine shrugs. 'Saved him any suffering he may have faced at the end, perhaps? If I had to lose him, and it seems I did, it was better to spare him that.'

A silence descends for some moments, before Faith chirps up once more.

'So, how did you end up working here?' she asks Christine, her voice slicing through the quiet.

Christine pushes her fingers through her hair, and reaches for her glasses. Puts them on. 'It was a while back. I'd closed the shop for the final time; was planning to sell up and move away, maybe join my son in France, when a leaflet came through my door. I'm guessing it went to all the residents of Dunwold. It was about the hotel opening the following October. They were advertising for a general manager.'

'And you applied?'

Christine nods. 'It was too good an opportunity to miss.

The money was amazing. So I came over for an interview with Cameron Patterson. But when I got here there were only painters and decorators on the premises – nice group of Eastern European chaps. They showed me round, and I was sold on taking the position, should I be offered it. Later Cameron emailed apologising that he'd got stuck in traffic, and after an email exchange, he said I was perfect for the position.'

'Just like that?' Alice says, her eyes widening. 'Didn't you think it was a bit odd? I mean where was Cameron that day? Where is he now?'

'To be honest, I didn't think anything of it at the time,' Christine says. 'I'd managed a shop for years, had a pilot licence for the boat. He said I was just what he was looking for.' She looks about her. 'But I don't know anymore.' She shakes her head. 'What with everything that's happened—'

'I'm with you on that,' Alice says. 'I keep wondering if Cameron brought us all here for a reason. I wonder if … well … Hugh Flynn looks so much like my father, and I know so little about my dad's past.' The words are out there, swirling like toxic fog in the air. The fear that had been burrowing away, that her father, the father she has always known as Adam Hadley, had lived in this house as a boy and as a young man, and never told her. That he had a sister he never mentioned. But if that was true, why had he kept it from her? Why had he changed his name? Why had he kept his past hidden?

Faith leans over and touches Alice's hand. 'Is this to do with the portrait, sweetie? Because, the resemblance could be coincidental.'

'Maybe.' But Alice is sure there's more to it.

'Lori said she worked here as a nanny, didn't she?' Christine says, cutting through Alice's thoughts. 'But I have no connection to this house that I'm aware of, unless you count that I lived on the mainland all my life.'

'And what about the Winslows?' Alice says. 'And what possible link could Gabriela have to Flynn House? I mean, she's Eastern European, doesn't speak any English.'

'Cameron doesn't know about her. She only arrived on Thursday. He left money in the safe to use for anything I felt I needed, so I took her on cash in hand.'

'What about Mitch?' Alice goes on.

'And me,' Faith says. 'I only decided to come at the last minute.'

Alice shakes her head. She feels like crap, her temples pounding, her body so tired it aches. 'I don't know, perhaps I'm wrong,' she says, sounding defeated.

'Maybe we should try to get some sleep,' Faith says. 'I know it won't be easy, but if we all have a little power nap.'

'OK. But one of us should stay awake,' Alice says. 'Just in case.'

'Nobody can get in here.' Faith leans over and grabs a throw from the bottom of the bed, covers herself with it, and shuffles down in the chair. 'I've pulled the bolt across. We're safe.'

Christine removes her glasses once more, and eases down the bed, curls her legs up like she's a foetus.

Alice wants to say, *But what if it's one of us?* She hates that she's even considering her friend as a possible killer. 'I'll keep an eye open, all the same,' she says. 'You two can go to sleep if you want.' A redundant comment, as both Christine and Faith have closed their eyes. Alice's eyes are gritty and sore, her lids heavy. She's exhausted, but her body buzzes like a beehive. She's not sure she'll sleep.

Five minutes later, Faith lets out a sudden shriek, and Alice bolts to her feet, races over to her. But her friend doesn't wake, has fallen silent once more. In fact, the whole house is quiet, and a suffocating fear settles around her.

There's no clock in the room, and without her phone, time seems to have lost all meaning. Surely it will be daylight in a few hours. She leans across to the bookshelf and grabs a book, sits back down, and opens it at the first page. But the words blur in front of her eyes. Her head is too full. It's impossible to turn off her fear, the sadness.

You kept so many secrets from me, Dad. A tear rolls down her face, and plops onto the page. *Didn't you?*

Chapter 34

1994

Tiger

The frothy waves roll towards me like big white wheels. I sit on the sand, legs crossed, halfway to Dunwold and halfway to the island, looking out at the sea on both sides of me. It looks like a giant grey cake with blobs of cream everywhere.

Daddy says I'm a good swimmer. That he is very proud of me. I want to make him proud again, so that he will love me. I'm wearing my swimming goggles. And I'm wearing my red shorts. And I'm wearing my yellow T-shirt.

Aunt Verity doesn't know I am out here today, but I know Daddy will see me from his window. His desk is there. Facing the sea. He sits at it all the time, writing. I want him to watch me from his window. I want him to watch me swim like a fishy, fish, fish.

The sea creeps across the sand, looking like watery fingers. It starts to rain.

I look up at the cliffs, at Daddy's cottage, but I can't see him at the window. I look up at the grey and swirly sky. The clouds are like puffs of smoke.

I wait. I wait for a very long time.

And now the sea is quite deep and I'm standing up, as it swirls around me, making me wobble. The rain is getting heavier, bouncing on my head, making it hurt. I can't see through my goggles so I pull them off, yelping as the strap gets caught in my hair.

I still can't see Daddy, so I try to walk back to the island, pushing my hands through the water that's getting deeper and deeper and deeper. I slip and slide on the sand, and my head goes under the sea. Water shoots up my nose, and when I come back up, I cough and cough and cough.

'Aunt Verity,' I scream, scared now. I've forgotten how to swim. It's too hard. 'Aunt Verity, help!'

I try not to cry. I try to be brave. I try to swim. Daddy will be proud of me if I swim. But I can't see Flynn House or Daddy's cottage, or which way to go. The rain is bouncing and bouncing and bouncing on the water, on my head.

I try to put my feet back down on the sand, and step, one, two, three, and whoosh – the sea lifts me up and I'm moving and moving, and I don't know where I am, and I cry and I cry, and the rain stings my face. 'Daddy, Aunt Verity.' And I cough and I cough, because the water is in my nose and in my mouth and in my ears.

Daddy doesn't care about me.

And then I feel someone taking my hand …

*

'Tiger, Tiger.' It's Aunt Verity. Her voice is all funny. High and screechy, like when I don't put my toys away but worse, and she's crying, and pressing down on my chest over and over and over and it really hurts. Water bursts from my mouth like a fountain, and

210

I cough again. I look up at her. Her hair is all wet, and hanging over her face, and her eyes look red and sore.

'Oh. Tiger,' she cries, lifting me off the sand, and she holds me so tight in her arms, wrapping me in a big, grey beach towel. And I'm so glad I'm here with her. But I'm so sad because there's no sign of Daddy.

'Oh, Tiger, my darling,' Aunt Verity says. 'I thought I'd lost you forever.'

*

'You can stay here, Tiger,' Aunt Verity says the next day. She's looking in her bag, mixing up the things inside, trying to find her car keys. 'You're still not completely well after yesterday.' She lifts out her keys, jiggles them, and zips up her bag.

I'm not sure if I want to be in the house on my own. It's never happened before, and it's a very big house, and sometimes I think there might be ghosts living here with us.

But then I think of my puppet friends. They'll take care of me while Aunt Verity is away. And it's better than going to Tesco. I don't like Tesco very much.

Aunt Verity has to go shopping when the tide is out, so she's in a big rush and is all flappy, and her cheeks are red. She kisses my head three times; she's been doing that a lot since I nearly drowned. 'Be good though, won't you, Tiger?' she says, as she races out of the kitchen.

'I will,' I say, following her into the hallway, holding my cuddly tiger by the tail. I'm wearing my slippers that are like fluffy rabbits, so I can't walk as fast as her. She waves and disappears through the front door. I wave too.

I stand by the big glass doors in the lounge, watching her car zoom along the sand like a racing car, before I take the key from the secret place.

I head through the hallway, running my hand over the gold

wallpaper – it's not real gold – in fact, it's peeling off in places – and up the stairs.

I'm panting by the time I get to the attic room because I've been counting all the steps, and my slippers are a bit heavy.

I unlock the red door, and push it open.

'Hello,' I say as I go inside. And the puppets all say hello back to me.

*

I've been playing for some time, when I hear a noise outside the red door. Footsteps, I think. I worry it might be a ghost, or Aunt Verity and that she'll be cross I'm in here, so I tell the puppets to be quiet. 'Shh,' I say, pressing my finger on my lip as I climb into Grandpa's magic box with my cuddly tiger.

The door to the attic squeaks open, and I curl up like a hedgehog, making myself invisible.

Chapter 35

Halloween Weekend 2019

Alice

Somewhere outside of Alice's nightmare a door swings open. She tries to escape the vivid dream, screaming into the void as she's dragged up the stairs towards the red door, away from everything she knows. She's only a child, gripping a toy tiger in her small fists, her eyes sore, her cheeks raw from crying – *Help me. Help me.* Suddenly her father takes her in his arms and holds her close. She feels tiny against his chest as he runs, blood on his shirt.

A woman's voice echoes, *'Don't go, Hugh. Please don't leave.'*

Leon

An orange flicker fights for life in some of the swinging lanterns that fringe the slope leading from Flynn Hotel down to the sea. Some have given up, no longer guiding the way. Light radiates from the house too, but visibility is poor. Leon huddles his arms around himself, as he makes his way towards the sea.

Quick footsteps startle him. He turns, heart thudding, eyes roaming the area. There's movement in the shadows. Someone is here, watching him.

More footsteps. Moving away.

'Lori?' he calls, hearing the tremble in his voice. 'Is that you? Gabriela?' He shudders, turns, heads in the opposite direction towards the jetty at speed.

He stands by the sea, his eyes flicking over the distant coastline. It's mainly in darkness, lights dotted here and there. It's about a mile to the mainland. Not far. The sea is choppy and restless, but it's doable. He swam the English Channel for charity a few years back. This short distance will only take half an hour at most. He'll be there and back with help within the hour.

He hates how upset Alice is. But if she stays in the room with Faith and Christine – keeps the door locked, bolted – she'll be safe. *Won't she?*

He strips down to his boxers and T-shirt, his eyes drifting towards the rocks where they found Alice's dress. He squints, returns his gaze to the shoreline, trying to focus on his imminent swim. He dips his toe into the frothy waves that beat a path up the rocks and cobbles.

'Shit!' *The sea is bloody freezing.*

Goose pimples rise on his arms, and a chill shudders down his back. He takes a deep breath, about to wade in, when he hears someone coming up behind him. He swings round, his eyes zigzagging across the darkness, dipping into the shadows. *There's nobody here.*

'Man up,' he tells himself, turning back to the sea, making his way in, the freezing water covering his ankles. *You're imagining things.*

The strike on the back of his head is excruciating. The sea

rises up to greet him within seconds. Water seeps into his nose, his mouth.

'Christ,' he mumbles, before everything goes black.

Alice

Alice wakes with a start, beads of sweat on her forehead, unsure how long she's been asleep. She rubs her gritty eyes, hauls herself to her feet, the book she was attempting to read earlier landing with a thud face down on the floor. She listens, her body trembling. The house is deathly quiet.

A scan of the room tells her Christine and Faith have gone. She looks towards the open door, ventures across the floor, hands pressed against her chest, heart pounding.

'Hello!' she calls, poking her head out into the hallway to the left, to the right. The glow from inside the room casts shadows, but it's too dark to see clearly – the wall lights on the landing are out. A shiver tickles her spine. 'Faith? Christine?'

She stands for a moment; they'd agreed to stay in the room until Leon could get help, hadn't they? Why have they taken off without waking her?

'Faith? Christine?' she calls once more.

Despite a voice in her head crying out for her to go back in the room, lock the door, slide across the bolt, she steps out, and heads towards the staircase, her heart thudding.

Someone's there, at the foot of the stairs, propped against the banister, legs twisted out of shape – so still.

'Christine!' Alice races down towards her, sees the red circles painted on her cheeks, the addition of a bow tie at her throat. She crouches down, takes hold of her hands. 'Christine, Christine.'

The woman stirs, opens her eyes.

'Christine, thank God. What happened?'

'Pushed,' Christine whispers. 'So much pain.' She swallows hard. 'Said I was a bully.' A tear rolls down her cheek, drips off her chin. 'Said ...'

'Who said? Who did this?'

'Said I deserved to be punished. Said we all do.'

'Who, Christine?' Alice squeezes the woman's hands, her eyes flashing from Christine's pale, distorted face, to her surroundings. 'Who the hell did this?'

Christine's eyelids fall over her eyes, her head tilts back. 'No, no, no,' Alice cries, searching the woman's wrist for a pulse – she's no expert – but she can't find one, however hard she tries.

She rises, rubs her clammy palms on her top, as she spins around, eyes searching. *Where's Faith? Lori? Gabriela?*

After a moment, she races back up the stairs, and along the corridor. Once inside her room, she pulls the bolt across, turns, and leans against the door, trying to catch her breath, fighting back tears.

Eventually, she heads over to the window, her heartbeat refusing to slow. Guilt rising. Could she have done more to help Christine?

She narrows her eyes, and peers closer to the glass, feeling sure she can see someone making their way down the hill towards the jetty. She blinks, and they disappear into the shadows. She moves her gaze to the sea. There are no flashing blue lights of a police boat. No sign of Leon.

She returns to the bed, sits down on the edge, and presses her fingers deep into her temples. Whatever happens now, she has to stay here until daylight. It's the only place she is safe.

Leon

'Leon. Leon. You OK?'

He hears the panicked voice infiltrating his dream, the broken sound of English. His head throbs; eyelids, like lead, seal his eyes.

216

He doesn't want to fully wake, to face reality. He wants to return to the spellbinding dream he was having, where the sun beamed down on him and Alice, as they strolled hand in hand along the river – deeply in love. The dream felt so real. He wants to go back there, where it's safe. He wants to go back there with Alice.

He attempts to lift his head, and groans. He's lying on a hard floor, a scratchy blanket covering him.

'Leon. You awake? Please.'

Gabriela?

The smell in the air is comforting, the warm orangey tang of wood, the sweet earthy smell of soil. He has to open his eyes, he knows that, but it's like lifting weights. He has never been good at weight lifting. Give him a swimming pool and his body has the kind of strength that can go on forever. Except … his mind jumps to the awful memory. He was about to swim for help, *wasn't he?*

'Gabriela?' His voice is weak. He barely recognises it as his own.

'*Tak! Tak!*' She grabs his hand, hers small yet strong.

He manages to peel open his eyes, but his vision is blurred, takes a few moments to focus, to see flickering candles highlighting garden tools, buckets, bags of soil, a sack over the window – a small rowing boat propped against the wall. *A boat! If he could gather his strength, this could be their way out of this nightmare.*

He's sure they are in the shed where Mitch found the boat oars earlier. Gabriela is kneeling beside him, her long dark hair falling over her young, pale face, her heavily made-up eyes sticky and smudged. She releases his hand.

He shivers, cold, his T-shirt and boxers soaked through. Pain slams into his head. He cries out as he eases up to a sitting position, and props himself against the shed wall. The blanket drops from his shoulders, settling around his waist.

'Someone hit you,' Gabriela says, and it's clear she knows more English than she let on earlier. 'I hide you.'

His mind jumps to Alice. He left her in the house, insisting she would be safe. Fear surges through him.

Gabriela's piercing blue eyes flick towards the closed door. Two bolts are pulled across it. Her hands twist in her lap. 'I hide here for now. Waiting. Then I hear you cry out. I …'

'You saved me,' he says, wincing as he moves.

'*Tak*. I save you.'

'Thank you.'

She smiles, but it doesn't reach her eyes.

'We have to get to Alice,' he says, unsure how much she understands. 'Save her too.'

'*Nie*. We wait. For now.'

Leon pulls himself to his feet, wincing in pain, his head throbbing, his legs like jelly. 'Help isn't coming, Gabriela.' He makes his way to the door. 'We have to get to Alice.'

'*Nie!*' Gabriela yells, as he pulls back one of the bolts.

He yanks across the second bolt his hand shaking, opens the door, and staggers into the damp darkness. He turns to ask her to come too, to help him, but she slams the door.

'*Idiota*,' she cries from inside the shed, the loud scraping of the bolts locking him out, jolting the silence. '*Glupi idiota*.'

He pulls on his jeans, picks up his coat, and shrugs it on as he staggers up the hill towards the hotel. But he's struggling; everything spins around him, spiralling like a macabre merry-go-round. Concussion. His legs go from under him, his vision blurs, and he tumbles sideways into the bushes, lands on the wet grass. *He's no use to Alice. He's no bloody use to the woman he loves.*

Alice

A loud anxious knock on the bedroom door invades the silence. Alice's body stiffens. *She's locked herself in. Bolted the door. She's safe. If she ignores it, they'll go away.*

Another rap on the door. Alice clenches her fists.

'Help! Let me in for Christ's sake.'

'Faith?' Alice jumps to her feet, approaches the door.

'Leave me alone!' Faith screams. *She's being attacked.* 'Oh God. Leave me alone. Alice! Please! Help me!'

'I'm coming.' She pulls back the bolt. Unlocks the door, and throws it open. 'Faith?' But the hallway is deathly silent. 'Faith?'

She peers down the dark hallway, narrowing her eyes. 'Faith?' The door to Faith and Mitch's room stands open.

Alice edges her way along the corridor, close to the wall, until she gets to their room. 'Faith?' she whispers, pushing the door open further, glancing over her shoulder, before stepping inside. 'Are you in there?'

The sharp wave of nausea as the sight of Mitch, and the stench of vomit, catches her unawares. He's on the floor, propped against the bed, legs out in front of him, back straight, arms rigid by his side. Red circles are painted on his chalk-pale cheeks, and his ponytail has been cut off, his hair oiled back from his face. His eyes are wide open – staring. Like Christine and Dane, he's wearing a bow tie. Alice moves her gaze to a half-empty brandy bottle standing on the bedside table. The churning nausea in her stomach won't subside – she must get out of this room. But her legs won't move, her eyes are back on Mitch. Mitch is dead. The Winslows are dead. Christine is dead. Everyone else has disappeared. She covers her mouth, heaving as she stumbles from the room.

'Alice!' Faith cries, her voice receding up the staircase. 'Help me, Alice. Oh God, please …'

Alice rushes from the room towards the sound of her friend's terrified voice. She reaches the bottom of the stairs, looks up into the semi-darkness. 'Faith?' She takes the stairs slowly, her heart thudding. 'Faith? Where are you?'

A scream comes from high above her – *the attic room?*

She continues up the stairs until she reaches the second floor. Makes her way past Gabriela's room towards the staircase that leads to the attic. Above her, the red door stands open, a light escaping from inside. She takes the steps slowly – one, two, three, four, five …

'A-lice.' The voice is chilling, and coming from inside the room. 'A-lice.'

'Hello?' She pushes open the door. 'Faith is that you?'

'A-lice … A-lice.'

A chill trails through her body, her heartbeat bouncing off her ribcage. She peers around the door, and catches sight of two ventriloquist puppets. One of them is the creepy thing she found on her bed hours ago, the other a raggedy, faded doll with wool for hair and freckles. They both have teacups in front of them, and a plate – a fairy cake on each.

There's a setting for one more.

Chapter 36

1994

Tiger

'Tiger, is that you?'

It's Daddy. I lift the lid. Spring out like a jack-in-the-box. I'm so pleased to see him, even though I shouldn't be here in the attic room behind the red door. It's OK, Daddy never tells me off. But he's not looking at me; he's staring at the puppets, his face all wonky.

'Oh God,' he cries.

'Daddy?' I climb out of the box and take hold of his hand. Look up at him. 'What are you doing here?'

Daddy pulls his hand away from me, and crouches down in front of Rosie. His cheeks are bright pink, his eyes really big.

'Do you like the puppets, Daddy?' I say, and he turns and stares at me for a long time. I can't decide if he's sad. His face is all funny. 'This is Paulo and Ralfie and Rosie.' I smile my biggest smile, trying to make Daddy happy. 'They are my puppet friends.' I clap my hands and spin around. I'm excited because Daddy is here in the big house, here with me. Excited he's meeting my puppet friends. I just want him to be happy too. *Please be happy, Daddy.*

He reaches forward, moving closer to Rosie, and takes hold of both her hands. 'What's your name, sweetheart?' he says to her, in his softest voice. 'Where did you come from, little one?'

But Rosie doesn't answer. She doesn't know Daddy at all.

'I told you,' I say. 'This is Rosie and she is my puppet and my best friend.'

He looks at me, then back at Rosie. 'Does Aunt Verity know about Rosie, Tiger? Does she know she's here?'

'Of course she does.' I nod three times. 'She comes up here lots of times.'

'Tiger,' he says, looking over his shoulder at the door. 'This … *Rosie* … you do know she is a real little girl, and not a puppet.' His voice has gone all funny like his face. 'Do you understand that?'

I shake my head. Look down at my cuddly tiger in my hands. Fiddle with his ears.

'Do you know where she came from? What she's doing up here in the attic room?' His voice is shaky now, and I don't know why. I feel a bubble of tears inside me, but I don't want to cry.

'She's a puppet,' I say. 'Not a girl.'

'She's a real little girl, Tiger. Can't you see that? Can't you see how she's different to Paulo and Ralfie?'

'No!' I stamp my foot, and my hands hurt because I'm squeezing them tightly. *Rosie is a puppet. She lives up here behind the red door, outside inside, with the other puppets.* 'Rosie isn't real,' I yell. 'Rosie is my puppet friend.'

'Oh, Tiger, we have to get Rosie out of here before Aunt Verity gets back.' Daddy stands up straight. He's so big and I'm so small, and I know I won't be able to stop him taking Rosie. 'We have to get you both out of here.'

He picks Rosie up, and she flops her head on his shoulder, and he grabs my hand so tightly it hurts, and then he runs from the room dragging me with him. And I struggle to keep up in my rabbit slippers. And I cry and cry, but Rosie doesn't cry. She's droopy and quiet in his arms, because she is a puppet.

We take the first stairs, and then the second stairs, and then the third stairs, and then we bump into Aunt Verity who is bringing carrier bags full of shopping from Tesco through the front door, puffing and panting.

She drops them to the floor, and a tin of baked beans rolls away. 'Hugh!' she shouts. 'What the hell do you think you're doing?'

Chapter 37

Halloween Weekend 2019

Alice

Faith appears in eyeshot, a wide, unnatural smile pinned to her face. Her ponytail is high – neat and tidy, as though she's brushed her hair; made herself look presentable for Alice's arrival.

Alice steps in, bewildered, eyes roaming the room, but before she can fully absorb her surroundings, Faith darts past her, pushing her so she topples, almost falls.

Faith slams the red door. 'A-lice, A-lice.' It's the same creepy voice, but this time it's clear it's Faith. 'Welcome home, lovely. Would you like a fairy cake?'

Alice spins round to see the woman she thought was her friend locking the door, pocketing the key. Shock ricochets through her as she notices a knife in Faith's hand.

'I'm so glad you're back,' Faith says. 'I almost thought you wouldn't respond to my kind invitation. But I knew once I sent you the photo of your father's portrait, you wouldn't be able to resist.'

'Cameron? You're Cameron?'

'Well no, obviously I'm not Cameron.' Faith laughs. Shakes her head so her ponytail sways.

Alice's eyes leap around the room once more; the bars at the window, the huge magic box, shelves crammed with tricks, the puppet tea party, the muddy-brown walls, the grass-green carpet – *outside, inside*. She knows this place – she's been here before. Suddenly, she's five years old – helpless.

'This is where she kept me,' she whispers, memories flooding in unbidden, her stomach churning, as the recollections fill her head. '*Verity*. This is where Verity kept me.'

'Mmm, outside inside.' Faith glances about her, not losing her smile. 'I loved coming up to see you when I was little.'

Alice stares at Faith, an avalanche of memories the room has triggered crushing, impossible to take in, make sense of. 'You visited me sometimes.' She takes a step forward. 'You made me tea, and fairy cakes. You called me Rosie.'

Faith claps her hands like an excited child. 'I'm so glad you remember.' She screws up her nose. 'It was only pretend tea.'

'Yes. Only pretend,' Alice whispers, reaching for more memories, catching the scary phantoms as they drift by, bile rising in her throat. And suddenly it's all there, as if it was only yesterday.

PART FOUR

'It's no use going back to yesterday,
because I was a different person then.'
Lewis Carroll

Chapter 38

1994

Hugh

'Who is this little girl, Verity?' The child was lifeless in Hugh's arms; her head flopped against his shoulder, the awful stench of the attic room still ripe in his nostrils, making him want to heave. 'She's so thin, for Christ's sake. Who does she belong to?'

'Calm down, Hugh, I can explain.' Verity picked up a tin of beans, shoved it back into the carrier bag. 'You're over-reacting.'

'But the kid hasn't said a word since I found her; she's so limp, lifeless.' He was shaking, afraid of what his sister had done. 'How long has she been up there? Who is she?'

'It's Rosie, Daddy,' Tiger said, in her usual bright voice, as she tugged on the hem of his jacket, staring up at Hugh with wide blue eyes. 'She's my puppet friend. I told you that already.'

It was obvious to Hugh that Tiger really believed that the helpless little girl in his arms was a puppet. What game had Verity been playing at Flynn House, while Hugh had hidden himself away from life at the cottage? Hugh's pulse whooshed in his ears, and a swirl of guilt and fear whipped through his body. *What had his sister done?*

Verity grabbed Tiger's arm and tried to tug her away from Hugh. Hugh pulled back, determined to keep hold of her, his knuckles white as he gripped the child's hand. Tiger let out a scream – ear-splitting. Their ridiculous game of tug-of-war was hurting her. Hugh released his grip, and Verity wrapped her arms around the child, pulling her close, as though her arms were chains, her hands padlocks.

The strange little girl from the attic room, still flopped in Hugh's arms, was around five or six, about the same age as Tiger, though tiny by comparison. 'Who is she, Verity?' he said again, pleading.

'Just give me a minute, and I'll explain.' Leaving the bags in the hallway, she raced away, dragging Tiger with her into the kitchen. Hugh followed to see them standing by the Aga. Verity crying, loud, dramatic sobs; Tiger covering her ears. 'Stop, Aunt Verity. Stop!'

'What the hell's going on?' Hugh cried.

'You'll never understand,' Verity said, dashing her sleeve across her face, before grabbing a bottle of whisky from a cupboard, and filling a crystal glass.

'Try me.' It was all he could think of to say.

She shook her head, before knocking back the amber liquid in one gulp.

'Whoever this little girl is, she's malnourished, Verity. For Christ's sake.'

'I can't help it if she doesn't want to eat.' She sounds flippant, her face grim. 'I gave her food every day.'

'Tell me who she is, Verity,' he yelled. 'Where you got her from.' Anger boiled inside him, and despite the weight of the child in his arms, he raced forward, lunged at his sister, and grabbed her by the throat.

Chapter 39

Halloween Weekend 2019

Alice

Faith's face falls from smile to frown in a fragment of a second. 'And then you were gone. Stolen away. And you never came back, and Verity – my mother – cried all the time. And I had to care for her all the time, and life was horrible all of the time.' She places one hand against her hip, like a handle on a milk jug; the other grips the knife so hard her knuckles are white.

Alice's head aches with confusion, her heart thudding in her ears. 'Why am I here, Faith?'

'Because this is where you belong, *Rosie* – here with me – and this is where you must stay, forever and ever.' She moves closer, runs her index finger down the flat of the blade, a peanut-size pulse thumping in her neck.

A whiff of her body odour catches in Alice's throat; a surge of nausea churns in her stomach. 'I don't understand.'

'My mother hanged herself in the stairwell of this house.'

A pause. 'She'd given up, you see. Given up her search for her brother – for Hugh. Ironic really, as things turned out.'

Alice feels a sudden surge of sorrow pushing through her fear, but stays silent.

'We lived in the cottage for years. Rarely came to the house. One day I woke and she wasn't there. Eventually I found her.' She looks down at the knife. 'She left a note saying she was sorry, along with the diaries she'd written over the years. I think she knew they would explain everything.' She shakes her head. 'There was so much pain on those pages, as though written with her blood.' She darts her eyes upwards, traps Alice in a stare. 'I had no idea what she'd been through.'

'I'm sorry.' Alice forces the words out.

'It's fine. All good.' Faith looks away. 'I'm making them all pay now, you see. Every last one of them.'

'Who, Faith? Who are you making pay?'

'Mitch—'

'Mitch?'

'He raped her when she was in her early twenties.'

Alice covers her mouth, holding in a gasp, tears blurring her vision. 'Mitch was a rapist?'

Faith nods. 'That's exactly what he is. Mum had tried to convince herself it was a mistake, *not rape*. That's what she wrote in her diary – but she'd said no, over and over – and still he forced himself on her.' She swipes the back of her hand across her mouth. 'You've no idea how sick to my stomach it made me having to be so close to that disgusting man. I was glad when it was over.'

A flash of memory: Mitch propped against the bed – *a puppet*. 'You killed him?'

'I knew it wouldn't be long before he drank the brandy – he loves, I mean loved his brandy – and that was a particularly decent brand. Shame to mix it with poison hemlock, really.' She laughs. 'It grows on the island all year round here. Ingested it

232

attacks the nervous system, causes severe seizures and convulsions, cardiovascular collapse.'

Shock pumps through Alice's body. 'You poisoned him?' Her voice cracks, eyes drifting to the ventriloquist dolls. 'You made him look like a puppet.'

'Of course! I packed the brandy in his holdall, though I didn't know when it would happen exactly. In fact, I was praying it would be sooner than it was, but hey ho.' She pauses, examines Alice's face. 'Oh come on, you detested him.'

'So when you went to check on him, after we'd been to the cottage, he was—'

'Dead – yes.' She taps the knife against her chin. 'Mother didn't even know his name, but she'd written in her diary that he owned a tattoo business in Bristol. It was a long shot, the chances of it still being there after all this time. But I travelled there, and there it was. Mum also drew his rose tattoo in her diary, wrote that it was on his lower arm. It meant I knew immediately when I'd found the right man.

'Mitch's rather naïve sister, who worked as a tattooist in the shop, pointed out his photo on the wall, told me her brother was a fan of LARPing. I went along to a festival she told me he would be attending.' She bites down hard on her lower lip. 'The rest is history.' She wiggles her head, as though proud of herself, her ponytail swinging. 'I admit I hadn't factored in that I would want to heave my guts up each time he touched me. Though I think you'll agree, I made a good job of masking my disgust.'

'And the Winslows? You killed them too?'

Faith's lips curve into another smile. 'They were nasty characters. They said it was a good thing Hugh was dead. Mother would have been devastated that they spoke of her precious brother that way.'

'And that's it?' Alice pushes down thoughts of how upset she was when she heard them talk about her father, but nobody deserves to be murdered in cold blood. 'You killed a young couple because they said that?'

'Oh come on. They were ogres. Present-day monsters. Always pulling people's lives apart on social media and YouTube, ruining reputations, small businesses. They had a huge following too.' Her voice is joyous; there's a manic gleam in her eyes. 'When Mitch mentioned them in the pub, and I listened to their crap – how they tried to ruin your father's reputation, how they'd destroyed so many people with their cruel words, while raking in money, I was so angry.' She clenches her fist. 'I thought why not invite them here too on the pretence of them reviewing the hotel, and kill them – in for a penny, that's what they say, isn't it?'

'Oh God, Faith.'

'They jumped at the chance of a freebie weekend. They were leeches, sucking the happiness out of people with their cruelty. Apparently a woman committed suicide after they destroyed her debut film. They won't be missed.'

She smirks. 'They were so easy to kill. Just stuffed their faces with free caviar and smoked salmon canapés, champagne – all laced with poison hemlock.' She furrows her forehead. 'Surely you of all people can see they deserved to die?'

Alice glances over her shoulder at the door, then back at Faith – she barely recognises the woman in front of her as her caring, fun friend. This woman's skin is pallid, her eyes dark, vacant, her body rigid. She's a stranger.

Faith darts forward, places the tip of the knife on Alice's throat. 'Nobody's coming, sweetie – it's just you and little ol' me. I just want you to stay here with me. Is that so much to ask? This was where we were happiest, wasn't it? You do remember those good times, don't you, Rosie? *Outside inside.*'

'Leon!'

His body jerks awake. Wet grass has soaked through his jeans; his bare feet are freezing. Through sore eyes he sees someone crouched down beside him.

'Lori?' He rubs the back of his throbbing head, shivering as he attempts to ease himself up. But his limbs are weak, and he drops back down onto the grass like a wounded animal. 'Gabriela helped me,' he says, his voice is husky. He shouldn't have left the shed when he did. His injury is far worse than he thought.

'I saw her,' Lori says. 'I saw her knock you out. She bashed your head with a boat oar. I wanted to help you, made my way down to the sea, but when I got there, you'd gone.'

'Who?'

'Faith.'

'Faith?' *Alice's friend?* His head spins. He left Alice with her – he tries to move once more, but he's dizzy, incapable.

Lori glances over her shoulder, then back to Leon. 'She came out of nowhere, whacked you, and then she was gone.'

'Why would she—?'

'I had my suspicions. She asked me about my time here as a nanny.' She shakes her head. 'I hadn't told her anything about it. She wasn't there when I spoke to Alice about working here, being Hugh and Verity's nanny. I knew there was something not right about her. I had to get away.'

'So you left us to it – never said anything.' His head throbs; he has to get up. *Must get to Alice.* 'You climbed out of the window?' He notices a gash on her hand. 'Saved yourself.'

'I was afraid.'

'Not an excuse, Lori – we were all afraid.'

'No you're right.' She lowers her head, her chest sounding wheezy. 'I was a fool, selfish. But people don't always act as they think they might in a crisis. You will always get heroes and cowards.' She closes her eyes for a moment. 'And it's not the first time I've been a coward. Those children – Verity and little Hugh – needed me but I was too afraid to stand up for them. I was no more than a child myself, I suppose. That's been my excuse all these years. And I had thought I was a better person now, that if I came back here it would give me some sort of redemption. But it seems not. In fact, I'm no better now than I ever was. At the first sniff of fear ...'

He stares at her for a long moment, the attractive woman of earlier windswept, exhausted, scared.

'It's Faith who's brought us all here, Leon. She's going to kill us all.'

'But why?' He attempts again to get to his feet, once more with no luck.

'I don't know.' She glances about her. 'I've no idea who she is. All I know is I received an invitation from Cameron Patterson to stay here. He said he knew I was once a nanny at the house and asked if I would like to attend the opening weekend. I didn't even question how he knew who I was.'

'Help me up,' Leon says, pushing on his haunches, fighting the pain, the dizziness. 'Alice and Christine are in the house with Faith. We have to help them.' Tears are close – pathetic helpless tears. He shouldn't have left Alice. What had he been thinking with his heroic swim to the mainland? He tried so hard to do the right thing, but failed miserably. He has to make things right.

Lori rises, pulls Leon to his feet. 'I'm with you,' she says.

At a sudden noise behind them, he turns to see the shed door crashing open, banging hard against the wooden building.

'Gabriela?' Leon whispers, peering into the darkness, as the young woman in black heads towards them with determined strides.

'Sit down, Alice.' Faith points the knife towards the vacant spot at the tea party. 'Now.'

Alice lowers herself to the floor, next to the puppets. *She remembers.* Her young life spent here. Here in this room. A tear rolls down her cheek, tastes salty on her lips, drips off her chin.

'You of all people must understand the power of grief,' Faith says, crouching down on her haunches in front of her. 'Once I started reading my mother's diaries, which were fascinating and heart-breaking in equal measure, I had to punish the people who ruined her life and mine. You can see that, right?' She tilts her head, stares long and hard.

Alice remains silent. She's a little girl again. Trapped. Afraid.

Faith drops down onto her bottom, dangles the knife between her legs. 'I'm not going to lie; it was a shock to find out Hugh wasn't my daddy.'

Alice looks up, stares into those vacant eyes.

'Oh don't look like that. Even I realise incest isn't the done thing. But when Hugh left with you, I thought he was my father. Mother never told me otherwise. She just said she wasn't my aunt, that she was my mother. What else was I supposed to think? But her diaries corrected that.'

Alice knows she has to keep her talking. 'You pushed Christine down the stairs.'

'That's right. I wasn't sure how Christine's death would pan out. But it just sort of happened.' Her lips curve into a cruel smile. 'You fell asleep. If you hadn't, Christine may still be with us. But once you were out for the count, it was easy to threaten Christine with a knife – tell her to get up – lead her out of the room. The woman almost pissed herself. Which is ironic really.'

Alice stares, waiting for Faith to continue.

'According to my mother's diaries, Hugh used to piss himself in fear when Christine and her friends bullied him as a child.'

Faith screws up her face. 'And the same woman, years later, swept me out of her shop like a piece of garbage when I was a child. If my mum hadn't had to traipse all the way to Tesco, Hugh would never have found you.'

'Did you kill Christine's husband?'

She nods. 'I had to. I needed Christine alone. Vulnerable. Though I was disappointed to hear he would have died anyway.'

Alice's stomach knots painfully. She looks again at the puppets, takes in the neat stitching at the base of their ankles. She swallows hard. 'Where are their feet?'

'I cut them off. It stopped them from running away.' Faith points at a saw hanging on the wall. 'Did you know our grandpa used to use that to chop women into three pieces?' Her gaze returns to Alice. A smile. 'I'm so glad I found you again, Rosie – so, so glad. I just wish Mummy and Hugh were here to see us back together again.'

Bile rises in Alice's throat, threatening to choke her.

'I read about your father's death in the media,' Faith goes on. 'Saw the photographs of him. I knew it was Hugh immediately from the endless portraits my mother painted over the years. Those eyes, that sharp nose – they could have only belonged to Hugh Flynn.' She tilts her head like a bird. 'I remember those eyes from when I was a child. I'd so wanted him to look at me through them and be proud I was his daughter. But I know now why that never happened.'

Thoughts of her father's death flood Alice's head. The moment the police came into her shop, told her the awful news.

'And that's how I discovered you too – from the pictures in the media. I knew it was you, Rosie.'

'Did you kill my father?'

Faith laughs, and shakes her head. 'Good God, no – I loved him. You loved him. My mother loved him – why would I kill him?'

'I don't know, Faith.' A tear rolls down her cheek. 'Why would you do any of this?'

She bites down hard on her lip, and then whispers, 'I know who did kill him. And it was no accident.'

The memory of losing her dad punches Alice's heart afresh.

'It was Tegan Matthews.'

'Tegan?' Alice's mind flashes to the news report she saw earlier that evening in the TV lounge. Tegan was dead: *police are treating her death as suspicious*. 'Tegan killed my dad?'

Faith nods three times. 'I heard her confessing to Leon in the pub in Whitby. I was standing at the bar. It was the day you met the delightful Mitch. Remember? You ran off when you saw Leon.' She smiles. 'And later I followed you.'

'That was you?' Alice recalls the car in the lay-by in Sparrow Lane, headlights on full beam. 'You were the one freaking me out that night?'

Faith nods. 'I didn't mean to scare you. I'd planned to tell you what I'd overheard. Then I saw Leon's car, so I left.'

'What did you hear?'

'Tegan telling Leon that the hit and run was an accident, that she hadn't meant to knock him down,' Faith says, oblivious to the turmoil inside Alice's head. *Tegan knocked her father down. Leon knew and he never told her.*

'Tegan was crying her little eyes out, saying she couldn't live with herself, and Leon was doing his best to console her. Not that she deserved his sympathy and understanding. He's such a sausage though isn't he? Leon. Shame about him really.'

Alice looks towards the door. 'What have you done to him, Faith? Where the hell is he?'

Faith shakes her head. 'I'd hoped he wouldn't come with you to Flynn Hotel. Though now I think about it, he probably would have come searching for you if you didn't return to your precious Whitby. He clearly loved you – so it's all worked out for the best.'

Loved. Past tense. The thought that Leon was hurt or worse swirls around her head. The idea of losing him is unbearable.

This is her fault. If she hadn't begged him to come, he would be OK. She lets out a sob.

'Oh, please don't cry,' Faith says. 'We'll be happy here together, you'll see.'

'Somebody will look for me.'

'Will they? I mean you haven't got anyone but me, have you?'

It's true. How had she let that happen? How had she become an island? Alice looks again at the closed door, tears streaming down her cheeks, cold against her skin. She goes to rise, but Faith leans forward with a jolt, pushes her down.

'Don't you want to hear about Tegan? It's too late for Leon.'

Bile rises once more in Alice's throat. She coughs, choking. But she doesn't move.

'That night, Tegan was spouting to Leon about how she'd chased after your father. Apparently he'd ended things with her and left. She got in her car, wanted to catch him up, beg him not to leave her. She pulled into Sparrow Lane. It was dark, she'd been drinking … she struck him … didn't even get out of the car.'

Alice covers her mouth with her hands, holding in a sob.

'That's at the very least manslaughter, don't you agree?'

Alice nods, feebly, imagining her father crushed against the tree.

'And that's why I killed her.'

'You killed her?' Alice pushes down a pang of what? *Gratitude?*

'Oh come on, Alice, surely you saw that coming. She deserved it. She killed Hugh – my mother's brother – your father. She needed to be punished.' She pauses for a moment, letting her words sink in. 'The news report you saw in the TV lounge, I'd recorded earlier. I was waiting for an opportunity for you to see it. I had thought you'd be pleased.'

Alice rakes her fingers through her hair, catching a tangle and wincing.

'Though I was grateful to Tegan for revealing your father's true identity. If she hadn't, I guess we wouldn't be sitting here together now.'

'Tegan told the media?' It doesn't come as a surprise; Alice expected as much.

Faith nods. 'Another little nugget I overheard that evening.' She looks down at the plates, each with a fairy cake. 'Eat your cake,' she says. 'Christine made it specially.'

'Christine?'

'Yes, though they were instructions from Cameron, of course. For someone who doesn't exist, he was one bossy man.' She laughs. 'Kept Christine busy.'

'Cameron isn't real?'

'Of course not. Think about it, Alice – I was the only one who saw the mysterious owner of Flynn Hotel. I made the website, the Instagram account, grabbed a few photographs from stock pictures to invent the man and his wife. It was easy really.' She pauses, looks once more at the cake. 'Eat up, Rosie. Don't let the cake go dry.'

'My name is Alice,' she whispers.

'No!' Faith yells, startling Alice, and then much softer. 'Your name is Rosie, and if you don't eat some cake, I'm going to have to force you to.'

Alice tries to get up, but Faith darts forward, holds the blade against Alice's throat. 'Take a bite,' she says pressing the sponge against Alice's lips with her free hand.

Alice's heart races as she opens her mouth, tears filling her eyes once more as the sweet taste of the pink icing makes her choke.

Chapter 40

1994

Hugh

'Daddy, please stop,' Tiger cried, and Hugh released his grip on his sister's neck.

Verity bent over, holding her throat, choking. 'Look closely at the kid, Hugh,' she said. 'She's your child. Yours and Pippa's.'

He froze for a moment. 'What?'

'It's a long story,' she said, straightening. 'But yes, the girl is yours.'

'I don't understand.'

'She's your daughter, Hugh.' Verity puts both arms around Tiger, and pulled her close once more.

Hugh shook his head, his body twitching with anxiety. 'No, Tiger's my daughter.'

Verity shook her head. 'You don't get it do you?'

'Get what, Verity?' Confusion bounced through him, his heart thumping, unable to comprehend what his sister was telling him. He knew he should grab both children and run away from the

242

place where poison oozed through the walls, and never come back – but he needed to know. He needed to know what secrets Verity had been keeping from him.

'When I came back from Europe, I had a daughter. Her name was Faith. She was two months old.' Verity's eyes are glassy, a layer of tears on her lashes. She strokes Tiger's hair. 'This is Faith.'

'What the …? I don't understand. When? Who—'

'I thought I'd actually fallen in love when I met her father, Mikolaj. That my life was changing for the better. And then he was gone.'

Hugh dragged his fingers through his hair, eyes flashing from Verity to Tiger. 'Why the hell didn't you tell me?'

'I was abroad when I found out I was pregnant. You were here, wrapped in your own happiness with Pippa. I couldn't turn to you, Hugh. I just couldn't. And anyway, I planned to get rid of it at first.'

'But you decided to keep it – her?' Hugh looked at the child being held in a vice-like grip by Verity. Had the little girl he struggled to bond with never been his? Was she really Verity's daughter?

'As time went by, the harder it was to go through with an abortion. So I kept her.' She stroked her hand over Tiger's hair. 'Best decision I ever made. Then, when you rejected your baby the day Pippa died, a child I knew you would eventually grow to love, I decided to make a swap.'

'Christ, Verity.' Hugh covered his mouth. 'What the hell were you thinking?'

'I wanted my baby to feel your love. It was easy to make you believe she was yours. You weren't interested, barely looked at her when she was tiny. But I felt sure one day you would, and when you came to your senses, my child would be your child – and we could be a family.' She paused for a moment. 'I intended to get rid of your daughter, but it wasn't as easy as that. I couldn't bring myself to hurt her. So I kept her in the attic.'

Guilt surged through Hugh. If he hadn't left Verity to bail him out, just like he'd done his whole life, none of this would have happened. If the going got tough, if he couldn't cope, there Verity would be – to the rescue – saving him, or picking up the pieces. But this time she'd gone too far. He'd gone too far.

'I cared for your baby, Hugh. I'm not evil. I'm a good person. I went through the motions, kept her fed, changed her when she was a baby, even sung to her a couple of times, but she was surplus to requirements.'

'Aunt Verity?' Tiger looked up at her with watery eyes, and Verity stroked the child's cheek, pushed back her dark hair.

'You can call me Mummy now, sweetheart,' she said. 'And I can finally call you Faith.' Verity turned her eyes back to her brother. 'The perfect name, don't you think? You've got to have faith, haven't you?'

Tears filled Hugh's eyes. What had she done? *What had he done?*

'To be honest, I never expected to feel anything when Faith was born. Nobody was more shocked by the overwhelming love that grew inside me for my daughter. And I wanted you to love her too, Hugh.'

'I would have loved your child, Verity.' He swiped his sleeve across his eyes.

She shook her head. 'No. Not in the same way I thought you would love your own daughter. I wanted you to be a father to her. I hoped, once you got over your terrible grief of losing Pippa, that your child – yours and Pippa's – would become the most important thing in your life. I thought if I substituted her for my daughter, she would become the object of your love and affection. Something I'd accepted I could never be.'

Hugh shook his head, the shock of what she was telling him bouncing around his head like a grenade waiting to go off. 'You're crazy.'

'All I wanted was for Faith to feel your love. But it never happened, did it? You've rarely wanted to see her over the years. That bond never came.'

Hugh looked at the little girl who had called him Daddy for so long. Verity was right. There was never a bond between them, never that surge of love he had hoped he might feel for the daughter Pippa and he had made. He liked the kid, a cute little thing, but she could have been anybody's child.

'I'm so sorry,' he whispered for the kid's ears. 'This was never about you, little one.'

The child broke free of Verity, headed across the room and held her cuddly tiger up in the air. 'This is for you,' she said to the child in Hugh's arms, but the little girl didn't respond.

'Thank you,' Hugh said, taking it from her.

'It will make her happy.'

'I'm sure it will.'

He turned to Verity once more. 'You kept my little girl in the attic room, Verity. How could you do that?' The words felt alien on his tongue, the shock, or perhaps a need to know, driving him on. Keeping him from showing the rage firing in his stomach. 'Felix used to take me up there, Verity. Do you remember? Do you remember how scared I was, how I cried? How those puppets haunted me? How father threatened to slice me into three pieces? And then you do the same thing to my child.'

'Not the same thing,' she said, as though that made everything right. 'And not at first – at first I had both babies with me always, but eventually, yes, I had to lock her away. I had no choice, Hugh. I was worried you'd come over to the house. And then, when Tiger started talking—'

'Tiger? Tiger? She never was Tiger though, was she?'

'Daddy! Please stop shouting.' Faith had wandered towards the back door, as though she wanted to escape, alone and helpless, her little arms dangling by her sides – eyes too big for her face as she peered at Hugh from under her heavy fringe.

'I'm so sorry, sweetheart, this isn't your fault,' he said, tears filling his eyes as he moved across the room towards her. But

Verity got there first, closed her arms tightly around her once more. Hugh knew she would never let her go.

'She's my daughter,' she yelled, and pulled open a kitchen drawer. She brought out a sheet of beige paper. 'That's what it says on here. Look.' She waved a birth certificate in front of him. 'Faith Flynn: Mother Verity Flynn. Father unknown. She's not yours.' She pointed at the child in his arms. 'That's your daughter.'

Hugh stared deep into his sister's eyes. He knew he must try for calm reasoning, for both the children's sakes. 'Let's get help for this little one, hey, Verity?' He needed to make his daughter safe. 'Then we can work something out. The four of us.'

'No! That *thing* in your arms is an impostor,' Verity snapped. 'She's not part of the plan.'

'What plan, Verity? What are you talking about? There is no plan.'

'She lives in the attic, Hugh. She's OK up there. It needs to be just you, Faith and me from now on. The way it was always meant to be. A perfect family.'

'This is ridiculous, V. You're sounding crazy.'

'You have to stay, Hugh.' She spun round, grabbed a knife from the kitchen side, and waved it at Hugh, her face flushed with anger.

Chapter 41

1994

Hugh

Within moments, Verity lowered her arm in defeat. She placed the knife on the kitchen worktop, and dashed her palm across her damp cheeks. 'I just don't want you to go,' she said, her voice breaking. 'Please stay.'

'I can't, V.' He took a deep breath, the girl heavy in his arms. 'I have to get the kid help. You must see that.'

'You will come back, won't you?' Verity said, as he turned and headed for the door. 'Promise us that.'

Hugh looked back over his shoulder, and into his sister's pleading eyes. Her arms were limp by her sides, like a puppet without strings; tears glistened along her lashes and rolled down her plump cheeks. She was defeated, and Hugh hated that. His sister had always been the fighter. The strong, feisty young woman, who'd battled to keep him safe throughout his life, was now a wreck. Had he done that to her? Should he stay?

'I can't,' he said. 'But I will be back.' And at that moment, he believed his words. He had no intention of deserting the sister who'd protected him all his young life, or his niece. She and her daughter needed help as much as the girl in his arms, and he would get that for them. He would make things right. 'I'll bring help, Verity.' He looked at the girl standing beside her. 'Faith will need psychological help.'

'No! She's doing fine, Hugh.'

'But you led her to believe I was her father, and she's been playing in the attic with a child she thought was a puppet. She'll need help, Verity, and I'll get that for her.'

'No, we'll be OK, Hugh. We don't need anyone here but us.'

'And we should sell the house.' His gaze roamed the kitchen. The place made his stomach heave. 'We must all get away from the poison in these walls. I know you feel it too. The past is still here, haunting us.' He shuddered. 'Felix Flynn damaged both of us. We have to get away from here, for these kids' sakes, if not for ours.'

'But I like it here, Daddy,' Faith said, and Hugh stared down at the child he now knew to be his niece. There was something chilling about the little girl's voice – as though someone else was speaking for her. *No, he was being ridiculous, overemotional.* 'I want to stay here for ever and ever. I want you to stay too, Daddy.'

His heart ached, as he looked at her standing next to Verity, cute in dungarees and a yellow T-shirt, her dark hair layered to her shoulders. 'You have to stay,' she said. 'You have to stay with us, Daddy.'

Hugh froze in the doorway, adjusting the child in his arms. 'I can't stay. And neither can you. This life isn't normal, sweetheart. You'll understand that when you are bigger. But I will get help for you and your mummy. I promise.'

'No!' the child yelled, and stomped her foot one, two, three times. 'Don't go, Daddy. Don't take Rosie.'

'But Rosie is sick.' Hugh hated that he was going along with the name. 'I have to get her to somewhere safe, and then I'll come back for you and your mummy.'

The moments that followed happened so fast. Hugh barely had time to think, let alone react. Faith grabbed the knife from the worktop and ran at him, plunging the blade into his side. 'You can't take Rosie, Daddy,' she cried as the knife clattered to the tiled floor. 'You just can't.'

Within seconds, Verity had grabbed a screaming Faith, and the girl's arms flapped and smacked, as she tried to get free from Verity's grip.

'You can't tell anyone, Hugh,' Verity cried. 'They'll take her away from me. I can't lose her. I can't lose her.'

Hugh stumbled through the kitchen door, and across the hall, holding his side, blood dripping onto the parquet flooring. He looked over his shoulder, expecting Verity to follow, but she didn't.

The keys to her car were in a dish by the front door. He grabbed them, and his coat, and lumbered into the warm summer's day.

Outside, with shaking hands, he strapped his daughter into the back seat, laid the cuddly tiger in her arms, and wrapped her in a grey beach towel he found on the seat. 'Everything's going to be OK,' he said to her, barely believing his words.

With wide-open eyes, the child stared up at the house, seeming to take it in – filing it in her memory.

Hugh limped round to the driver's side, wincing in pain as he folded himself inside. He hadn't driven much since he lived in Bristol, and crunched the gears several times before pulling away at speed.

He drove fast along the causeway, tyres churning sand, desperate to get away, blood oozing from his side, the pain intolerable. But he had to keep on going. He had to.

He glanced in the rear-view mirror, adjusted it slightly to see his daughter on the back seat. Her eyes were still wide open as she looked about her. He moved his gaze to the reflection of Flynn House framed, captured, a tiny version of hell, before pressing his foot down on the throttle, and pulling off the causeway onto the country road, and away. He had no idea where he would go, but knew he would never be back – *not even for his sister, not even for the child he once thought was his own.*

Chapter 42

Halloween Weekend 2019

Alice

'Your lips are so pink, Rosie. Rosie-pink.' Faith giggles. Fake. Childlike. 'Christine must have put too much colouring into the icing.' A pause. 'She didn't know what else I put into the mixture, of course.'

Alice looks down at the cake; the yellow crumbs sprinkled across the plastic plate, and at the puppets, each with their own pristine, uneaten fairy cake in front of them.

'I still can't believe Hugh was a best-selling author,' Faith says, her tone chatty. 'I've read all his books. Though I didn't realise at the time who he was. Ironic now I think about it.'

'The police will be here soon.' Alice's voice is weak.

'Oh dear, you still believe that?' Faith leans forward, runs her finger over Alice's lips. 'I didn't call them. It was just pretend. I'm good at pretending.'

'Let me go, Faith, please.' Alice hears the slight slur in her voice, notices the gradual heaviness of her limbs.

'No!' Faith cries. 'You must stay. Eat more cake.' She rests the knife blade against Alice's cheek. 'Well go on, eat up.'

Alice nibbles at the sponge, knowing it's laced with something toxic – *poison hemlock?*

Faith moves the blade, turns to look at the barred window, and Alice takes advantage of her distraction, crushes the remaining cake in her fist, feeling it reduce in size, stodgy in her fingers.

'Mum thought she'd found you and Hugh once, in Devon. You must have been seven – eight, perhaps.' Faith shrugs, eyes back on Alice. 'Then you vanished. Mother cried for weeks after that.'

'I saw her,' Alice whispers. *Why had her father said she imagined it?* But she knows the answer to that before the question barely enters her head: she could never know about his past. She takes a gulp of air. 'Why didn't you just tell me who you really are?'

Faith makes a weird puffing sound. 'You would never have come back here, stayed with me forever.'

Alice sways, her head swimming, her mouth dry. She hasn't eaten much of the cake. *I can fight this. I can fight this.*

'Though I planned all of this long before I found you. You're just the icing on the cake, as it were. When mother left the house and money to me, it was in dire need of repair,' she says. 'I decided to do the old place up. Make it the perfect setting to hold a last supper, as it were. Revenge is the best medicine, Rosie. It's rewarding. Uplifting. Perfect.'

'But why Lori and Gabriela? Please tell me you haven't killed Gabriela,' Alice says, thinking of the girl who looked so lost – afraid. 'She's just a girl – an innocent girl.'

Faith shrugs. 'To be fair, Gabriela shouldn't be here at all. Bloody Christine took her on. She has nothing to do with any of this. Of course I will have to kill her. I can't have any loose ends. She and Lori are somewhere on the island, and I will find them before the tide goes out.' She laughs, rubs a finger across her chin.

She's deranged. How hadn't Alice seen it? She needs to keep her talking.

'But why Lori?'

'Nanny Bell? Well, that's simple. She hated my mother. Made life impossibly hard for her. There were other awful nannies, of course. I tried to find them all. Some were in care homes, others dead. In fact, Nanny Bell was the only one I could find who would remember us. She'd moved back to Suffolk only recently, and will wish she hadn't. She will die for them all.'

Alice's head swims, her hands are clammy. *Keep her talking. Keep her talking.* 'My yellow dress?'

Faith laughs. 'Now that's a very funny story.' A pause. 'When I delivered Paulo to your room, I saw your dress screwed up on the bed. I thought it might creep you out to find it outside on the lawn, so I opened the window and threw it out. I never dreamt it would all become so dramatic. That the wind would catch it and it would end up on the rocks. That Leon would see it. It was all rather marvellous, almost theatrical.' She screws up her face, her eyes wild. 'Why did you leave me, Rosie?'

'I was five years old.'

'But you never came back.'

'I had no memory of any of this – until now.'

'I hope you understand why I must make sure you'll stay this time.'

'But people are dead, Faith. How do you think you'll get away with this? The Winslows, Mitch, Christine. Their families will miss them. Don't you see that? They'll know they came here. They'll contact the police. Leon's parents know we're here. They won't rest until they find him.' A beat. 'Let me go, Faith. Please.'

'Sorry, no can do – you will stay with me.' Faith puts down the knife, unzips both Alice's ankle-boots, pulls one from her foot, then the other.

'What are you doing?' Fear knots inside her as she watches Faith push her leggings up her leg, away from her ankles, her fingers icy cold.

Faith rises to her feet, reaches up and takes the saw from the wall, its wide sharp teeth glinting like they belong in the mouth of a wild animal – a predator.

'As soon as the drug fully kicks in,' Faith says, turning back to Alice and smiling, 'which it will very soon. I will make sure you never leave me again. And we will all live happily ever after.'

Chapter 43

Halloween Weekend 2019

Alice

Let your mind and body combine. Find yourself in a beautiful stillness. Rest in peace.

Alice tries to control the fear rising in her body. *Steady.* Quell her pulses. *Steady.* Manage her breathing. *Surrender to the stillness.*

'I don't want to hurt you, Rosie,' Faith says. 'But I have to do this. I hope you understand. I promise to sew you up neatly, like I did to Paulo and Ralfie when I removed their feet. You'll be sore for a while, I expect. But I'll take good care of you. I promise.'

Alice's mind is fading. She's losing her grip on the moment. *Keep alert.*

'And in case you're wondering, the drugs I put in your fairy cake were Mummy's pills. They will wear off in a few hours. They always do.'

Alice feels Faith's clammy hands on her ankles once more. 'You're shaking. Relax, Rosie. Relax.'

The chill of the metal against Alice's skin sends a shriek of terror through her body. She has to move. She has to take control. She attempts to move, but the drugs impair her movement. The pain as the blade tears through her flesh is unbearable. She lets out a scream. Feels the cold trickle of blood on her ankle.

A sudden hammering on the door startles both women. 'Faith? Alice?' The voice is familiar. 'Alice?'

Faith rises, places her finger against her lips. 'Shh!'

Loud thuds follow. Someone is ramming the door over and over. 'Faith?' they call. And then there is silence.

Faith crouches down once more. 'Now, where were we?' she says, pushing a tear-damp, straying hair from Alice's cheek.

Within moments, something hard is being bashed against the lock.

'Go away,' Faith yells, rising up once more, leaving the saw on the floor. 'Leave us alone. We're happy here.'

The lock smashes. The door swings open.

'Gabriela!' Faith reaches for the knife, but the young woman lunges at her, pushes her. Faith stumbles, falls to the floor, cracking her head against the wall.

'You poisoned my father,' Gabriela yells. 'You left him to die. You pay for this.' Her accent is strong, her face pale. She looks at Alice through fired blue eyes, then back at Faith who is lying on the floor, holding her head, crying out in pain. 'You tell me why. You tell me why you do this.' She picks up the knife, points it at Faith. 'Or I kill you.'

'You're Mikolaj's daughter?' Faith whimpers from where she cowers, eyes widening in shock.

A beat. 'Tell me. Tell me why you do this – why you do something so horrific to my father.' Tears fill Gabriela's eyes.

Faith takes a long deep breath. 'My mother loved him. She said in her diary that her time with him was the happiest she'd ever been.' Her eyes are shimmering with tears. 'And then he walked out.'

'So you find him?' The young woman's voice trembles. 'You

poison him for this?' Her knuckles turn white as she grips the knife, points it towards Faith, her arm shaking.

'There was a photo of him in the pages of her diary.' Faith rubs her head; blood trickles down her forehead. 'It took months to find him. I wanted revenge. He abandoned my mother, abandoned me – he was my father too.'

'He had no idea of this.'

Faith shrugs. 'I know. He was shocked when I told him. But he abandoned my mother when she was at her most vulnerable.'

Alice is sluggish, her ankle throbs in pain, she can do no more than listen to their exchange of words.

'Poland's a beautiful country.' Faith lowers her head. 'Mother loved it there. For a short while.' She closes her eyes. 'I told Mikolaj I was his daughter, that my mother died because of him. He said my mother was deranged – a stalker.'

'He told me who you are – that you wanted him to come to Flynn House. That when he refused, you pretend to accept this, make him drink—'

'How do you know? I left him to die. There is no antidote for poison hemlock.'

'*Nie.* This is true. When I arrive to see him in agony. But still he tell me about you. What you do.'

Faith's move is sudden. She lunges towards Gabriela, attempts to grab the knife.

It all happens so fast. Gabriela's reaction is whippet-quick – she plunges the knife into Faith's chest.

Alice's chest tightens as she watches her once friend – *her cousin* – fall to the floor. She reaches for her hand, her own arm heavy, thinking of the child Faith had once been – a little girl called Tiger who visited the attic room when Alice needed a friend most. She hears a struggle for breath and then nothing. Faith is gone.

Leon

Leon's heart thumps as he takes the final stairs to the attic room.

He's left Lori with Christine.

He staggers into the room, taking shaky breaths, eyes wide, bewildered, as he falls to the floor, pulling Alice to him.

He blinks rapidly, his gaze roaming his surroundings. Faith is lifeless, blood saturating her dungarees, a knife in her chest; Gabriela stands, arms rigid by her sides – frozen, pale. Two ventriloquist puppets look macabre, awaiting a tea party that will never happen. The walls are muddy brown, the carpet grass green.

'There's a rowing boat in the shed,' Leon says after a silence that stretched and stretched, his voice shaking. 'We need to get to the mainland.'

'Faith thought I was her best friend,' Alice says, her face expressionless, her voice slurring. 'She wanted me to stay.'

Alice

The boat bobs on the salty sea, churning Alice's stomach. She feels sick. Her brain is foggy from whatever Faith put in the cake, her mind a scrambled mess. She blinks, trying to focus on the sun rising on the horizon; its rays glinting on the water, dancing with the joy of a new day.

They are halfway to Dunwold. They are halfway from Seafield Island.

Safe now.

Lori rows, strong and steady, the oars splitting the still water. She hasn't spoken since they left Flynn House – nobody has.

Christine is curled in the base of the boat, covered to her neck with an old, grey blanket. Lori found a pulse when she and Leon discovered her at the foot of the stairs, but it's only faint – Christine will need to be taken straight to hospital when they reach the mainland.

Alice leans against Leon, his arm around her shoulders. She's still woozy, and her ankle throbs, wrapped tightly in a towel. She will need stitches.

Gabriela sits on the other side of her. Alice isn't scared. Gabriela isn't a threat to them. She killed Faith because of what she did to her father.

The thought of what the police will find at Flynn Hotel doesn't bear thinking about. A twisted, desperate woman who was stabbed, after wreaking revenge on the people she believed ruined her mother's life – her life.

She glances back towards Flynn Hotel, blinks, adjusting her eyes to the Victorian Gothic building standing on the cliff edge, grand and imposing, with its steep, high roof rising to a point, and its arched windows. A shudder runs down her spine. She swiftly moves her gaze back towards the coastline, towards safety, towards home, towards the future.

Chapter 44

November 2019

Detective Sergeant Short isn't one for letting things get to him – a hefty bloke in his late forties, he worked in Kansas City in the US for thirty years after growing up there. He thought he'd seen pretty much everything by the time he moved to Suffolk with his English wife in 2014. *'It'll be a chance to wind down,'* she said. *'You don't get any less stressful than Suffolk,'* she said. And now look what he is faced with: two bodies propped up like life-sized dolls in one of the bedrooms, another victim – a middle-aged man – in another room, and a creepy attic room. The whole scenario is off-the-scale weird.

The body of Faith Flynn had been taken from the attic. The odd, footless puppets have been bagged, along with a saw, a knife, and the remains of an apparently drugged fairy cake.

'It looks as if there's a grave in the wood, boss,' Detective Constable Martin says, and the DS startles and looks over his shoulder at the young officer framed in the doorway. She's red-faced and wheezing a little from climbing the stairs. She takes out an inhaler. Takes two puffs. 'Just a small wooden cross with a "P" on it.' She shrugs, pushes her ginger hair from her face. 'Could be a pet. Could be nothing. Could be something.'

'You should be a detective,' Short says, trying for humour, but not feeling it. 'Right, get the area cordoned off.'

'Will do, boss.' DC Martin disappears from view, and then pokes her head back round the door. 'Oh, and they're about to go into the cottage.'

'OK.' DS Short nods, and flicks his eyes around the attic for a final time. 'This place,' he whispers to himself, as a shiver runs down his spine. 'It's as though someone's still here. Watching.' He shudders, and leaves the room.

Back in the hotel's reception, DC Martin appears through the double doors of the bar, her face drained of colour.

'You OK?' Short says, stopping at the foot of the stairs.

'Yeah, fine.' Her voice holds a quiver. 'Just a weird place, is all.' She shakes her head, glances back over her shoulder towards the bar. 'It's creepy, right?'

'Let's get over to the cottage,' he says.

*

The team are searching the place when they arrive, and the DS and DC clamber into fresh protective gear, and enter.

'Who's this guy, do you reckon?' Short picks up a picture of a young couple from the dresser in his gloved hands.

'Cameron Patterson, I think,' DC Martin says, as Short puts it back down again. 'There's a picture of him in reception. The owner, according to that, but I'm not sure where he is.'

The DS shakes his head, and furrows his forehead. 'Odd. Alice Hadley said the owner was Faith Flynn, the woman we found dead in the attic. Bag the picture.'

'Will do.'

Short heads up the stairs two at a time. Four doors greet him at the top.

He peers into a bathroom. A polka dot shower curtain is stretched full length across the bath. A greying flannel hangs over the sink taps.

Floorboards creak as he retreats and makes his way across the landing.

He searches the first bedroom, decorated in blues and yellows; finds nothing of interest. A second room has an easel and a chair facing a small square window looking out over the sea. A palette of paint, and a jar full of brushes are on a table, some paintings propped against the wall.

The next room is locked. 'We need to get this open,' he calls down the stairs.

A thud with a ram is all it takes to shatter the doorframe, allowing Short access. It's a baby's room, painted pastel lemon. There's a white cot in the centre etched with lemon roses, a dusty mobile above it, a rocking chair by the window.

'What is it with these horrendous puppets?' he says under his breath as he heads towards the chair. This one is wearing a yellow and blue striped jacket. But it has one major difference from all the others.

'Christ, that's freaky,' DC Martin says, entering the room, and coming up behind him.

'Well, at least he's got his feet.' Short picks it up and hands it to the DC for bagging.

'Not a lot of use if you've lost your head though, is it, boss?'

Chapter 45

May 2020

Alice

Alice senses Leon shudder as she shows him her latest creation – a macabre ventriloquist puppet tea party moulded from twisted copper.

'It's brilliant,' he says. 'But I'm not going to lie, after everything that's happened—'

'I started it before we went to Flynn Hotel.' She puts it down on the table, and Henry pads over, sniffs it, and looks up at Alice with deep brown eyes.

'And that's not freaky at all, is it, boy?' Leon laughs, ruffles the dog's head as though they are in cahoots, and Henry wags his tail.

Leon turns and splashes white wine in one glass, orange juice in another. They are in the kitchen at Butterfly Cottage – safe, happy.

'I found it quite therapeutic finally finishing it.' Alice turns from the sculpture, picks up the orange juice.

'Well your customers will love it.'

She's glad Leon is here – that he's moved in – that, if fate

263

allows, they will always be together. They've been so close since everything happened. The thought of losing him shifted her perspective – she's not sure what she would have done if she had.

She strokes the curve of her stomach. They are on the same page now. The thought of bringing up a child no longer holds the fear it once had.

Flynn House is hers now, but she will never return. It's up for sale, but with everything that has happened there over the years, she's not expecting many offers.

'I went to the cemetery this morning,' she says, heading over to the cooker to reduce the heat under the bubbling saucepans. She can hear the sadness in her voice. She always feels low when she's visited where her father is now with the love of his life – Alice's mother, Pippa Larkin. The police had found her remains on Seafield Island, and once they'd released her, revealing she died of natural causes, it seemed fitting to bury her with her father. It's what he would have wanted.

'You should have said you were going. I would have come with you.'

She nods. 'I know. But sometimes I like to talk to them alone, you know? Try to get to know my mother.'

He nods, seems to understand.

'I had an email from Christine, earlier.'

'How's she liking France?'

'She misses Suffolk, but glad to be close to her son.' A beat before she adds, not for the first time, 'I still feel desperately sorry for Faith.'

He shakes his head, takes a mouthful of wine. 'Alice, if she'd done what she intended, you would have bled to death. Can't you see that?'

'I know, but in her mind she never saw it that way.' She lets out a sigh. 'She just wanted us to be together.'

'She killed so many people, Alice.'

'I know.' Another pause. 'They've released Verity's diaries.' Alice nods towards a pile of books, ranging from exercise books to leather-bound hardbacks, stacked on her father's desk in the corner.

'The ones they found at the house?'

'Mmm, they arrived this morning. As her next of kin they came to me.'

'Have you read any of them?' His eyes are fixed on the books.

'I skimmed through a few, but it makes for difficult reading.'

'Does it say whether Verity killed her father?'

'Not exactly, though she mentions pushing his body into the sea – can you imagine that? She was just a kid.' A pause. 'I need to put the diaries in the loft,' she says. 'I can't carry on reading, it'll break my heart.'

'Oh, Alice.' Leon takes her in his arms. 'I'm sorry this is so hard for you.'

She rests her head against his chest for some time, tears spilling down her cheeks.

*

After they've eaten, Leon and Alice head into the lounge and snuggle on the sofa together. Henry stretches blissfully by the fire.

She clicks on the TV, bringing up Netflix, and hands the remotes to Leon, knowing he likes to scroll through the endless options.

Despite everything that has happened – the trauma of what took place at Flynn Hotel, the loss of her father, the fact Leon kept things from her – something good has come from the horrific nightmare. She knows what she wants from life, and that her father would want her to make every moment count.

She looks up at Leon and smiles. He kisses her hair.

Epilogue

1994

Hugh

Hugh drove for miles, staying on familiar roads as he travelled through Ipswich and Colchester, the pain in his side easing the further from Flynn House he got. Eventually, he pulled into a lay-by on the outskirts of London, to check his wound. It didn't seem as bad as he first thought. The knife had missed any organs, and because of the little girl's lack of strength and size, the blade hadn't gone deep. It was nasty, yes, but not life-threatening. He unbuttoned and removed his shirt, stripping down to the blood-soaked T-shirt beneath. He ripped the shirt to bandage-sized pieces, and pressed the fabric against his injury.

'Tiger?' The voice in the back of the car was tiny, hopeless. He looked over his shoulder, where blue eyes stared up at him from a drawn, pale face. 'Where's Tiger?'

'We won't be seeing Tiger again, sweetheart.' Tears burned his eyes. 'Tiger is staying with Verity.'

'Verity,' the girl said, and her heavy lids fell over her eyes once more.

The thud of pain Hugh felt at that moment didn't come from his injury. It came from his heart, as though it had splintered into pieces and he would never be able to put it together again. He'd let this happen. Hugh Flynn with his selfish indulgence and self-pity – he'd let this happen.

Forgive me, Pippa.

Forgive me, Verity.

Forgive me, Tiger.

He glanced in the rear-view mirror once more, at the now-sleeping child, her arms folded around the cuddly tiger. *Forgive me, daughter. I'll make this up to you. I promise.*

He sat for some time in the lay-by. Cars whooshed by. The sun went down. The hot day turned to a warm evening, as darkness fell.

He had money – plenty of it, stashed in a bank account that Verity had set up for him years ago. But a bloke covered in blood arriving in a strange place, with a child who had been so desperately neglected, was going to cause attention. He was her father, but he had no way of proving that. He had no clothes for her. No food. What the hell was he going to do? Where could he go?

He knew the answer wasn't to tell the truth. He couldn't go to the authorities and let them know what his sister had done. He just couldn't. Verity had been his salvation. Protected him. He owed her. This was Hugh's fault, and she would go to prison if it all came out, and her daughter would be taken from her, placed into care. *No.* That wasn't an option. He couldn't do that to his sister.

He started the engine, and pulled from the lay-by. He would keep driving, head around London until something came to him. But first he needed petrol, to grab something to eat for the child.

He drove into a petrol station, dragged his overcoat over his

268

bloodied T-shirt, and filled the tank, before locking the car, and making his way into the little shop, where he grabbed a couple of packs of sandwiches, a milkshake, some coffee.

*

'Is that nice?' he said, as the child pulled her sandwich apart, and nibbled at the cheese, like a mouse. She didn't answer, and he wondered again at the damage his sister had done.

When Hugh started the engine once more, he knew exactly where he was heading. The only place he had ever travelled to outside of Flynn House. He would go to Bristol.

After travelling for more than five hours, exhausted, Hugh pulled the car onto the wide drive of Clara McCloud's house on the outskirts of Bristol, and dragged on the handbrake. He prayed she would be able to put him and his daughter up.

The Edwardian house felt familiar, and his mind skittered back to happier times with Pippa. He'd escaped Flynn House then too. His life had been on track. He closed his eyes, imagined himself sprawled on the grass, Pippa in his arms. Would things have been different if he hadn't returned to Flynn House?

Hugh climbed from the car, and pulled on his overcoat, buttoning it to the neck. He stepped out towards the front door.

Clara McCloud had been in her late seventies when he and Verity had rented there. She would be in her eighties now. He glanced at the two annexes at the side of the house, in darkness. Students, if they still rented there, would be home for the summer break.

As he stepped onto the porch a security light sprung on. He pressed the doorbell.

It was some time before Clara opened up. 'Can I help you?' she said. She looked the same, but wasn't as agile. Her stout body supported by a walking frame. She narrowed her eyes. 'Hugh?'

'That's right.'

'I thought so. I never forget my lodgers.' Her voice was soft, her eyes lifting upwards as though searching for memories. 'How are you and that sister of yours, Vivian?'

'Verity.'

'That's right.' She screwed up her life-worn face. 'Are you all right, dear? You look terribly washed out.'

'I'm OK. Thank you.' Hugh looked back at the car. 'The thing is, I need somewhere to stay. Only temporarily.' He looked over at the annexes. 'I wondered ...'

'Well you're in luck, Hugh. It being the summer break, you can take your pick.'

'That's fantastic. Thank you.'

Clara turned, and plucked a key from a row of hooks by the front door, and handed it to him. 'Now please don't think me rude, but I'm in the middle of a Hitchcock film – the one about the birds.' She turned in the hallway, moving slowly with the aid of her frame. 'But if there's anything you need, dear boy, you know where I am.'

'Thank you,' he said, knowing Clara wouldn't bother him while he worked out how to repair his life.

*

The following month was traumatic. Hugh's injury should have been stitched, and was taking a while to heal. His trips out to get food and clothes were torturous.

The child barely slept, and when she did she would often wake in tears following recurring nightmares about being dragged back to Flynn House.

It had taken a lot of coaxing to get the little girl to eat, but with the aid of food supplements, she was gradually gaining weight.

At times Hugh wondered if he had made a mistake – was he really up to caring for the child? Was he really any better than

Verity or Felix, trapping this little girl in a tiny annex, where nobody knew of her existence?

But slowly things improved. A milestone was seeing her smile for the first time; another was a small tinkling laugh when they sat in the park together, and a brown Labrador raced up to her and licked her face.

'I like dogs,' she said, as the sun beamed down on them, and Hugh gripped her hand. It felt like a sign from Pippa. *They'd planned to get a Labrador, hadn't they?*

'I like dogs too, Alice.' He had no idea why he called her Alice, but it suited her, with her long blonde hair and that lost look. She was no Tiger, no Rosie. She was a little girl who had fallen down a rabbit hole, and got lost in a strange world. Hugh had saved her from danger, hadn't he? He hoped it wasn't too late.

At that moment he had no idea what the future would hold, but the intense feelings that ran through him were overwhelming. Was it because she was his daughter, or had he simply needed to protect her, a little someone who would finally give his life meaning?

*

At the end of the university summer break, Clara needed him to give up the annex for students. Hugh packed up the few things they had, tracked down an old friend who arranged fake birth certificates for Adam and Alice Hadley, and headed to Woolacombe in Devon. By then Alice was a good weight, growing into a happy, healthy child. The recurring nightmares she'd had when they'd first arrived at the annex were growing further and further apart. Life would never be easy, Hugh knew that, but then he didn't deserve easy.

He would always be haunted by his past. Never be free from the grief of losing Pippa, the shock of what his sister had done, or the trauma of being bullied at Felix's hands. He would always be grateful to Verity for getting him out of their lives – thankful that she did that for him.

But now Alice must come first, and he would keep her safe *until the day he died.*

Author's Note

I'm not the first author, and I'm sure I won't be the last, to use poison hemlock in murderous fiction. Agatha Christie springs to mind as the most famous writer to use the plant in her clever murder mystery *Five Little Pigs*.

When I was researching for a suitable poison that would suit my plot, I found what I learnt about poison hemlock fascinating.

It's a beguiling plant, with an intriguing history, going back as far as Ancient Greece when it was used to execute prisoners. In 399 BC it was attributed to the death of Greek philosopher Socrates.

There are macabre tales of children using the stems of the plant as peashooters or whistles and reaching a sticky end. And a grisly story from the nineteenth century tells of two children innocently collecting the plant for a sandwich for their father, who never lived to tell the tale.

Extracts from poison hemlock were once used as a sedative, though this was discontinued by the early twentieth century because of its toxins. The plant contains the neurotoxin coniine, which can cause the central nervous system to shut down. Victims stumble about until their limbs become paralysed and their heart stops. Not a very nice death at all.

There are many names for the plant, including spotted

hemlock, bad-man's oatmeal, poison snakeweed, deadly hemlock, skarntyde – but I feel poison hemlock sums it up perfectly.

The plant can grow up to eight feet tall, and is related to the innocent carrot. The irony that two members of the same family can be so different hasn't gone unnoticed on me.

Hemlock gives off a musty smell and the stems are hollow and speckled with blotches of purple. If you see it, I would very much advise keeping your distance.

Amanda Brittany

Acknowledgements

Big thanks to my brilliant editor Belinda Toor. I'm so grateful for all her support with *The Island House*. And thank you to my agent Kate Nash – who is amazing and absolutely nothing like the literary agent in my book.

Thank you to Audrey Linton for all her help, to Caroline Lakeman for her fantastic cover design, to my copy-editor Helena Newton, and proofreader Helen Williams, and all the team at HQ, and all the team at The Kate Nash Literary Agency.

Sending big thanks, as always, to my lovely friends Karen Clarke and Joanne Duncan for their brilliant support.

Thanks to everyone on Facebook, Twitter, Instagram, and, of course, in real life, for being there and cheering me on. I appreciate every single one of you.

Thank you to everyone who reads and enjoys my books. I still find it amazing that people are reading my words as far away as Australia, and always appreciate the lovely messages I receive from happy readers. Thanks too, to the brilliant blogging community and lovely reviewers who take the time to give such wonderful reviews.

I'm lucky to know so many amazing writers who make writing not only less lonely, but a pleasure. Having contact with them, especially throughout the pandemic, has made such a difference to my writing world. Special thanks to Vikki Patis and all the fabulous authors at the PSAA; to Keri Beevis, Heather Fitt and the team at The Paperback Writers, to Wendy Clarke and everyone at the amazing Fiction Café; to all the amazingly supportive writers at Authors Support Network, and KN Lit Authors – and an extra special thank you to Diane Jeffrey, Charley Crocker, Sherri Turner and Sue Blackburn.

Big thanks to my daughter-in-law Lucy, who again bravely read an early draft of *The Island House* and gave me great feedback. Thanks to my eldest and middle sons Liam and Daniel, who always tirelessly support me, and to my youngest son Luke who brainstormed the early plot with me and came up with some brilliant ideas. Thanks too to Amy for cheering me on.

Thank you to my mum for always rooting for me, and to Cheryl and my dad, who my acknowledgements would never be complete without.

Keep reading for an excerpt from
I Lie in Wait …

Prologue

Now

Me

'Maddie? Maddie, is that you?' It is. I know her voice. She's in the next room. 'Maddie! Maddie, please help me!' I tug at the chain trapping my wrist to the bedstead. It cuts into my flesh. Makes fresh wounds.

'We're heading back to Drummondale House on Friday,' she's saying. 'It's the anniversary of Lark and Jackson's disappearance.'

'Maddie, please!' I yell. *Why can't she hear me?*

'Robert feels there may be something we missed that night. I'm not sure what to think, but I'll keep you updated. Wish us luck!'

'You're wasting your time, Maddie,' you say. And of course, you are right.

The sound of your laptop snapping closed brings me back to reality. Maddie isn't there at all. You were listening to her vlog.

I close my eyes, fatigue washing over me, my usual thoughts carrying me to nightmares: *How did I let this happen? How could I have been so stupid?*

*

I have no idea how long I've slept, but I'm now alone, and the place is in darkness. I shuffle up the bed, ears pricked on alert for the sound of tyres rolling over the ice-packed ground. My sore, watery eyes pinned on the window, waiting for a glimpse of your car's headlights to cut across the grubby glass. But it's silent, and I wonder if you've gone back there – back to Drummondale House.

Chapter 1

Present Day

Amelia

He took her. Jackson Cromwell – my mother's lover. He took my teenage sister. He took Lark from us. I know he did. And sometimes, looking back – eyes wide open – I wonder if I should have reacted when I saw the way he looked at her, the way he flirted.

It's the anniversary of her disappearance this Friday. Twelve long months of not knowing where Lark is – whether she's alive or dead.

My ex-partner William couldn't cope with my outpourings of grief following my sister's disappearance. It couldn't have been easy for him listening to me repeat the same tragic words, desperate to explore my feelings, desperate to cope with what had happened. I went from numb to feeling too much, to numb again, all with the aid of too much wine.

In fact, I still hadn't come to terms with her loss when, seven months later, my mum died. Imagine a car wreck – well that was me in human form.

But a few weeks after her funeral, life took an upward turn. I discovered I was pregnant. For three months a tiny baby had been growing inside me and I'd been too swept away by grief overload to realise. It was a miracle, and for the first time in ages, bubbles of happiness fizzed.

'It can't be mine,' William said, when I broke the news over his favourite meal of guinea fowl and gnocchi.

'Of course it's yours,' I said, placing the little stick telling me the best news ever onto his side plate, and trying to smile despite his tactless comment.

'That's got your pee on it, Amelia,' he said, pushing it away. 'Are you positive it's mine?'

'OK, for one …' I held up my index finger '… I've only slept with you in all the time I've known you. And two …' I burst into tears.

William jumped up, grabbed a serviette – he always insisted we had them on the table, as I had, still have in fact, a habit of getting 'stuff' on my face when I eat – and thrust it into my hand.

'OK, great, I'm going to be a dad,' he said, and left the room. He'd barely touched his gnocchi. I guess the pee on the stick hadn't helped.

So this portrays William in an awful light. But, in fairness to him, he'd been through my hell with me, and was no longer 'Fun-Loving Will' the man with the amazing smile who I met on a night out with the girls three years ago. He was a faded, tired version. In fact, I couldn't recall the last time he'd smiled. He wanted out of our relationship, but, at the time, he didn't have the heart to leave a woman weighed down by a bucket-load of tragedy. And now, a baby – our baby – would trap him forever.

*

Things improved after that. We began picking up the scattered pieces of our relationship, and I tucked the loss of my mum and sister into a little velvet box at the back of my mind, determined to move on with my life – our lives. It's what Mum and Lark would have wanted, I told myself. And I desperately wanted to make William happy.

But that small snatch of happiness lasted no time at all. My life, the life I thought was back on a safe, even road, plummeted into another deep dark ditch, and I wasn't sure I'd be able to climb out this time. After awful stomach cramps I prayed were IBS, I lost our baby at five months pregnant.

So, it's been a tragic year – a year of heartache and loss. I've heard people say bad things come in threes. But how does anyone stay strong when said bad things hit one after the other? One! Two! Three! Wham! Bam! Slam!

Lark vanished.

Mum died.

I lost my baby.

I'm not going to lie; I wondered what I'd done in a previous life to deserve such sorrow.

I tried so hard not to be *that* woman who everyone felt sorry for. '*Poor Amelia – nothing goes right for her.*' '*Oh, Amelia, love, it could only happen to you.*' Or worse, the woman people crossed the road to avoid, fearing her misery was catching. But it was impossible. I *was* that woman wallowing knee-deep in self-pity, and I hadn't got a clue where to find the strength to pick myself up; still haven't. In fact, I fully understand how some women lose their mind following a miscarriage, as I'm pretty close to losing mine right now.

With the loss of our baby, my life with William was over. He'd seen the worst of me – not a pretty sight. Couldn't take any more. Wasn't strong enough. He said, as he touched my cheek gently a week after our loss, his fingertips drying my skin, 'I can't do this anymore, Amelia.' He'd lost his baby too, he said – he was in pain too, he said – but I know he never felt the same kind of screwed-up agony I felt.

He stayed around for two months after that, spending a lot of time at his mum's, or crying on the shoulder of an ex-girlfriend. He never did tell me her name. Did he think I would knife her on a lonely street?

For a while it was as though my baby – the little girl I had so many plans for – was still with me. But eventually, with time, I accepted there was an empty place inside me where I once felt her flutter – a timid butterfly trying out her wings for the first time. I'd felt so sure she was happy. I'd held my belly so often, talked to her, sung to her. But we can never be sure when happiness will be snatched away from us. I know that now.

*

'Amelia, have you got the contract for Jennings and Jennings?'

I look away from the office window, and up at Malcolm. My boss is out of breath, and needs to lose a few pounds before he keels over. His tone, as always, is anxiety-tinged, his face stretched into a shiny-cheeked smile. He won't make old bones at this rate.

'You need to shave off that ridiculous moustache, Malcolm.' I've wanted to say that for years, if only to help him find his soul mate. No wonder he's single. 'You look like Hitler.'

His eyes widen, as much as they can in their puffy sockets, as he touches the hairy culprit under his nose. 'You need more time away from the office, Amelia.'

'I need forever,' I say. I haven't even turned on the computer and it's almost midday. I've spent most of this morning gazing out at the grey day. Thinking. 'Can you give me forever, Malcolm?' I ask, in a maudlin tone – that's pretty much my only tone right now.

'Take more time out if you need it. You're no use to us here.'

'Cheers for that.'

'I think you know what I'm saying, Amelia.' He strides off, in his creased shirt and too-short trousers.

I've got to go home, or hide in the loos for the rest of the day.

I fidget in my swivel chair. I won't get paid if I go home. I've had way too much time off already. The thing is, I can't afford the apartment now anyway, not since William left. I need to do something – something else, something to make life worth living again. But then how can I do that without Mum, without Lark, without William, without my precious unborn child?

I look out of the window once more. The tall buildings of London surround me, and The Gherkin feels so close. I'm tempted to open the window and lean out – try to touch it. I would fall, of course. Tumble to my death, and possibly make headlines in *The Metro*. But then nobody would care. Not a single soul would miss me – except perhaps my dad, and possibly my brother Thomas.

I roll my chair back over the plush carpet, put the photo of William in the bin, and my Thor figure, that Thomas bought me a few years back because I told him I *love* Chris Hemsworth, in my bag. I grab my jacket, rise, and head for the door, throwing one look over my shoulder at the rabbit warren of desks. Nobody looks my way. I'm right. Nobody will miss me.

Outside, I dash towards London Bridge Underground, pushing through the crowds. I won't cry, I tell myself. I'm all cried out.

*

'William, it's me. Pick up, please.' I'm pissed, sobbing into my phone, my cat curled on my knee, her purr giving me comfort. Drunk-me is far too needy, and I seem to turn to her too often lately. 'Call me, please. I need you right now.' It's the tenth time I've called and it's only seven o'clock. Ten times he's ignored me.

I throw my phone across the room. It hits a photo of us in Rhodes. It clatters on the dresser. The glass cracks. Were we even happy then? I know it was difficult when Mum got cancer, and everything that followed was impossible – William struggled with me struggling, which made me struggle even more.

I look at the empty wine bottle, before burying my head in

my hands until the tears stop. And then it hits me. I need my dad, to feel the comfort of his arms around me. But I can't take off to Berwick-upon-Tweed and leave my cat – who now looks up at me as though she knows what I'm thinking. 'But if I stay here, sweetie, I'll go crazy,' I say, tickling her soft ears.

Later, after crying on my neighbour's doorstep – a kindly twenty-something with pink hair – she gives me a much-needed hug. 'You've been through hell, Amelia,' she says. 'Of course I'll look after your cat. Take as long as you need.'

'Thanks so much,' I say, wishing I knew her name – but it's far too late to ask her what it is; we've been chatting for months.

I return to my flat and call Malcolm, realising, after apologising profusely for letting him down at such short notice, that he sounds relieved I'm taking time off.

'Great. Super,' he says. 'Brilliant!'

'I'll be taking an early train to Berwick-upon-Tweed and probably won't be back for a while. Is that OK?'

'Of course, Amelia. Please, please don't hurry back.'

I end the call, flop down on my bed, and close my eyes.

Dear Reader,

We hope you enjoyed reading this book. If you did, we'd be so appreciative if you left a review. It really helps us and the author to bring more books like this to you.

Here at HQ Digital we are dedicated to publishing fiction that will keep you turning the pages into the early hours. Don't want to miss a thing? To find out more about our books, promotions, discover exclusive content and enter competitions you can keep in touch in the following ways:

JOIN OUR COMMUNITY:
Sign up to our new email newsletter:
http://smarturl.it/SignUpHQ
Read our new blog www.hqstories.co.uk
🐦 : https://twitter.com/HQStories
🅵 : www.facebook.com/HQStories

BUDDING WRITER?
We're also looking for authors to join the HQ Digital family!
Find out more here:
https://www.hqstories.co.uk/want-to-write-for-us/
Thanks for reading, from the HQ Digital team

ONE PLACE. MANY STORIES

ONE PLACE. MANY STORIES

If you enjoyed *The Island House*,
then why not try another gripping
thriller from HQ Digital?